THE SINKIANG EXECUTIVE

"Quiller is tops!"
— CHARLOTTE OBSERVER

"You can't go wrong with Quiller."
— HARPER'S

"Quiller by now is a primary reflex."
— KIRKUS REVIEWS

ADAM HALL

"Hall tops ninety-nine percent of all writers of
spy books."
— ST. PAUL PIONEER PRESS

"When it comes to espionage fiction,
Adam Hall has no peer!"
— Eric Van Lustbader
bestselling author of THE NINJA

"Nobody writes better espionage than Adam Hall."
— THE NEW YORK TIMES

Other books by Adam Hall

THE VOLCANOES OF SAN DOMINGO
THE MANDARIN CYPHER
THE NINTH DIRECTIVE
THE STRIKER PORTFOLIO
THE TANGO BRIEFING
THE KOBRA MANIFESTO
THE WARSAW DOCUMENT
THE QUILLER MEMORANDUM
THE SCORPION SIGNAL
THE PEKING TARGET
QUILLER

ADAM HALL
THE SINKIANG EXECUTIVE

A JOVE BOOK

This Jove book contains the complete
text of the original hardcover edition.

THE SINKIANG EXECUTIVE

A Jove Book / published by arrangement with
Doubleday & Company, Inc.

PRINTING HISTORY
Doubleday edition published 1978
Jove edition / September 1986

ISBN: 0-515-08678-9

Jove Books are published by The Berkley Publishing Group,
200 Madison Avenue, New York, N.Y. 10016.
The words "A JOVE BOOK" and the "J" with sunburst
are trademarks belonging to Jove Publications, Inc.

PRINTED IN THE UNITED STATES OF AMERICA

To Pat Murphy

Contents

THE SINKIANG EXECUTIVE

1

Katia

The winter rain had driven everyone off the streets and half London was down here in the underground trying to get home in the dry. My train was packed and we stood crushed together, swaying from the straps as the thing moaned through the curves. Flashes came now and then against the black windows as the contacts hit some dirt on the rail, making it look as if lightning had struck. We stood with the patience of cattle, our clothes steaming from the deluge that had drenched us up there in the streets.

The man had got on at Knightsbridge. I was standing next to him now.

We stood reading the advertisement panels and watching the lightbulbs dim and flicker intermittently. A couple of girls along at the end were getting some furtive attention, one of them still managing to look sexy under a colourless plastic mac and with hair like seaweed; but we were mostly men on this train: The typists had gone home punctually an hour ago, leaving the department and managerial staffs to goad their ulcers into overtime.

In the window I watched the reflection of the man standing next to me. I had forgotten his name, but I knew who he was. It was two years since I'd last seen him and at that time I hadn't thought I would ever see him again.

"Is this Piccadilly?"

I looked down at the plump woman. "No. Hyde Park."

"I've got to get off at Piccadilly," she said, looking worried about it.

"I'll let you know."

"You can't see what the names are, can you, with the windows so dirty?"

"Not really."

The train rocked again and the man swayed against me; I eased away from him slightly, not wanting him to bump me too hard, in case he felt he should apologise. I didn't want to look at him, for any reason whatever. He was jammed into the corner between the glass partition and the doors, so that I was the only person close to him. I could feel the draught slicing through the gap in the doors where the rubber had warped; they said it would freeze to-night.

"Is this it?" the plump woman asked me.

"No. This is Green Park."

"Are you sure?"

"Yes."

The train was stationary now and I turned away from the man by a few degrees more, because that would suit his book. I didn't want him to feel worried about me.

"When's Piccadilly, then?"

I looked at the woman. "The next stop." I didn't want to tell her I was getting off there myself, because the man would hear, and behave differently from the way I wanted. "I won't let you miss it," I told her.

The train began moving again and I took a series of slow breaths, inhaling the smell of wet overcoats. When we were going at full speed I shifted my feet an inch for the sake of balance, and waited.

The woman was standing sideways-on to me with her shoulder against my chest; she had to turn her head quite a bit and look upwards when she talked to me, but that wasn't good enough. I went on waiting.

Lightning came again on the black windows.

"Is it the next stop?" she asked me. "Piccadilly?"

"Yes."

She nodded, turning back to stare at the windows. Then the train lurched and the waiting was over and I reached up with my left hand to brace myself against the partition; and now the woman couldn't see my face anymore because my arm was blocking her view.

The only sound was the moaning of the wheels, and someone saying, on the other side of the compartment, that it was going to snow. There was no other sound, of any significance. But time was going by, and my right arm began tiring. I would have liked to rest it, but couldn't.

Katia, I thought, Katia, remembering her name but not her face, or not very much. Just a girl standing there under the lamp with the two men on each side of her, standing there looking at me and smiling. It was all I needed, this thought. And the memory of her name. Katia.

The train began slowing.

I kept my eyes on the opposite side of the compartment now. *The Glow of Wundalite,* a panel read, *For a Festive Christmas!* It was already late January. Perhaps they meant for next Christmas too, for every Christmas. That would be the message, really: that you could have a Festive Christmas with those things lit up all over the tree. I let my mind, or part of it, consider these ideas, surprised that I needed so desperately to hang onto something ordinary and acceptable as a focus for thought while the soundlessness went on, and the fierce primeval satisfaction.

The train came to a halt and as people started moving I pushed against the plump woman, forcing her towards the doors on the opposite side as they opened and some of the passengers got out.

"Is this—"

"Yes," I told her, "but we'll have to hurry." I took her arm and stopped her falling as we reached the doors.

"Are you sure this—"

"Piccadilly," I said, and made certain she didn't turn round. "I'll look after you, don't worry."

But as soon as she'd got her feet on the platform I turned away and didn't look back. I was one of the first through the gates and a minute later I was walking fast in the blinding rain with my head down and my hands dug into my pockets and a kind of laughter coming that I tried to stop, but couldn't.

"What the hell for?" I asked him.

Holmes shut the file and went back to his desk and sat down and said: "It's all I know. You're on standby. Signal ends." He picked up the phone.

"Put that bloody thing down," I told him, and he did, looking up at me with his totally expressionless face. "I want to know who sent for me."

Gently he said: "I was going to phone Tilson, to see if he knew."

Holmes is like that: he manoeuvres you around till you shit on your own doorstep and then says now look what you've done.

"Tilson won't know," I said with an edge. Tilson was in Briefing, and therefore one of the last people you go through on your way out to the field. "Only a director could have slapped me on standby when I'm due for leave and you ought to know that. How long have you been here?"

"Longer," he said, "than you."

I went out of his office and left the door open, going along to Debriefing. I passed Matthews near the stairway, leaning backwards behind a stack of files he was carrying.

"Who's got in?" I asked him.

"Where from?"

"Anywhere."

He didn't answer right away and I couldn't tell whether he was considering the question or deciding not to say anything. He kicked open a door and called back: "Have to ask Tilson."

He kicked the door shut behind him and I began worrying again. Matthews normally told you things, if he knew them, and if he didn't know them he simply said so. This morning he was being evasive, like Holmes, giving me the same Tilson routine. Tilson was the traditional backstop for questions of any kind except those concerning your briefing: You might just as well ask a brick wall.

I found the big square-headed character in Debriefing and he was surprised to see me and I could understand that, because he knew I wasn't in from a mission, and that's about the only time you ever go in there.

"Hello, sir," he said brightly. "How are things going?"

"Who's just got in?"

He thought about this, without taking his eyes off me. He was an ex-Yard man with the knack of looking at you as if you'd got a lump of custard on the tip of your nose and he didn't like to mention it.

"I expect you're looking for Briefing, aren't you? This is—"

"Oh for Christ's sake, it's a perfectly simple question." I leaned over his desk. "Has someone just got in from a mission?"

He folded his square freckled hands and his eyes went stony.

"Well, sir, they come and go, don't they?"

He didn't have executive status and this was his way of telling me to get the hell out of his office.

"You must be a pain in the neck to your dentist," I told him and went out and tried to find Thompson. Someone said he was down in the Caff for a tea-break. He wasn't.

I sat down at one of the tables and ordered a cup and didn't drink it because the last thing my nerves wanted at the moment was caffeine and in this place the stuff tasted like something out of a horse.

"Is it too cold?" Maisie asked me.

"It's fine."

She went away.

The thing that worried me was that someone had slapped me on standby and they wouldn't do that without checking the records and the records showed that I'd got back from Turkey a week ago and was due for special leave. Special leave is granted when you come in looking like something the dog has found in a rubbish dump, and we nearly always get it because no one ever comes in looking very fit: It's in the nature of the job.

Being on standby isn't the same as being on call. When you're on call it means they've got a specific mission lined up for you and you have to be ready to hit the field at a moment's notice, so you don't go far from a telephone and you don't leave your pad without telling them where you're going. They let you see one of the girls but it's on the understanding that if her phone rings you've got to put down the tiddly-winks and get to your car in zero seconds flat, so it's no use complaining. Standby is less demanding and more general: It means they may have a job for you but you can leave home and travel around the metropolitan area providing you call them at twelve-hour intervals.

The one alert phase often leads to the other, of course: From standby you can suddenly find yourself put on call and then you're in line for briefing and transport, within minutes or hours or sometimes days: it depends on how soon the directors can work out things like access, cover, liaison, so forth. The one thing I knew at this moment was that they wouldn't be putting me on call, because the Turkey thing had developed a lot of problems and we'd lost a courier and blown the escape route and I'd had to get out under fire from the frontier guards at Kâzim Pasa. I'd had no cover for Iran and it had meant holing up in a freightyard for three days in the snow before I could reach the embassy. That was all right but I'd lost some blood because one of the guards had made a hit and it was the wrong time to go on a fast in a freight-yard at five below zero.

"Hello, old horse."

Tilson sat down and began a little tattoo with his fingertips on the plastic table, not looking at me but gazing around at the tea urns and Maisie and the liverish yellow walls.

"Who put me on standby?" I asked him.

"I wouldn't know." Then he turned his pale watery eyes on me and said under his breath: "What have you been up to, for Christ's sake?"

I went instinctively deadpan and felt the heart rate increasing suddenly, whipped up by the shock. He hadn't said much but it was enough. In the Bureau people talk so little that if someone says good morning you feel like dashing into Codes and Cyphers to find out what he meant. The Bureau doesn't exist, so you don't exist, and nobody else exists, so there's very little to talk about.

I looked at Tilson.

"You want some tea?"

He shook his head, looking away again. "I've got a message for you, old fruit, that's all. You're requested not to leave the building. Okay?" He got up and wandered off in his red plaid slippers, saying a word to Maisie as he went out, leaving her giggling.

I sat at the table with the cold cup of tea and didn't want to move. My stomach had gone sour and I tried not to think about what Tilson had said—what Tilson had *meant*. But I'd *have* to think about it and I left the Caff and went up to the fourth floor and looked for Woods, because he might know the score. He was in Signals, perched in front of the mainline Asia console trying to get a director in the field some kind of access before his executive ran out of information—they were so *bloody* good at kicking you into a red sector and leaving you there like a sitting duck while they sat around here in London working out the material they should have worked out before you were even briefed.

Not true. They *sometimes* did it. Only sometimes, or no one would ever get back with his skin on. I was just feeling paranoiac, that was all, and when Woods turned round from the console to look at me and turned right back without saying anything I gave it up and cleared out. I hadn't expected him to say anything except hello or something because he didn't have time: The yellow was flashing and the director was asking for a signal and Woods had one for him because he hadn't got the phone in his free hand; but it was his face that had rattled me: the quick surprise in it and then the shut-down as he looked at me for a moment without any expression at all before he went back to the set.

I was beginning to get the message.

For the next hour I hung around the upper floors but couldn't find anyone to talk to. There was a lot of pressure on this morning and everyone looked as nervous as a cat on moving day. Harrison might have spared me some time but he was sending a group out to one of the African states and asked me to leave as soon as I went in there. In Room 12 there was a dental mechanic installing a three-phase micro-receiver in a wisdom tooth for one of the Moscow couriers, and I didn't stay. Young Gray was fiddling about next door with a couple of Dinky Toys and the model of a street intersection. One of the buildings had a little flag and the whole thing looked terribly like a long-range elimination setup for telescopic sights and I didn't interrupt him, except to remind him to lock the door as soon as I'd gone: We get a few visitors to the Bureau and although they're usually deep-screened people from the Foreign Office or DI6 we ought not to be seen playing games like that on the fourth floor, which is now the executive action complex.

I was sitting around in Monitoring with one ear on some stuff going out on the Chinese-speaking propaganda programme from Moscow when one of the phones rang and someone picked it up and looked around and said: "Yes, he's here." He passed it to me and I gave my name and listened very intently because this was the call I'd been waiting for: It couldn't be anything else.

It was one of the girls from Admin. asking if I could be in Mr. Parkis' room as soon as possible and I said yes I could and put the thing down and went out, keeping my breath steady and my pace steady but finding it difficult, having to work at it. Because I knew what had happened, and I'd spent half the night and all this morning trying to tell myself that I didn't.

A copy of the *Telegraph* was lying on the desk with the front page turned towards me as I came in. Parkis was looking down at it, his pale fleshy hands in the side pockets of his jacket with the thumbs hooked over the top. He didn't speak.

When he saw I was looking at the newspaper he turned away and began walking in a short straight line between the window and the Lowry on the wall, his soft elegant shoes leaving traces of dark and light as they disturbed the nap of the carpet. I didn't spend long looking at the paper: I'd seen it already.

Parkis stood still and looked at me with his ice-blue eyes. He is made entirely of ice, this man, and one day when I blow my cover at the wrong time or spring a trap in the wrong place or walk into a red sector without checking it first I'm going to go out cursing Parkis. This I promise.

They're all ruthless bastards, the London directors: They've got to be. They wouldn't survive if they weren't, and nor would we. But most of them understand what this kind of work does to us, and what it can do to us if it's allowed to get out of hand. Most of them regard us as human beings even when they're directing us into operations that no human being could be expected to bring off and keep his sanity. So we usually manage to get back, give or take a few exceptions; and this is partly because when we're out there in the field we know there's someone doing his best to look after us from London Control.

Parkis is different. He is like Loman, but infinitely worse. I've worked three missions under his control and since a year ago I've refused him and I'm going to go on refusing him. Parkis doesn't think we're human beings. He thinks we're robots. And the only reason why he's still among the top-echelon directors is because he plans his operations so meticulously that nothing can go wrong: providing you're a robot. But there are situations in the field that even Parkis can't control: It can rain and your foot can slip; a plane can be late; a shot can ricochet. Then if you're still alive he'll throw you to the dogs because there's nothing else he can do: His operations are designed to tick with the precision of a watch, and they are thus too sensitive to accommodate the unpredictable.

So he wins on points: He brings back as many of us as the other directors do, and he does it by skill; but it's the skill of a toymaker. He finishes the paintwork and winds us up and sets us going and nine times out of ten we don't hit the wall. It isn't the odds I mind: They're pretty good. It's Parkis.

He spoke.

"I've been waiting for you."

"Not for long," I said.

They could have found me in five minutes, wherever I was, since I'd come in this morning.

"What were you doing in Monitoring?"

"Keeping an ear open." We're not supposed to wander about on the fourth floor unless we're on call or briefed.

I looked down at the *Telegraph* again, just for a second. They'd got a picture of the train, empty and with the doors open. The headline was across the three right-hand columns: *Murder in London Underground.*

I turned away from it and looked at the rain on the windows.

"Time is very short," Parkis said thinly.

"Then let's get it over."

He said in a moment: "I have a question for you, Quiller. How many men have you been obliged to kill in the course of a mission?"

"What? God knows. Not many. Half a dozen."

Bangkok. East Germany. Warsaw. Tunisia. Hong Kong. The States. Other places.

"Half a dozen," he said tonelessly. "Possibly more."

"Possibly." Zade had taken one or two with him, in that jet.

Parkis swung round and said with soft fury—"Do you think that gives you a *licence?*"

"Not really."

He waited to see if I was going to add anything. I let the silence go on.

"This man Novikov," he said at last.

"Is that his name?" I looked at the paper again.

"Yes. His cover name was Weiner."

"I didn't know."

There must have been someone else there. Or they'd—

"You didn't know his name?" he asked sharply.

"No. I only—"

"But you knew who he was?"

"Oh for Christ's sake, Parkis, I don't go around doing that sort of thing to strangers. If you—"

"Very well. I am now asking for your explanation."

I took a breath and wondered if there was any point in giving him some carefully considered lies. I didn't think there was. And some remnant of human faith was averse to my playing Judas to the dead.

"It was a personal thing," I told Parkis. "I—"

"Personal?"

I shut up again. If he wanted an explanation he'd have to let me give it in my own way, without interruption. But this wasn't going to be my game anyhow: I'd already lost. I knew it and they all knew it—Matthews, Woods, Tilson, and all the rest of the people who'd looked at me this morning as if I were some kind of zombie. And Parkis knew it.

"Be good enough to proceed."

"Without interruptions?"

He stood gazing at me in silence and I could feel the chill.

"It was in Czechoslovakia," I told him defensively, "a couple of years ago. The Bratislava thing. Mildmay handled that one, with Loman in the field." I looked away from him. "Well, there was a girl."

He waited. I was trying to remember things about her, but all I could think of was her name. Katia.

"It was the end phase," I said in a moment. "I'd been in there and sent the stuff out and London was satisfied and my orders were to save myself if I could. Loman was still directing me in the field, with signals through Prague. But they had the girl, so I made a deal. I said they could take me for interrogation if they let the girl go."

I was trying to remember the details but it's often hard to go back over the end phase of a mission: We're usually concerned with saving our skin and I suppose there's a certain amount of retrogressive amnesia that sets in to protect the psyche; otherwise we'd never go out again. Today, talking to Parkis in a different environment, I found that particular scene was still in sharp focus, fogging out most of the background: Katia standing there under the lamp, scared to death and still smiling for me because that was the way she wanted me to remember her; and those two bastards standing one on each side.

"They agreed to the deal," I said absently, "and I saw her walk away, free."

He asked too casually: "You submitted to interrogation?"

"What? Of course not. I knew I could get out: Loman had a plane lined up and I'd got papers for Austria. So that's what I did."

I listened to the rain on the window. It had been raining then, in Bratislava; she'd been wet with it, her hair shining as she'd walked away, out of the lamplight, free.

"When I was back in London I heard what they'd done to her."

That was all I wanted to tell him.

I watched the streaks running down the window, distorting the skyline across Whitehall; it looked as if the roofs were slowly melting out there in the January cold, and the buildings dissolving.

"You failed to keep this 'deal' of yours," Parkis said.

"So did they."

"Did you ever imagine they'd keep to it?"

"I think they would have."

"If *you* had."

"Yes."

"So the blame was yours."

"Indirectly. But I didn't kill her. They did."

He looked at the carpet, his feet together, his hands coming out of his pockets and clasping themselves in front of him. It looked as if the bastard was praying for something. Patience, probably.

"So I am to believe that for the sake of avenging this girl you speak of, you killed a man in a public place and put the Bureau in extreme hazard."

"Believe what you like," I told him.

His head came up sharply. "But she wasn't even working for us! The Bratislava operation was—"

"She was liaison. She'd been helping us to—"

"Not *Bureau* liaison. Loman would have—"

"Of course not. She was Czech, working through their—"

"But if you were on the point of getting out, her work must have been finished! You had no further use for her!"

"*Use* for her?" I realised I was backing off a little, in case I hit him. It wouldn't do any good. "You mean she was expendable?"

He turned away impatiently. "They had no reason to kill her in any case, did they?"

"She'd blown one of their cell."

"That would be no reason."

"I thought so."

But this was why I'd lost. If it had been anyone but Katia I would have chanced it. The risk wasn't high: but the risk was to *her*. And I couldn't tell Parkis because he wouldn't have understood.

"How deeply involved were you, Quiller, with this girl?"

"That's none of your bloody business. I went into Bratislava, I did the job and I got out again. That's all Control was concerned with."

He turned away and took a couple of steps and turned back and asked tonelessly: "How did you kill him?"

"Windpipe." My arm still felt the strain: I hadn't been able to use my left hand to increase the force because the plump woman might have turned round again and seen his face. He'd gone down slowly, sliding against me as I eased him to the floor. My strength had appalled me, because I knew it was abnormal, fired by the rage; but I had exulted in what I was doing. The only unpleasant thing was that he'd had bad breath.

Parkis wasn't looking at me. He said: "He'd been following you. Did you know?"

"Of course I knew!"

"Where had he first got onto you?"

"Knightsbridge."

He swung into movement again and said with sharp emphasis: "We received a complaint."

"Oh really? So you weren't certain it was me."

"Not until you admitted it. But surely that's academic?"

He meant I would have admitted it anyway, if he'd asked me point blank. I suppose I would have.

"Yes."

We're allowed some kind of a private life outside the Bureau; and this thing between Novikov and me had been a private matter. Parkis wouldn't normally have the right to question me on it but of course I'd stirred something up and there was a risk of the Bureau's being involved unless they could put out a massive smoke screen. I thought there must have been another man on that train, someone who'd seen what happened; and I was relieved there hadn't been because I'd been thinking I must have missed him.

"You realise of course," Parkis said, and one of his phones rang, "that the police are looking for you at this moment, and with great energy?" He picked up the phone and spoke with his back to me. "No. No clearance. No briefing. The first available. I would say within ten minutes." He put the receiver back and faced me. "Well?"

"Looking for *someone*," I said, but I didn't feel so casual as I sounded.

"You killed Novikov," he said with soft anger, "and they are looking for his killer. They are looking for *you*, don't you understand? And you were seen on that train, by a great many people. The Yard is now questioning every passenger they can trace, asking for a description of anyone acting strangely."

"No one saw me do it. They—"

"How far do you think you'd gone before they saw him lying there dead? You imagine—"

"Descriptions are notoriously vague, you know that."

He came up to me and stared into my face with his ice-blue eyes and his voice was soft, though not quite steady. "Even if the police never found you by routine investigation, they'll receive every possible help from the Russian Embassy, however anonymously. Don't you *realise* that?"

I didn't say anything; it wasn't really a question. He was just getting rid of some shock and setting me up for the pay-off, in whatever form it would take. Of course he was perfectly right about the Russian Embassy: They'd give my description to the police out of sheer indignation. On any given day there are scores of people moving around London with a tag on their tail, with the action concentrated at the embassies and consulates; the Foreign Office and the headquarters of MI5 and DI6 are also under uninterrupted surveillance. The tags are second-class material for the most part: trainees, executives earning their pension after action in the field, sometimes an odd spook who's after someone specific. All the services do it and everyone knows about it and we settle for that; it's the routine chore of keeping tabs on each other in case the pattern changes and we can learn something new. And the thing is that we could all knock each other off if we wanted to, but there wouldn't be any point; we're doing our job and they're doing theirs and if anyone really wants to go somewhere in strict hush then he first makes bloody sure he's got a clean tail.

It's been an unwritten law since the services became organised, and last night I broke it.

"Have you anything to say?" Parkis was asking me.

Wearily I said: "What like?"

"In your own favour."

I thought about it.

"Not really."

He went and sat down behind his desk and now I caught so much of the chill in the air that it reached my spine. I suppose I'd been holding back from the brink that I knew was there, hoping for some kind of luck that'd save me. As Parkis began speaking I knew it was strictly no go.

"I wasn't able to see you the moment you arrived here this morning, Quiller, because I was in emergency conference with Administration. Two decisions were reached. One: that you should be sent out of London as soon as possible and in the utmost secrecy. Two: that your immediate resignation would be received with our unqualified approval. You will draw an overnight bag on your way out of the building, and there is transport waiting for you at the door. Your escort will facilitate your passage through London Airport Immigration as best he can." He paused briefly. "Unless, of course, it's already too late."

2

Cockroach

The black widow dropped lower, until I could see the red hourglass pattern on its abdomen. Soon it dropped lower again, stopping at intervals, the long thin legs spreading out.

The thread was visible now, very fine and very dark.

I moved my hand.

"Don't do that," Charlie said quietly.

I kept still. In a moment the spider dropped again, this time to the surface of the bench. Charlie turned the reel quickly, catching the thread fast enough to wind it into a helix on the twin rods.

"They're sensitive," he said, his voice quiet. "They don't mind slow movements, but if you move quickly they get upset." He took the probe and coaxed the spider onto its tip, endlessly patient. It was five minutes before he could lift it onto the reel again, and another five before it began dropping, letting out its thread. "She's good for one more spin, this one. She's made four today."

The long pointed legs splayed suddenly and the widow stopped.

"I can feel a draught," I said.

"So can she."

He began winding the long reel as the spider dropped at regular intervals, sensing its environment.

"She's out of sorts," Charlie said, softly crooning. "They're not normally active in winter."

The widow began moving towards the edge of the bench and he teased it into the jar, giving it a fly to catch.

"They'll only take living food—they don't eat carrion, like us."

"*¡Carlos!*"

"*¿Sí?*"

"*¿Quiere usted leche?*"

"*¡Por favor, Pepita!*"

We could hear the woman going down the stairs.

"Voice like a foghorn, heart of gold. Does everything for me. Lost her son in the civil war. Now she's got another one—me." He wheeled his chair across to the other bench and took a handframe out of the drawer, holding it up to the light. "I told you I'd show you. This thread's four days old—it's dried now, lost its stickiness. This thing's a micromanipulator. You put the lens in here—they come already grooved. All I have to do is lay the thread into the grooves and Bob's your uncle. Five dollars a go, okay? That little sweetheart spun me fifty bucks' worth just now while you were watching."

He dropped the lens into the foam-lined box and shut the drawer gently. "Next time you find yourself behind a long-distance rifle, you'll know what the crosshairs are made of—if it's a good one. This stuff's stronger than platinum wire and about ten times as good as the plastic hairs they've got on the market now—they're too brittle and they're not really *black*. Of course, I don't get much call for this kind of thread these days—they're making everything of cold crap, aren't they? No wonder civilisation's falling apart. What are you doing in Barcelona, anyway?" He was looking at me over the edge of his half-moon glasses.

I didn't answer.

"Silly question," he nodded.

Charlie was one of our sleeper agents in the Mediterranean theatre, originally Codes and Cyphers, then operational for two years until the El Fatah took him for a Shin Bet executive and blew a Porsche from under him when he was nosing around in Cairo.

"I got thrown out of London," I told him.

This must be the cleanest window in the whole of Barcelona: I suppose that was Pepita. A few dried brown leaves were still on the platanas down there along the Ramblas, and a wind from the harbour pulled at them. *¡Feliz Navidad!* a torn banner said in red-and-blue letters.

"*Thrown* out?" He sounded concerned.

"Slung out, kicked out, what d'you want me to say?" I swung round to face him.

"What we want," he said gently, wheeling his chair across to the living quarters, "is a nice little drop of Carlos Primero, which by good grace they named after me." He picked up the bottle and poured two shot glasses.

"I'm on the wagon," I said.

"Oh, that's right. Never been off, now I come to remember."

I knew he wouldn't say anything more about the other thing so I poured myself some Orangina and tipped his glass by way of apology and said: "I blotted my copybook, that's all. They had to get me out of London so fast that *that* is what I'm doing in Barcelona—it was the first available plane to anywhere."

"Dear oh dear." He stared upwards from his chair. "I suppose that's fairly typical. You tend to leave a suitable uproar behind you when you skip town."

"This time it's not quite as funny as that."

"I wish I could do something," he said in a helpless tone. "Wouldn't you like to sit down?"

"You're doing your bit," I told him. "You're my contact here."

"Be my guest."

Then I decided to tell him.

"My neck's on the block, Charlie."

He swung his chair round so that he was facing me.

"Spell out," he said.

"I'm being fired."

He sat perfectly still, looking up at me over his glasses. By the way I'd said it he knew I wasn't joking.

"Did you say 'fired'?"

"Invited to resign. Same thing."

Very quietly: "What in Christ's name for?"

"Breach of security."

His large greying head tilted sideways, and I remembered his good ear was the left one.

"You?"

My mouth tasted awful and I wished I hadn't started this: in the course of sixteen missions I'd learned to keep things to myself, and what I was doing now felt like a confession under interrogation and I didn't like it because I'd experienced interrogation a good few times and they'd never broken me.

But my voice went on. "It wasn't anything professional. I mean I didn't make a slip or blow cover or lose information." I had to turn away from him now. "It was something I did in hot blood."

Again he said, and as quietly: *"You?"*

It made me turn back to him. "All right, I'm ten-tenths reptile, is that what you mean?"

"How else could you do your job?" he asked gently.

"I'm not looking for excuses. I am what I am and I do what I do and"—a fractional hesitation in my mind while I asked myself exactly what I was, what I did—"and it's too late to make any changes."

"Of course," he said after a while. "It's the same with most of us." He didn't glance down at the rug on the wheelchair but I sensed it was what he meant. "Who was the woman?"

I went across to the window, subconsciously looking for escape. I wanted to stop talking and get out of here: He knew me too well. I don't like being known.

"How's business?" I asked him.

"Can't grumble."

I heard his chair moving behind me, the rhythmic squawk of the tyres on the polished floorboards.

"You ever get out of this place, Charlie?"

"What do you think I am, a fucking cripple?"

"Not with those arms." They were enormous; I'd seen the weights and pulleys in the corner when I'd come in here. He couldn't run anywhere but if anyone got within reach of him and he didn't like it I'd say they'd be better off with a black widow.

"We could have a meal," I said, "sometime."

"Delighted."

"After it's official."

"Oh," he said cheerfully, "That's a lot of balls. They can't do that to you—you're one of their top men, still in your prime."

"I've heard it's the best time to quit: when you're winning."

I watched the man selling roast chestnuts down there in the winter sunshine, and realized it must be all written down somewhere. A mission was one thing, but life was another. In a mission you went in with everything worked out for you and all you had to do was stick to the instructions and watch out for traps, and by the time you'd been a few years at it you could handle pretty well anything because your mind turned into a computer, scanning the data and keeping you out of trouble. But life wasn't circumscribed by the limits of your own experience, and you could run smack into a land mine because you couldn't see it: because it was all written down somewhere that you should do just that.

Katia. Novikov. Two names. Take them separately and you'd got two elements of a mission; one on our side, one on theirs. Put them together and you'd got the two components of the bomb that had blown me apart. Question: Did I regret it? No, I would do it again, my arm round his neck, tightening, tightening, tremendously strong, stronger than Charlie's. All that was left, really, was the shockwave of knowing it had cost me everything I'd got.

"Where are you sacking out?"

I turned around.

"What?"

"Where are you staying?"

"The Internacional."

"Ah. Just up the road."

"Yes."

"I'll give you a buzz if they signal."

"It won't be anything I want to hear."

"*¿Carlos?*"

"*¿Sí?*"

"*¡Tengo su leche!*"

"*¡Pase usted, Pepita!*"

She came in, a vigorous dark-eyed woman still in black for her son, a birthmark livid on her face, her gold teeth flashing. She pulled the carton of milk from the bag of groceries and put it onto the table, eyeing me with the courage of her kind and daring me to think of her as anything but beautiful.

"*Pepita, este es un amigo mio, Señor Turner. Señora de la Fuente y Fuente.*"

"Mucho gusto de concerla, Señora de la Fuente," I said formally.

"Igualmente, señor."

Then the phone rang and Charlie spun the wheels of his chair and answered it.

"Yes," he said. "Half an hour ago." He looked across at me and held the receiver out and I took it and said hello and that was when everything started.

"Can you do anything with suede?"

"No entiendo, señor."

"Suede. These things," I said more loudly, pointing at them.

"¡Ah—sí, sí! ¡Sientese, señor!"

"What?"

He motioned me into the chair at the end, taking the crutch away and leaning it against the bar, getting a wire brush and looking at my shoes with his head to one side. There wasn't much suede left: I hate buying new shoes.

The man at the bar looked English.

"He could pretty well use polish on them," he said with a silly laugh. I looked up at him. "No offence," he added quickly.

"It's his problem," I told him shortly, "not yours."

"You're absolutely right."

"¿Americano?" the woman asked me.

"What?"

"You American?" She picked a piece of fluff off her sweater, just over the left nipple.

"No. And I haven't got any money. Or I wouldn't be in this stinking hole."

"Too bloody right!" the man at the bar said. "By the way, do you happen to know where I can get a gas refill for my lighter? They don't seem to stock any here."

"Christ," I said, "I wish I had your problems." The bootblack had got the rest of the suede off by now so I stopped him dead with fifty pesetas and told the Englishman, "There's a place round the corner—I'm going past there now."

He put some money on the bar and came with me into the street.

"You seem to know your Barcelona pretty well," he said, as if impressed. "It's my first trip here." We crossed over to the central boulevard, where the goldfish hung in clusters from the surface of their bowls, trying to get oxygen. The *chico* said we should buy some for our girlfriends.

"I've been here before," I said. "The thing is, I took a calculated risk. I mean it wasn't anything clumsy, or slack or anything. I could understand them blowing their bloody stack if I'd dropped a pad or something." That would be dangerous, any kind of mistake. You can make a few mistakes when you're new to the game, but not when you're a veteran. At my age it can only mean you're losing your grip, and they'll sling you out before you can blink. "How did those bastards pick it up anyway?"

"It wasn't difficult. He was tagging you on orders. When he was reported killed, they didn't need to look anywhere else, did they?"

He wandered away from me and put his foot on something and I saw a yellowish splodge on the paving stones as he came back. "I wish to Christ you wouldn't do that," I said.

"I know." He gave a soft laugh.

Ferris isn't specifically a bastard, like most of them; but he's got a thing about insects. About bigger creatures too, for all I know. I'd hate to see him with a mouse: I can't stand that kind of thing.

"How did *they* get the complaint?" I asked him. *They* for Bureau.

"The Russ told MI5, and they shoved it over to Liaison 9."

"It's getting too bloody easy. We used to be totally nonexistent, and—"

"And that's what you relied on. But they didn't send me out here to ask for excuses."

There was a bench and we sat on it, both of us checking the street for ticks from force of habit. It wasn't necessary because yesterday they'd smuggled me out of Heathrow like a leper and I'd made a thorough check when I'd got off the plane.

Obvious question: "Why did they send you after me?"

He sighed gently, pushing back his thin sandy hair with his fingers and for a moment glancing at me, though nothing showed in the pale amber eyes. "To help you frame the wording of your resignation. They're fussy in Admin., as you know; they don't want to feel they're being unfair to a trusted employee after years of good service and all that sort of thing. On the other hand they insist on your record showing you'd broken the rules and had to go."

"Screw them," I said.

"Point taken." In a moment: "I told them I'd rather not come out here."

"They could have done worse." I got up and stood helplessly with my hands dug into my pockets, looking along the boulevard past the flower stalls and goldfish man and the stacks of cheap multi-coloured comics on sale by the roadside. Ferris had local-directed me in quite a few theatres: East Germany, Hong Kong, the States, Tenerife. He'd been very good: underplayed everything, the way I like it, no dramatics, plenty of leeway when the odds were short. I suppose, as a director in the field, he'd saved my skin more than once by watching the way I was running. Today he was going to take it back on a salver to London.

"No formal enquiry," I said.

"It's been made." He got slowly to his feet.

"No appeal."

"On what grounds?"

I didn't answer that. There weren't any grounds.

I'd broken the First Rule and I'd confessed to it. The Bureau is the Sacred Bull and I'd violated its sanctity. While Ferris and I were standing here in the pale sunshine in Barcelona there was a full-scale murder hunt going on in England and if I went back there I'd risk being caught because people *had* seen my face on that train and they *had* been interviewed by the police, and if the Russ could leak the fact that it was one of their spooks who'd been on my tail at the time he'd been killed then they'd do that— and the hunt would at once concentrate within the closely circum-scribed limits of the secret service *milieu*. And the Sacred Bull could find itself in the limelight: a non-existent shadow organisa-tion responsible solely to the Prime Minister and with extra-ordinary powers in the international intelligence field that would be brought into immediate question in the House if they were ever acknowledged.

The outcome would be unequivocal. The Bull would be sac-rificed. *Finis.*

I didn't like those people in London because they were ruthless and they were implacable but I'd worked with them through sixteen operations and we'd learned mutual respect of the kind a wolf learns for the rest of the pack and there'd been no complaints on either side—until now. And now I knew they were doing the only thing they could do, choosing to sacrifice a disciple of the Bull to protect the Bull itself. I wouldn't expect them to do anything else.

Ferris had wandered over to look at the magazine stall, giving me time to think. Now he came back. I got off the bench and said:

"Why *Parkis?*"

He said with a wintry smile, "Nobody else had any stomach for it."

"He enjoyed it, of course."

"What else would you expect?"

I looked along the perspective of the boulevard, catching at a stray thought or two, finding nothing of value. I felt disorientated: Time and place had changed and I was lost and it hadn't happened to me before and I wasn't sure how to handle it. Sixteen missions, then *phutt.*

"How many people knew?" I asked Ferris.

He considered this. "Three."

"*Three?*"

He looked up. "Parkis and two others. Why?"

"Christ, the whole place was like a funeral home when I went in there yesterday morning."

He said: "That was about something else."

"You're lying."

He looked surprised.

I said: "They were all looking at me as if I'd shit on the rug. Tilson—Woods—Matthews—everyone I tried to talk to."

Another faint smile. "You're a little paranoiac, remember."

I swung away and swung back. "So it was something else. What like?"

"They've had a wheel come off," he said quietly, "in Central Asia."

I waited before I spoke again. It had been a mistake, telling him he was lying. They don't lie to you. If you ask them something they don't want to answer, they say so or say nothing. We call it uninformation and it covers a large and specific area in the work we do: They tell us as much as we need to know so that we can operate efficiently, and nothing more.

But this wasn't an operation. Ferris didn't have to tell me *anything*. Parkis had been appointed to tell me as much as I had to know, and there wasn't going to be any appeal because there weren't any grounds. Ferris had been sent out here for one purpose and all I was doing here in the winter sunshine of a Barcelona street was dodging around in the dust while he waited to put his foot on me.

So I didn't want to keep still.

"What kind of wheel?" I asked him.

"I don't know."

"Who was running it?"

He looked around him with his yellow eyes screwed up against the sun, as if he wasn't really listening. But he was listening. And so was I. "It's not in my area," he said at last.

"Did anyone get hit?"

"It's possible." A dead leaf blew against his shoe and he looked down at it with quiet attention.

"Are they switching controls?"

He smiled wearily. "They don't really know what they're doing."

The leaf blew away and he watched it go, and noticed the cockroach swivelling through the maze of dust round the manhole cover not far away. He walked over there and I swear to you I heard the faint crunch above the noise of the traffic.

He came slowly back.

Taking a breath I asked him: "Are they going to send someone else out there?"

"They'd like to. But they can't get anyone to go."

"It's that bad?"

He shrugged slightly and began walking and I fell into step and didn't say anything more in case he was going to answer.

"It's not so much a question of its being bad," he said reluctantly, "although that has a lot to do with it. They're also stuck for someone with peculiar qualities, and there's almost nobody at base who could tackle it, even if they could be persuaded to have a go. We're trying to get Flack in from Delhi, but he's not responding to signals."

I was slowly getting cold.

They're like that, in London. Two-faced, devious, treacherous. They are worse, really, when you're between missions than when you're working, because then you're relaxed and not looking for traps or thin ground or a rigged bang or a missing stair in the dark. You shouldn't ever relax: It can be fatal.

"Why can't those bastards put it on the line?" I asked Ferris suddenly, and he stopped walking.

"I'm not sure what you mean."

And of course he'd go on like that. Those would be his orders: to deny any suggestion that they were asking for me. I had to volunteer, for the sake of their conscience. *I* had to ask *them*—if I could muster the guts. There wasn't even any room for bargaining: I wasn't in any position to do that, and they knew it.

"Tell them to go to hell," I said.

"All right."

He stood gazing at me with his quiet cat's eyes, until I looked away.

"They're bloody usurers, you know that?"

He smiled faintly. "But they don't advertise."

He meant you had to go to them, when you were broke. And I was broke. They'd done this with Tucker and Wayne and Fosdyck and not many people knew about it but I was one. They'd been for the high jump, all three of them, and at the last minute they'd been thrown a final chance on the principle that letting a man go out doing something useful is sound economics: There's a chance of some profit in the stuff he sends back before he blows up and it saves the expense of the end-of-the-line debriefing that has to be done before he can be sent out to grass without any risk to the Bureau. It worked with Tucker and it worked with Fosdyck: They never got back. The last I saw of Wayne was in a clinic in Northampton, where they were teaching him to write with his foot.

I looked at Ferris.

"There's one thing I've got to know," I said, "isn't there?"

"I could think of several."

"Just one. I don't care about the rest." I looked around at the bare trees, the coloured magazines, the goldfish hanging from the surface in their bowls, while I tried to think how to put it, so that he couldn't fox me. He wouldn't lie, because if he lied this time it would amount, in sensitive and subtle ways, to attempted murder. "If I *don't* take this thing on, are they still going to fire me?"

He didn't hesitate because he knew I'd have to ask.

"Yes."

"With no other chance?"

"With no other chance."

I turned away from him and we walked on through the shadows of the bare boughs.

"All right," I said.

He nodded. "I'll find a phone."

Something small was moving along a crack in the paving stones and Ferris took a step towards it and I caught his arm and said through my teeth—"Leave that one, for God's sake. Just *that* one."

3

Finback

Then the whole thing fell out of the sky and I shut down and checked the trim and noted the emergency jettison switch on the left of centre before she began yawing badly across the runway with the tail coming up and the wheels bouncing and taking her in a series of wild leaps that forced my shoulders into the harness leaping again so I throttled up a degree but it looked like no bloody go.

The tower was trying to tell me something but it was just a lot of squawk and I didn't take any notice. When I pulled the canopy control the thing slid back with a bang and I glimpsed a blob of yellow to my left, then another, the emergency vehicles coming up to run parallel as the ground speed came down to ninety, eighty, seventy while she gave another leap and the tail came up so high that I hit the throttle harder than necessary and waited for the kick in the back, but the power was gone and that was that: I'd got some brakes and steering but one of the tyres must have burst because she was dipping badly to one side and trying to start a ground spin and I got worried because if she started doing that at sixty knots I'd be sitting in a centrifuge.

Stink of burnt rubber and kerosene and my own sweat as she

went dipping again, dragging, freeing and dragging as I tapped the brakes at short intervals to see what would happen. They had the sirens going outside now and the two yellow blobs came back into the picture as they began closing in. The speed was still dropping and she had all three wheels on the deck but we were still doing forty knots when the burst tyre came off and she dug in and began spinning to the left in a series of sickening swings that blacked me out as the blood piled to one side of my head: There was a rhythmic screeching as the undercarriage took the strain and the bare wheel went gouging across the runway, and at some time or other I saw the two yellow blobs grow very big as we took a swing towards them. Blacked out again.

Sirens dying away.

A face looking down.

"You all right?"

"Shit," I said.

They helped me out. Nearly fell over.

"You had some wind shear," Gilmore told me. We started walking over to the buildings.

"You're a bloody liar."

"They were trying to tell you." He linked his arm in mine and I shook it off. "Didn't you hear them?"

"I suppose so. I was busy, that's all."

"You guys wanna hop on?" someone called out. A Jeep was alongside us, still rocking on its springs.

"I'll walk," I told Gilmore.

"We're okay!" he called back and they shot off, leaving a lot of dust.

"It could've been a lot worse," Gilmore said cheerfully.

"Oh could it? I don't know how anyone ever manages to drive those bloody things."

"They're not easy, are they? But that could have happened to anyone at all—you know what wind shear means, as well as I do." He stopped suddenly and pulled me round. "Before we get in there and start putting it all down on paper you ought to bear it in mind that I'm your instructor, and as far as you're concerned that means Almighty God. I'm going to report wind shear as the cause of that accident and if you've got any other ideas I'd like to hear them now, not later."

"You're running this show," I said and walked on again, making him catch up. "There wasn't anything wrong with the controls; I don't mind telling them that."

"That's all I need."

"Not really. A pilot might help."

"Jesus," he said with a forced laugh, very annoyed, "you've been flying these kites for just three weeks! You think you can bring them down on a dinner plate?"

"Yes."

"Oh," he said, "you're one of those."

Later I went out and watched them haul the plane clear of the runway and start taking the wings off. There wasn't a lot of damage but they were going to have to replace the undercarriage and make stress tests, alignment checks, so forth.

"Squadron-leader Nesbitt?"

He looked down at me: I was sitting on the grass at the edge of the runway with my back to a numbered sign.

"Yes?"

"Joe says you have a ride into town tonight. Okay?"

"Okay."

Joe was the officer commanding the USAF base at Zaragoza. A ride into town meant a flight into Barcelona, a hundred and sixty miles east of here. One of the little things I'd learned since Ferris had sent me here was that Barcelona had *not* been the first available flight out of London. They could have put me on board a plane for Berlin or Paris or Rome about the same time or even earlier: There was a forty-five minute wait for the Iberia 149 and they'd shut me in the loo with a sack over my head because someone said the Yard had come out with an Identikit picture as a result of their interviews with the train passengers and it might look a lot like me.

But Berlin or Paris or Rome weren't within a hundred and sixty miles of the USAF base at Zaragoza, and Barcelona was. And there was another thing I'd learned since I'd got here: The RAF unit attached to the air base by courtesy of the American forces comprised only fifteen men, and their sole concern was with getting one pilot refresher-trained in advanced fighter handling. They *might* have got here before I was shot out to Barcelona—I wasn't sure, because whenever I started asking questions they pulled the zip—but the pilot they'd been sent out here to train was me, and no one else. Ferris had talked about "peculiar qualifications" and I was the only shadow executive in London between missions and with an updated degree of experience in military jet operation: I was only three months out of the routine simulator course at Norfolk.

And throw this in: Ferris had said the target area was "still undefined" but they needed someone with fluency in metropolitan Russian.

They normally put Egerton on to me when they've got some shit to shovel and can't find anyone to do it: He has that Old World fustian charm that cons you into believing you're dealing with a league of gentlemen; but this time they'd got their foot on my neck because there was a murder hunt going on throughout the British Isles and the Yard would have contacted Interpol and even here in north-east Spain I was already vulnerable.

The only hope I had of keeping out of sight until the Novikov thing blew over was by doing what the Bureau told me to do and going wherever it sent me. This was still my thinking, three weeks out of London: that I was on the run and would use the Nesbitt cover for all it was worth as my only means of staying free. But of course this was much too subjective. The larger truth was that London had a mission on the board and I was the executive and we were moving near zero.

I peeled off from Joe and his group in the Plaza de Madrid some time about eight o'clock. They said they'd heard of some sensational girls who could do things I'd never dreamed of, and I said that was quite possible but as a matter of fact I'd got an elderly aunt near the consulate who was worried about her drains and I'd promised to go and poke around with a coat-hanger.

Ferris was waiting for me when I arrived.

"Five-ten," I told him, "twelve stone, black eyes, dark skin, black moustache, beret, otherwise dressed like a clerk."

"Where?"

"Still outside the building. I had to come in the back way, over the dustbins."

"Oh," Charlie laughed, "that's Ignacio. He's sweet on Pepita." He rolled his chair to the window and looked down over his half-moon glasses.

"Are you sure?"

"Takes her to *Los Caracoles,* I can't say more than that."

I got a glance from Ferris meaning everything was all right, but it still wasn't easy to relax: The Interpol connection was still on my mind. Charlie was a sleeper and this place had the status of a safe-house and we were a hundred per cent secure according to the book; but we'd had a sleeper in Tehran on the top floor of the radio station building and London must have put half a dozen operations through there before something blew and the SAVAK sent in six armoured cars to surround the place and put a helicopter down on the roof and took seventeen minutes to do the snatch: two spooks and their field director and the communications man who'd been using Tehran radio for years, tinkering with aural cypher patterns on the Coca-Cola programmes.

The only one they didn't get was Sinclair and that was because he took a capsule: He was on his way through to Bahrain with his head full of stuff on a Near East network project the Bureau was going to run through Crowborough and the embassy and he obviously didn't trust himself because he couldn't stand pain. It was Sinclair, of course, they'd been after, and at the other end of the line we'd all breathed again and wished him peace but the point is that a safe-house is a safe-house until it's blown.

It can happen anywhere, and at any time.

"Oh Christ," I said when Ferris dropped the picture onto the table. It had everything: the non-committal eyes, the sharp nose, the lopsided jaw and the go-to-hell line of the mouth. "Where did you get this?"

"Liaison asked the Yard for a copy."

"Going a bit close, weren't they?"

"They knew what they were doing." His yellow cat's eyes lingered on me. "Which is more than you can say."

"Leave the poor sod alone," Charlie told him. He was putting a tie on, his huge hands losing track of it.

I looked at the picture again, avoiding Ferris. The Novikov

thing had been a gross breach of security and it had shaken the Bureau and they'd lost their faith in me and that was why they were kicking me into a shut-ended mission and Ferris thought they were right, and so did I. But he didn't have to look at me like that. I've done a bit of good, too, along the line.

"It's in the London papers," he told me in disapproval.

"I don't give a shit!" I said and my voice cracked and I saw Charlie look up quickly, shocked. "It was something I had to do —understand?" Ferris went on watching me, pleased to have drawn so much blood from such a small scratch. I watched him back and thought of other things to say and heard myself saying them in my mind, enjoying them, things about Novikov, like he'd never made a sound, things like that. Then I slid the Identikit thing across the table to him and turned away and saw Charlie reaching for a jacket, blue serge, the cleaner's tab still on it.

"Very sharp," I said, knowing better than to help him on with it. "Are you cutting out Ignacio?"

"No. Little Sevillian dolly. Mastectomy." He jerked the lapels straight. "That's why she goes for me." The rubber tyres squawked across the floor. "Lots of Carlos Primero for the good Mr. Ferris. Help yourself," he said to me, "to whatever you fancy."

By the show he was making I assumed he'd been asked to leave the two of us alone and that would be logical because the tower had confirmed wind shear and Gilmore had told me he wanted ten more flying hours with this type so we must be getting pretty close to it and I hadn't had any briefing. We could trust Charlie, of course, or we wouldn't be meeting here; but no one—strictly no one—is given access to information that doesn't specifically concern him. The risk of being picked up and put under implemented interrogation is always present at any time and in any place, and the less we know the less we can give away when it comes to the breaking point.

When the door was shut Ferris stood for half a minute with his sandy head tilted and his eyes moving by degrees around the room, looking at nothing. We could hear the sound of the tyres on the landing outside and the whine of the lift as it came up from below; then the door rattled shut and the whine began again, rather lighter than before: Presumably the counterweights were less heavy than the lift cage plus Charlie and put less strain on the motor.

Ferris went on listening. The door of the lift may have closed by now—I couldn't tell; there were other sounds from below: street traffic, someone on a phone, the voice of the chestnut vendor, a dustbin lid banging in the rear. Ferris waited another fifteen seconds and then padded across the floor and opened the door and looked out, listening again.

He wasn't normally like this: The field directors aren't executives and they take security for granted; all they have to do if something blows is to get out as fast as they can, and perhaps that makes them less cautious. Tonight Ferris was nervy and I didn't like that: One of the things your director in the field is supposed to do is to assure you, by his whole attitude, that things are running perfectly and you're going to come out all right.

He closed the door and came padding back in his soft green shoes, looking at the spiders in their transparent plastic boxes as he passed the bench.

"They've got a lethal bite, haven't they?"

"It depends on your condition," I said. "They pack about the same kick as a rattlesnake." Charlie had filled me in.

Ferris peered down at them, fascinated. "They're so small."

"For Christ's sake don't tread on them. He has them flown in from Arizona."

He tapped a box to make one of them move, then lost interest and padded past me and sat on Charlie's bed. "How are the flying lessons?"

"All right."

"Nearly through, I'm told."

"Another two days."

"Did you get any prelim briefing out there?"

"Only on flying."

He looked up quickly. "Well they wouldn't have briefed you on anything else, would they?"

"How the hell should I know?" I was getting fed up with his studied reproofs. "Nobody's told me who that chap Gilmore is—he could be Bureau for all I know, couldn't he?"

"Unlikely," he said after a moment. "You see, we—"

"Oh for Christ's sake do your job, Ferris. If you're my director in the field for this one then bloody well say so, and if you're not then tell me who is."

I went over to the fridge in the corner and found some milk and drank it from the carton, bringing it with me, calcium for the nerves. All right, a lot of it was characteristic paranoia and a lot of it was guilt, but he ought to understand that: it was what he was for, to guide me and send me out with my armour shining and my head held high and some—at least some—of the fear assuaged in the pit of my shrinking gut.

Because this was likely to be the last go, and we both knew that. Not because there wouldn't be a chance in hell of getting out at the other end—there's always a chance—but because they didn't want me back. And I don't know how those poor devils do it, standing on the trap with a good breakfast inside them and a parting joke for the priest, I'm not like that, I don't intend to go out doing *nothing,* I'm going to fight like a cat in a sack, and if you've ever tried drowning one you'll know what I mean.

"You're rather touchy," Ferris said.

"Didn't think you'd notice."

He waited five seconds and then said: "All right, I'm your director and this session has got to be your field briefing, because you obviously can't get back into London and there isn't enough time anyway. Time," he said and swung a glance at me, "is very short as things are. Otherwise we'd have extended your flying hours by another fifty, which Gilmore has been bleating at us to do."

I couldn't think of anything useful to say. The gut just shrank a little more.

"A wheel has come off, as I told you, in Central Asia. But we're not sending you out there to put it back on; this isn't the situation you had to face in Tunisia. This is *your* mission exclusively and not the tag-end of someone else's. Incidentally, the code-name for the mission is Slingshot. Time is short but that doesn't mean Control hasn't been able to set everything up satisfactorily while you've been learning to fly those things in Zaragoza. We've got total access"—he gave an amused snort for some reason—"and we've got reasonable cover. The target is precise and the field hasn't any *specific* opposition deployed." He got off the bed and put his thin freckled hands into the pockets of his mac and wandered about. "The get-out point can't be defined because it'll depend on local conditions, but you'll be close to a neutral frontier. You won't be, for instance, anywhere like Moscow. I hope all this makes you feel a little better."

It looked all right. They weren't going to drop me into a mess someone else had made and there wasn't any opposition—except of course for the entire population of the U.S.S.R., including the Army. But they were non-specific.

"Let's start with the access," I said. "What frontier?"

"In effect, there won't be any. You'll be going too fast."

I felt another slight squeezing of the gut. "I'm not going in with one of those things?" I meant the FM-30's I'd been flying at Zaragoza.

"Oh no. You wouldn't get very far, would you? No, they've got a Finback lined up for you in West Germany, complete with markings."

"A *Finback?*"

"That's right."

NATO designation for the Soviet MiG-28D, duo-syllabic F group: Fishbed, Foxbat, Flogger, so forth. I said: "Jesus Christ, where did they get it?"

"One of their defectors put it down in Alaska, in July last year. We—"

"*That* one?"

"That one."

I suppose he was enjoying himself in a way. The field directors get a certain amount of glory spilling over from London when Control comes up with something exotic or spectacular: Access is a phase where the planners can use their creative imagination and they always try for something elegant—it's a sophisticated exercise and the spotlight's on them and they can rake in a lot of kudos if they devise something effective, especially if the heat's on and they've got the clock to beat. The one we like was when they dropped Dawkins smack in the middle of the sports stadium in San Salvador by parachute in broad daylight and dressed up as a clown, five minutes before President La Paz was due there to make a speech—Dawkins said he was advertising for the local circus. It was an anti-terrorist thing and London had had exactly *three hours* to get a man in there so they'd used a private plane and one of our sleepers, unsuccessfully because La Paz took a magnum in the rib cage before we could do anything, but that didn't spoil the score for the access.

Of course they don't work at the spectacular for its own sake: The prime requirement of access is that it's the *best* way in to the target area, meaning quickest, safest, most discreet, so forth. If the best way in is through a main drain then you've got to crawl through the bloody thing and hope there's more than one end.

This was the first time they'd thought of putting a man into Russia in a MiG-28D with Russian markings and that was why Ferris was looking pleased.

"How long have I got with it?" I asked him. Time was short, fair enough, but it hadn't got to be *that* short.

"You mean to train with it?" He was looking away.

"Yes."

"They've got a simulator for you."

"All right, but—"

I left it but he didn't say anything.

"Well how long?"

"We can't actually let you *fly* it," he said a little impatiently, "till you go in."

"You're joking."

"No. Sorry."

"You mean *no* training?"

"No training. I realise it doesn't—"

"Have you gone out of your bloody mind?"

"These are not," he said with a sigh, "my instructions."

"All right, who's running this? Who's my control?"

He hesitated.

"Parkis."

"*Parkis?*"

He turned away. I began saying something else, then shut up.

This really wasn't looking terribly good. They'd thrown me a last-ditch operation to give me a chance of going out with a good record; fair enough, at least I knew the score. But I hadn't known they were putting me into a potent, sensitive fifteen-hundred-mile-per-hour fighter-interceptor without even one hour's familiarisation with it in the air. And this was for the *access* phase, when mission-risk is normally at a minimum.

And Parkis was my control.

"Why don't they just send me a letter-bomb?"

Ferris came wandering back in his soft shoes, keeping his voice low and speaking in short sustained bursts: "You'll have to stop taking things so personally, Quiller, if we're going to get this off the ground. There *are* personal considerations, of course: they're reluctant to fire you summarily and they obviously feel you can do this job better than anyone else available at the moment—all well and good. But don't make the mistake of thinking they're just giving you the first bit of work that's come along." He stopped moving around and stood facing me, very concerned. "This is a major operation, and they've been working the clock round on it for more than a month. You know Parkis—anything he takes on has got to be big, and it's got to work. Above all, it's got to *succeed*. Am I getting anything across?"

"Sales talk."

"I hope you're joking."

"Not really."

I wanted to make him work for it. I wanted him to tell me more than I needed to know. Because I didn't trust London, not on this one.

"There were three planners," he said with forced patience. "Parkis, Mildmay and Egerton. That alone shows you the size of this operation. They had to rope in the RAF and carry out screening in depth. They had to get facilities from NATO and provide an extensive blackout on God knows how many security movements. And they had to ask the USAF for that Finback, in good condition and ready to fly. I want you to understand that everything has been worked out, exhaustively—including the access."

This was impressive but it didn't change anything.

"I've still got to take that thing off the ground without any training in it."

"You're being trained with the FM-30 at Zaragoza because it's the closest thing we've got to the Finback. The two particular planes you've been using had their cockpit layout modified to resemble the Finback as far as possible. What I'm saying is that Control is fully aware of the risk in the access phase, and has tried to do everything to decrease it."

"Good of him."

But of course it had to be true. If Parkis lost me on the run in he'd lose the mission and he knew that.

"There are always certain areas of high risk," Ferris said reasonably, "in any operation. They're not usually in the access phase. In this one they are. It's possible that Parkis wanted you for this one because he knows you do your best work when the risks are high."

I turned away and looked out of the window and didn't like the view but it was better than Ferris. "Parkis wants me for this one," I said, "because he's got his boot on my balls and he knows I can't get away. So don't give me any bullshit." I turned round again. "Is that thing in Europe now?"

"Yes. It's waiting for you at Fürstenfeldbruck, ten miles from Dachau."

"How did they get it there?"

"In a transport plane."

"Where was it before?"

"In California."

"They make a model of it?"

"That's right."

It looked logical enough. London wanted to inject me into Soviet airspace without getting me shot down, so it had to be in a Russian plane; and I couldn't fly the thing anywhere in the West without people noticing, because that Finback had made the front page when it had dropped into Alaska and everyone knew where it was—and where it ought to be. That's why they'd made a model.

That bit didn't worry me. But both shoulders were still bruised and I could still feel those sickening swings this afternoon when the FM had begun spinning, and the primitive brain was afraid and wouldn't give me any peace. I stood a good chance of finishing up as a lump of brawn compacted into the front end of a tin can on a mountainside maybe three days from now and the organism was scared sick and it affected my thinking.

"Cockpit layout's one thing," I told Ferris. "What about actual handling characteristics?"

"You'll have the simulator at Fürstenfeldbruck, and Gilmore's going to be with you the whole time, right up until take-off."

"Good old Gilmore." I wished I could stop sweating.

"He's told us, in any case, that the handling characteristics aren't too different. He chose the FM-30 himself, right at the beginning. The least dissimilarity is in level flight and on fast turns. On take-off you'll find less lift, because the Finback can use larger outboard fuel tanks than the FM."

He was trying to sound very reasonable, very relaxed.

"What about landing?"

"You won't be landing it anywhere," he said. "This is a one-way flight."

4

Fürstenfeldbruck

"Haben Sie etwas zu melden?"

   "Nein, Her Hauptmann."

   "Ist jemand vorbeigekommen?"

   "Nur der amerikanische Offizier der Wache auf seinem Rundang."

   "Um wieviel Uhr war das?"

   "Mitternacht, Herr Hauptmann."

   "Nun gut. Das hier ist Herr Nesbitt."

   "Ihren Ausweis bitte, mein Herr."

   "Jawohl, hier ist er."

   "Danke, mein Herr."

He gave it back to me.

   "Wissen Sie was die Losung ist?"

   "Katapult," I told him.

   "Schon richtig, mein Herr."

The two dogs leaned against their harness, scenting, their eyes luminous in the lamplight.

"They are war-trained," Böcker told me. "Please don't make any sudden movement." He motioned the guard to hurry: It was freezing tonight and a drizzle was coming down, webby against

our faces. The hangar loomed above us, the heights of its
camouflaged façade lost in the rain-haze.

The two dog handlers stood firm while the guard went back into
his box and used a telephone, giving his name and service number
and repeating the password; then he asked for the door to be
opened.

"How long has the weather been like this?" I asked Böcker. As
a courtesy he always spoke to me in English.

"A week. Perhaps ten days. It's rather like London, don't you
think?" He had an almost soundless laugh that made his little
jokes seem confidential, a mannerism he might have developed
during his career in West German Counterintelligence. He called
to the guard.

"Haben Sie sich jetzt beschäftigt?"

"Ich habees ihnen gesagt, Herr Hauptmann."

We sank lower into our collars and I studied Hans Böcker while
his head was turned away to watch the guard. I needed to know
all their faces, and who they were, and what they did. Böcker was
a jolly sort, overweight and blond with a red face and small bright
eyes shining from puffs of flesh; his manner was confidential and
he spoke softly, a plump hand on my arm to remind me that this
was for my ears only. His dossier, which Ferris had got for me
through NATO channels, showed that his cover identity as Army
captain was for the Fürstenfeldbruck assignment only.

Ferris had said: "You'll find security's pretty good up there.
They don't know what we're doing but they know London's asked
for strict hush. And Böcker is first-class: We've checked him out."

Ferris was joining me here in the morning.

We could hear a jingle of keys from inside the hangar, echoing;
then the small door near the guard hut pulled open and a beam of
light struck across us, blinding me.

Then the whole thing started all over again except that this time
it was in English: Böcker introduced himself and presented me
and I showed my security card and told them the password and
we went inside and I heard one of the dogs give a low sound in its
throat. I was glad when the door was shut because I can't stand
those bloody things; they've got teeth like sharks.

I suppose I was a bit on edge in any case, because here it was:
the Finback.

It was standing all by itself in the middle of the hangar, draped in black shrouds under the cluster of lights. I couldn't see anything of its surfaces, just the general shape under the covers; and it stood there in a silence so total that it was hard to understand, considering the noise it was going to make when we took it into the open; but I could smell it: the subtle aromatic amalgam of metal, rubber, plastics, oils, fuel, coolant, and the after-smell of the heat that had burned in it on its way through the sky.

"You would like the covers removed?" Böcker asked me.

"What? Yes."

Two of the guards began work on it. There were four in here, two German and two American, all of them in uniform and carrying side-arms. A telephone rang and one of them went to answer it and came back but didn't say anything to Böcker.

"It's quite pretty," he said to me, and gave a secret laugh.

"Is it?"

I didn't think that was the word: The thing just looked tremendously potent, like an edged instrument for cutting the sky into swathes, though it had a slightly old-fashioned look, because of the way it stood high on the undercarriage and because of the rectangular air intakes, which looked like a couple of boxes stuck onto the sides. But that was because it was on the ground, out of its element like a landed fish. In the air I knew it would look blade-sharp and effective; but I would never, of course, see it in the air.

Basically it was a low-aspect-ration design with high-mounted delta wings and the twin air ducts starting from below the cockpit and flaring back to the engines and beyond them to the six-foot-diameter exhaust nozzles halfway along the tail unit. I walked round it, and Böcker and the guards stayed where they were, for which I was glad: I felt a sense of assignation with the machine, because I was going to be the last man ever to fly it and if I got things right it could do a lot for me and if I got things wrong it would kill me.

It was very quiet in the hangar and my footsteps grated on the concrete as I ducked under the plane and looked at the other side. It didn't have a lot in common with the FM-30 as far as the configuration was concerned, though that didn't mean its handling characteristics were as different to the same degree. This model had a retractable airbrake mounted well aft, almost underneath the exhaust nozzles, and the undercarriage folded backward and inward instead of forward and inward; there were also six underwing missile pylons, which had been adapted to sling centre-line fuel tanks to complement the wing pods.

When I climbed the steps I heard someone move closer, but it was probably a coincidence: They knew I was allowed to look into the cockpit and maybe I was touchy, anticipating some kind of opposition. They would also be touchy, since this machine had tighter security wraps than any other in Europe and it was going to be their neck if someone got through.

Ferris hadn't been selling me short: When I pulled the canopy back I saw that the cockpit layout was very like the FM-30's; and for the first time I relaxed a little and thought there might be just a chance of pushing through with this and coming out at the other end and giving those bastards in London the stuff they wanted.

I didn't know what it was, yet. Ferris had played it very close to the chest in Barcelona and I'd got the impression that the planning stage wasn't finished even now and that he was standing by for new instructions to pass on to me as soon as they were ready. There was also the smell of sealed orders about this operation and I didn't like it but there wasn't anything I could do about it. Our feelings vary on this subject: Some of the executives like leaving it all to Control, so they simply go for the selected targets and get there and do the job they've been told to do. These types work well for people like Parkis because Parkis is good at winding them up and pointing them in the right direction with everything already built in at the start so that all they have to do is respond to negative feedback till they hit the objective. His rationale is that if they knew the size of the background politics it'd give them purpose-tremor so that right at the critical time when they were meant to be making a document filch or blowing a cell or getting a contact across they'd just go to pieces and stand there doing it in their trousers.

The rest of us prefer to know what's happening behind the scenes because it gives us a chance of switching tactics or changing course according to the run of events: We like the responsibility and it makes us feel a bit less like a robot on its way to a toy fair but the fact remains that if Control or your director in the field doesn't want to tell you anything then it's a waste of time asking.

All I knew about this one was the access, and even the info on that was incomplete. All I really knew was that in approximately fifty-six hours from now they were going to send me into Soviet airspace in a Soviet aircraft and hope no one would notice.

"All right, we'll try putting her down now."

"We can skip that bit."

"You mean landing?"

"Yes."

"Why?"

Watch it.

"I'd like to get those turns right."

"You're not doing badly. I want you to put her down during this session because that'll just leave us evasive action to go through."

"If you say so."

You've got to watch security every second and I'd nearly blown it. All right, Thompson was career RAF and London had deep-screened him and he knew what a Finback was but he might *not* have been told it was a one-way flight and that I wasn't going to make a landing. And I'd almost told him.

Watch everything.

And concentrate.

"Okay, we'll go into the approach."

"What altitude?"

"Get down to three thousand feet and we'll start from there. But make a full circuit."

I put the column forward and used twenty degrees of bank to the left, watching the horizon and altitude.

"That's fine."

I could see Thompson in his glass-panelled control box in front of the simulator. He sat crouched with his headset on, watching the slave screen on the console; he never looked up at me through the windscreen, even when he had to give a sharp command.

"You're going too wide."

I corrected.

We'd been working for two hours on this session, nearly seven hours so far for the day. Thompson had wanted more frequent breaks but I'd kept him at it because for me any kind of learning has got to be intensive. I think he was getting fed up.

"What have you got now?"

"Three thousand five."

He'd got the same reading but he wanted to hear how fast I answered so that he'd know I was watching the right things. During the first hour I'd looked all over the control panel for missing FM-30 features and he'd got worried.

"Make another circuit. Don't forget that you've got a twelve-thousand-foot runway, two thousand feet longer than at Zaragoza."

We kept at it. The clock on the facia said 18:05.

"Right. Level out. *Level out now.* Less lift than the FM, remember?"

I overcorrected and the nose came up too high and I said shit and pushed it down again and thought Ferris might have told me it was a one-way trip because these bloody things were unlandable.

"Watch your altitude."

There wasn't any lift at all: We were dropping out of the sky and I trimmed again and brought the flaps down and saw her hit a wall on the air-speed indicator.

"Too soon. Ease off."

It took another ten minutes and I made the overcorrections and hit the power too late because she was going down like a stone and I panicked and Thompson went on talking into my headset, repeating himself so often that I didn't have enough time to assess anything for myself. The angle of approach was all right and we were lined up with the wings level but I cut the power too soon and we hit the deck and lit up the failure sign and I sat there thinking Christ we're going to go through all that again till I've got it right and it's going to be a total waste of time because I'm never going to need it and I can't tell him that.

"All right, here's the first one."

I watched the screen.

"It's a MiG-21 and it's seen you and it's closing. What's the distance?"

"A mile."

"A mile and a half at this point. Okay, we'll stop the action. Don't forget to turn *into* the missile's trajectory. It's the only way you can beat it. You just go into a very high-g turn, as tight as you can. Right—action."

The shape on the screen began moving again and a thin white cylinder shot forward from it.

"Missile fired."

I used the rudder and ailerons and glanced across the dials to check the degree of turn and pushed it a bit more and concentrated on the missile.

"More g's."

The cloudscape swung on the screen but the white cylinder went on growing.

"You're too slow. You've got to turn on a sixpence."

Pushed everything hard over but the missile kept coming in.

"More g's. But it's too late anyway."

I was braced forward against the harness and this was the limit of turn but the thing on the screen was rapidly filling it and the screen went white and a word jumped into the frame:

HIT.

I looked up through the windscreen and saw Thompson taking a gulp of tea.

"You're a goner," he said in a moment. "We'll try again, and look—the idea is to leave it as late as you can, so when you go into the turn you're as close to the missile as you can get in safety. The distance has got to be so short that it can't make the turn when you do: You don't give it enough room to manoeuvre. Okay? But you did two things wrong: You left it too late and you turned too wide. You're working on a very narrow margin, you see, between hit and miss. Let's try it again."

The screen showed a cloudscape and the silhouette of the MiG.

"Course is converging. But hold it."

The white cylinder shot forward of the plane.

"Missile fired. Wait. Wait. *Wait.*"

The thing was curving in fast and I didn't look at anything else.

"Turn. All you've got."

I braced myself and the g's piled up on the dials till I could almost feel them.

"Tighter than that."

Gave it the limit but too late and the red letters jumped into the frame:

HIT.

For the first time he looked up in his glass-panelled booth.

"Mr. Nesbitt, that Finback is very rugged. You couldn't make this degree of turn at Mach 1 in the FM-30 but you *can* do it in a Finback. I realise you think you're going to break the wings off but that won't happen. Now we'll do it again."

We did it again and we got HIT.

This was at 19:22.

MiG-19 and much slower, coming at Mach .98.

HIT.

"You should have beaten that one."

Shuddup.

MiG-23 and much faster.

HIT.

MiG-25—the Foxbat and very fast indeed at Mach 1.8.

HIT.

MiG-19 again. *Wait. Turn.*

MISS.

"More like it," Thompson said.

We went on trying.

HIT.

HIT.

MISS.

HIT.

MISS.

"Evens," Thompson said, and drank some more tea.

20:06.

HIT.

MISS.

MISS.

"Twice running."

Shuddup.

Concentrate.

MISS.

HIT.

MISS.

MISS.

MISS.

"You've got it now all right."

MISS.

20:51.

"Give me the Foxbat again." That was the fastest.

"Fair enough. Coming at Mach 2.6."

HIT.

"Again."

MISS.

"Again."

MISS.

"Again."

MISS.

"Right-ho. Call it a day." He sounded exhausted.

"I think that wraps it up," Ferris said.

He pulled the collar of his mac a bit higher. It was still drizzling, and colder today at this time: an hour after first light.

"All right," I told him.

We stood for a while not speaking again, looking around us. About a hundred yards away one of the USAF crew was dragging a pair of chocks towards the F-111 at the end of the line. Half an hour ago a BfV security man had walked across the tarmac to check on us, wondering what we were doing standing here in the middle of nowhere in the rain. We didn't spell it out for him.

I began clumping my feet up and down. They'd given me a heavier flying-jacket than the one I'd brought here from Zaragoza, but it was still bloody cold.

"Recap," Ferris said, and crouched down on his haunches to ease his legs. I did the same.

"Right. I'm to expect the Soviet radar stations to start picking me up as soon as I begin climbing. At that point I shall be heading south, parallel with the border and twenty-five miles into their airspace. As Colonel Nikolai Voronov I can—"

"You start climbing near a military field."

"Right. Near enough to give the impression I've just taken off from it. As Colonel Voronov of the Red Air Force I'll respond to any radio calls with the cover story that I'm carrying out a fuel-range test, which will explain all those extra tanks. Testing has to be done between thirty and forty thousand feet and any request to fly lower than thirty thousand or make a landing should be resisted for this reason."

"Use a lot of authority," Ferris said, and pulled his collar higher. "Yell at them over the radio. They're shit-scared of authority."

"Noted."

I recapped on the main elements: communications, cut-off points, rdv procedures, local direction, so forth; but most of this stuff was abstract and I'd stopped asking him for specifics because he'd said it was too early. It was beginning to look like sealed orders all the way and I assumed London was hog-tied by the security demands of the USAF, the RAF, NATO and the BfV, since all four parties were contributing to the mission.

It was the first time I'd taken on an operation with so much exposure at the outset. The first phase of any mission—the access— is normally sacrosanct in terms of secrecy, simply because the most effective way of blowing up a project is to hit it before it can start. With this one the access was blown if anyone talked: any one of those people who knew that a front-line Soviet aircraft was parked here under wraps at Fürstenfeldbruck. At a rough guess there must be more than a dozen of them, including the crew of the Lockheed C5-A Galaxie that had brought the Finback across the Atlantic and the guards now protecting it. Already at this stage of the briefing I could see why London couldn't find anybody to take this one on. It was much more, and much worse, than sensitive. It was vulnerable.

This was probably why Ferris looked so bloody sour.

"Photographs," I said, "of X and Y at low altitude. The film—"

"You'll be given the actual locations at flight briefing," he said, looking away.

"Thank Christ for that." I like as much data as I can get as early as possible, so that I've got time to feed it in. I hate being thrown a mass of stuff at the last minute when I'm busy working on the access.

"I don't like this one," Ferris swung a sharp look at me, "any more than you do."

"Bad luck. Did you volunteer for it, or did they catch you knocking off some bastard in a train?"

We crouched like a couple of half-drowned monkeys in the rain, snapping at each other, while in the background Parkis and his people were completing and perfecting their glorious brainchild that we were expected to take over when they were ready. I wished them luck. They'd come up with an access that was going to be about as safe as a duckshoot with me as the duck, and the target area they'd picked was about the most desolate bit of waste ground on the face of the planet: latitude 47° N by longitude 82° E in the middle of winter; work that one out.

"Signals," Ferris said.

"Through Chechevitsin in Yelingrad for London via Moscow. What about alerts?"

The man was nearer now. I'd been watching him.

"Use your contacts in place."

"Or cross the border."

"Or do that."

The man had a waddling gait; I know people by their walk.

"Get out through Sinkiang."

"If you're pushed."

"Otherwise try Pakistan."

"The end phase," he said, "is likely to be rather fluid."

I didn't follow up. It was my belief that while Parkis and his people were completing and perfecting their glorious brainchild they were building into its complexities a small but deliberate flaw designed to cut me off in the final hours of the mission and remove me from the London intelligence field as an expendable embarrassment.

"Böcker," I said.

"I beg your pardon?"

"Herr Böcker is coming."

Ferris looked up. "Now what does he want?" We straightened our legs and went on talking while we waited. "You're finished with the simulator, Thompson says."

"Yes."

"I hope you're feeling more confident."

"I'll be all right once I've got the bloody thing off the ground."

"Your flight briefing starts this evening at six o'clock. Why don't you hop into town today and shake yourself loose a bit? Get rid of the tension." He sounded terribly casual.

"Fair enough."

"I am sorry to disturb you, gentlemen!"

"'Morning, Hans. Not disturbing."

"Your embassy in Bonn was on the line. The cultural attaché would be obliged if you'd call him back."

"All right."

Ferris left us, hurrying through the drizzle with his head down and his mac flapping.

"No one seemed to know where you were, Mr. Nesbitt. I always find that a distinct advantage myself—to be difficult to find." A soundless laugh, his cheeks wobbling with it.

"How right you are. That limousine, by the way."

We began walking towards the buildings.

"Ah yes." He was right on to it. "They are our friends, of course."

It was a large black Mercedes and I'd seen it standing there at the boundary fence for most of yesterday. There were two men leaning on it, identically dressed and watching the aircraft on the north side of the hangars.

"Are they always there?"

He shrugged amiably. "Nearly always."

"I don't think much of their cover."

He bubbled happily at this. "You are familiar with their thinking, I am sure. In Russia only the *nachalstvo* drive about in large black limousines, and no one dares to question their movements. They believe it is the same in the West, and therefore station their cars where they please—quite often near airfields and missile sites." His hand rested for a moment on my arm. "You may be quite sure, Squadron-leader, that when your aircraft leaves its hangar before dawn tomorrow, these two gentlemen will be safely at police headquarters on a minor charge."

I saw Ferris for a few minutes in the base operations office. He said the embassy call had conveyed a London signal asking for confirmation that Slingshot was ready to go into access phase at first light tomorrow, 7:47 local time.

"Except for flight briefing and clearance," I said.

"We're giving you those tonight."

"Then we can go."

"That's what I told them," he nodded.

5

Swallow

"You like that?"

"Yes," I said.

"Tell me what you like. Tell me," she said, taking her mouth away for a moment, "what drives you crazy."

"You drive me crazy," I said, "whatever you do."

She started again and I shut my eyes and stroked her short thick hair, listening to what she was doing. The glare of the wintry light from the window was white against my eyelids, and I kept seeing the red word jump into the screen: HIT.

But we'd beaten that one: The last three had been misses, even with the Foxbat. There wasn't anything to worry about.

"This is the way?" she asked me.

"Yes. That is the way."

I wouldn't have been able to take it much longer if I hadn't been letting the brain run on. The thoughts in the brain weren't very sexy. If they were going to cut me off in the end phase and leave me hanging on the wire then I would do what I could to confound their bloody enterprise: get out and go to ground somewhere, and if possible leave evidence of death.

"You do not touch me," she said, and took her mouth away to

get her breath back. So I touched her and she jerked her thighs as if I'd released a spring. She'd come into the car park outside the hotel just after me, and we'd noticed each other and that was that. She was young, pretty, blonde and sun-tanned, with nothing very interesting about her; but I agreed we should go up to her room because that was what I was here for. She said she would speak English, because it was very bad and she would like me to correct her as often as possible so that she could improve.

"Oh God," she said on her breath, "you are fantastic. . . . I have never known a man like you. . . ."

It was a strictly sales-training compliment and I'd realised by now that she was practised to the point of pretending she was virginal and inexperienced: "You like this?" and so forth. I didn't think she was run by the hotel but she may have been free-lancing with a pitch here, on commission.

"Halt, bitte! Ich kann nicht mehr!"

She was forgetting her English now. At first I'd thought she was a lesbian and professional enough not to let it show; but now she was getting involved and her honey-brown shoulders had slid to the floor and she was arched upside-down across the edge of the bed, so I buried my mouth in the thick triangle of hair that reached almost to her navel, and she began thrashing about and saying things in German again.

"Noch einmal-mach' es noch einmal!"

At some time I thought I heard a knock at the door but I let it go because I'd checked for security on my way here and it was satisfactory; the only trouble I'd had was in flushing the man Böcker had obviously sent along on my tail when I'd left the airfield; it was good security but I don't like being mothered.

"Du bist so schön," she was gasping, and the choice of the word was lesbian so I assumed she was a bi, which was why she'd been able to get involved. We started all over again and I stopped thinking about the screen and the silhouette and about the high degree of risk on take-off and about the fact that for the first time in my life I was considered expendable.

Later we found ourselves lying across each other on the floor, our eyes shut and our sweat cooling, the quietness coming back.

"God," she whispered, "I need to drink."

"You need 'a' drink," I said and she laughed softly.

I fetched her some water and she drank and asked for more. She'd seen me at the airfield, she said: She had a brother working there as a technician—did I know him? His name was Max.

I said I didn't know him.

"You are pilot?"

"Yes and no."

"Yes and no?"

"More water?"

"No thank you." She got off the floor and kissed me and got a comb from her big leather bag and went over to the mirror, leaving the bag open. "Max knows all the pilots, because he is technician on airplanes. How long will you be at Fürstenfeldbruck, darling?"

"I can't really say."

She lit a cigarette and followed me as far as the shower. "You must stay a long time," she told me, "and we will meet with frequency. Are you here on special work?"

"Not really."

"Max said there was an Englander here on special work."

I turned the tap to cold and took the shock and turned it off. She handed me the towel.

"Well you see," I said, "I mustn't really talk about it."

She rubbed my back dry, dropping some ash on my foot.

"But I never tell about things. Max tells me many things, and he knows it is safe with me. You must be special pilot, or maybe technician." She threw the towel onto the linen basket and walked into the bedroom with her arm round me. "I think you are someone very important in your work. I guess good at these things, darling."

" 'I'm good at guessing things,' " I said, and she repeated it slowly.

"You are beautiful teacher." She put her hands down and stroked me. "You will teach me about this too." Some more ash dropped and she went over to stub out the cigarette. "Now tell me what is the work that you do—it must be exciting. I will never tell anyone, never." She came back, walking with a swing of the hips that started me thinking about bed again, so I started putting my clothes on.

"I promise," she said. "You can trust me, darling."

I looked into her eyes. "I really believe I could."

"But of course!" She kissed me generously.

"The thing is," I said doubtfully, "you might not understand, even if I told you. It's rather technical."

"You forget my brother is technician."

I pulled the zipper up and got my polo-neck sweater. "That's perfectly true, of course. Well, I'm at Fürstenfeldbruck to work on a new system they're developing. It's called the Directional U-beam Kinetic Sensor. We call it the DUKS for short." I pulled the sweater over my head. "The key component is the ARS, which is short for Annular Reciprocating Speculum."

"But I have heard of that!" she said excitedly. "Max has talked to me of it."

"Really? Then I'm not telling you anything new."

"Oh yes! He is only on the outside—outside part—"

"On the fringe."

"Yes. Fringe."

"Well, the big question in all our minds over there is to do with the actual *fit* of these components." I picked up her tortoise-shell comb from where she'd left it near her bag, which was still open a couple of inches. Going across to the mirror I said: "Expressed technically, the big question is: Exactly how *tight* is a DUKS ARS?"

In the mirror I watched her listening intently, her blond head on one side. "Of course," I told her, "we're already onto a theory. But that's *Top Secret*, and I ought not to—"

"But darling, you said you would trust me!" She came up behind me and put her arms round my waist, resting her head on my shoulder. "You promised."

"I suppose I did." I stroked her head. "Well, our theory is that it must be watertight, or it wouldn't float."

"What about over there?" Ferris said.

The Galaxie transport was standing on the far side of the tarmac from the hangars, only just visible in the slanting rain. We pulled our collars tight and trudged across to it under the main perimeter lamps, looking for movement and not seeing any. It was only 6:15 in the evening but the weather had grounded all aircraft, and the crews were off duty.

At the top of the steps I asked Ferris: "Have you got permission to board this thing?"

"No, but that doesn't matter."

"As long as they don't set those bloody dogs on us."

The main fuselage was cavernous and we sat like a couple of half-drowned Jonahs. "We'll only be here five minutes," Ferris said, "because you've got most of it."

I didn't ask him if he'd had any new signals. In final briefing and recap the thing is to listen as hard as you can because it's your last chance to get it right and if you don't get it right you can blow the whole thing anywhere along the line.

Ferris lowered himself onto a stack of life-jackets and brushed some of the rain off his mac. The only light in here came through the small round windows, and we could hardly see each other.

"There are one or two things we didn't spell out," he said in a moment, "like motivation, the rationale for various phases and things like that. You ought to know, for instance, why they planned this kind of access. You're being put into an area that nobody can reach from the West without an awful lot of complications; any form of public transport or the use of your own car would need months of form-filling for Intourist plus elaborate and substantial cover. A moon-drop wouldn't work because you'd be shot down the minute you crossed the frontier—*any* frontier. You could go in by road through Sinkiang from China or Afghanistan or Kashmir, but apart from frontier difficulties you'd have to spend half your time in ox-wagons if you could find a road that wasn't closed by snow at this time of the year. So despite the delays we've had because of training procedures, the *fastest* access is military plane, and that plane has to be Russian."

My eyes were accommodating now and I could watch his face. Ferris was a talented director in the field and could put you through a maze without hitting a cul-de-sac, but he wasn't an executive and he didn't have a poker face and that was why he was worth watching. All I could tell at the moment was that he was having to force himself through the business of getting me to the start line, without any stomach for it. Even though we could now see each other he avoided my eyes, and this was uncharacteristic.

"The plane has to be Russian, and so has the pilot. The only way we could get the plane was by going through NATO and the USAF. Our debt to NATO is being repaid by taking some pictures for them at X and Y: The current satellite photoscans show two villages that weren't there before, and they're believed to be missile sites for the Soviet six-MIRVed SS-9 with the built-in three-hundred-yard Circular Error Probable capability. The United States is also interested in air-surveying these two points, obviously, and the only way of getting really detailed resolution is by using a low-flying aircraft. Making sense?"

"In a way."

"How d'you mean?"

"Fair enough, it makes sense. It's just that I don't like going into a mission with so many armies in the field. What the hell are we doing, Ferris, operating in the open like this with—"

"We're doing," he said sharply, "what we've been told to do, and we don't have any choice; or at least, *you* don't. And remember that within a few minutes of taking off from this airfield, you'll be working in complete isolation."

I shut up and let him talk about mobile cover, local facilities, action phases. "You are to explore area Z, having photographed it." He still didn't want to look at me, but this might only have been because he'd obviously had new signals from Control. They'd thrown that Z at me without any warning and I didn't know where it was. "We've got an agent in place there and you can contact him any time after reaching ground."

"Where is it, for Christ's sake? I don't—"

"You'll be informed."

"Oh, shit."

Because you normally get the whole picture given to you with everything made perfectly clear before you leave London, and here I was in West Germany at the jump-off point and they were still chucking new directives at me through Ferris and the reason was clear enough: Those bastards were still in the planning stage while the clock was going round to zero in less than fourteen hours from now.

Sealed orders all the way.

"Do they want any elint?" I asked Ferris. I'd looked for fancy electronics in the cockpit of the Finback last night and hadn't found any, but that didn't mean there hadn't been a whole gang of deep-screened boffins putting the stuff in all day today.

"There's nothing you can pick up on this flight that the satellites aren't already getting, from radio programmes to rocket launch signals. All they've asked for are the pictures."

He went over general considerations: alternate routes, backup facilities (there was a man in Tashkent who *might* local-liaise, if sufficiently harassed), and end-phase decision-making. He asked for any questions on the last subject and I said there weren't any: I was damned if I was going to spell out what kind of decisions I was going to make when the show was winding up, because that was when they'd try to throw me to the dogs if they could.

"Have you got everything?"

I let him wait, while we listened to the soft roar of the rain along the enormous fuselage and the occasional creak of metal as the wind came in gusts under the wings. I'd been briefed enough times to know whether he'd left anything out but I went over it twice because on this one I was going to hell on a handcart and I wasn't sure of the way.

"I've got everything," I said, "that you've told me. Christ knows it's not much."

"You're going straight into flight briefing," he said impatiently, "when we leave here. That'll fill in the rest."

"Is it security?"

"Is what security?"

He knew what I meant.

"This lack of data."

"Yes."

I didn't expect that.

"From London?"

"Mostly from this end. These people are extremely security-conscious, partly because their eastern frontier is the Iron Curtain. You've no idea how difficult things have been, just to get their permission to take off from here. Parkis had a bed put into a spare office near Signals, three weeks ago. It's been like that."

"The bastard's actually been *sleeping*?" I got up from the crate I'd been sitting on and wandered farther into the tunnel of the fuselage and came back and said: "All right, I've got all you gave me. Now get me cleared."

"Very well."

It took less than a couple of minutes. I never draw a firearm but on this trip a Soviet-made senior officer's revolver was part of the cover and there was no point in objecting. The code for the overall operation was a one-time pad and he gave it to me. "You can use the local codes or cyphers if our contacts have got a reliable system going. Your discretion. But for all alerts and priorities you'll use the pad."

Travel and cover had been built into the access and that only left accounts and there was no change from the established records. Unless we're cleared in London, where there's a witness, we have to make the attestation verbally before we sign the form. Against the rain's drumming and the creak of the shadowed fuselage my voice was only just audible, because I was due out soon and this sounded less like a statement of faith than of despair.

"No dependents, no next of kin. No monetary assets or final bequests. If remains available, use them for medical research."

In the soft ashen light from the perimeter lamps he turned his head and looked at me, though his eyes were in shadow and I couldn't see them.

"Roses," he said, "for Moira?"

"Yes."

6

Nerves

When we left the Galaxie and walked through the rain to the main buildings I realised that Böcker must have seen us go into the transport because he'd thrown a substantial surveillance net round the area to seal it off. There was also a military escort of two corporals waiting for us at Base Operations and they took us down to an office on the floor below ground level and mounted guard at each end of the passage as we went in.

There were three men sitting round a briefing-table and they got to their feet as Ferris made the introductions.

"This is Major Connors, flying instruction; Captain Franzheim, navigation; Captain Baccari, signals, U. S. Air Force. Squadron-leader Nesbitt, RAF."

They put down their coffee and shook hands.

"Hi, I'm Chuck."

"I'm Bill."

"Call me Omer. Still raining out there?"

"Pissing down." I took off my soaked jacket.

"Would you like some coffee?"

"No thanks."

Connors looked at Ferris and said: "Okay, why don't we get started?"

"Do you mind if we take navigation first?"

"Let's do that." Connors sat down and looked at Franzheim, who went over to the map on the wall and picked up a pointer.

"Okay, this is an oblique parabolic equal-area projection with a scale of 109 miles per inch, and as you can see, it covers the whole of Asia and includes peripheral countries. We're right here." He moved the pointer.

This was at 6:35. The navigational briefing took just short of an hour and Franzheim spent most of the time on the access.

"You can't go in at night without the help of highly sophisticated terrain-mapping radar, because there are hills and you could hit one with only a few degrees of deviation. You can't go in at high altitude like they did in the days of Gary Powers because they'd shoot you down the minute you crossed the border, even if you were flying at sixty thousand feet—which the Finback can attain. So you go in by daylight and you go in very fast and very low."

He moved the pointer again. "We've routed you through Hungary, since there's no Soviet frontier between East and West; you have to go through either Poland, Czechoslovakia, Hungary or Romania. Also, you can go down to practically zero feet across these plains on either side of the Hungarian-Russian border and then head for the course of this river here, the Latorica, almost due east. Your speed should be less than Mach 1 from take-off till you're across the Carpathian Mountains, to avoid sonic boom. You'll be seen—and certainly heard—overflying the town of Mukachevo right here, but you are now in the Soviet Union and flying a Soviet airplane. How does it sound so far?"

"I like it."

"Great."

I liked it because the map had the countries in pretty colours and didn't show any surface-to-air missile sites and the Carpathian Mountains didn't look like anything you could smash into with an aeroplane.

The pointer moved. "We're now in Soviet airspace and still flying close to zero feet and radar-undetectable. When you're clear of the mountains you start climbing in the vicinity of the military airfield here, just west of Zhmerinka, and you turn south-east, parallel with the Romanian border."

He glanced at Ferris and went on with a rather shut face: "At this point you'll be picked up on Soviet radar, and since you're still inside ADIZ airspace they'll—"

"ADIZ?"

"Sorry. Air Defence Identification Zone."

"Thank you."

"They'll call you up and ask you to identify yourself and prove you're not a border violator. You now begin using your cover as a Russian colonel."

I began looking round the room for bugs because this was strictly cosmic material but the place looked more like a deep shelter than an office and had probably been designed as a briefing-room for NATO flight missions. These three officers had obviously been fully screened and Ferris was looking quite satisfied with the whole arrangement. This was the kind of situation where you had to remember that your control in London was God and that your director in the field was the Son of God and they'd got everything worked out, including a method for getting you to the end of the mission alive.

"Question," I said. "How many alternative routes did you consider and throw out?"

"I'd say twenty or thirty. The point we finally chose is where the terrain-masking afforded by the mountains is greatest, and the Soviet radar coverage is weakest, according to intelligence reports. Also the ground is virtually flat on both sides of the border and you can cross it at Mach .95, or 600 knots calibrated ground speed, just below military power and sonic boom."

"And very low."

"We estimate that with the handling capabilities of the Finback you'll be going in at 100 feet AGL."

"Christ, how high are the church steeples?"

"There aren't any on the route we've planned for you."

"You've checked on the *steeples?*"

He gave a brief grin. "The base commander said we had to do a good job, and we're kind of scared of him. We checked on steeples, power grids, radio masts, factory chimneys, the whole bit. At one hundred feet on that precise course you won't hit anything, and you can have that in writing."

I said I was impressed and he thanked me.

"Naturally, we couldn't allow for pilot error. You'll have quite a job staying on course. There *is* a navigation control system fitted to the Finback but the guy who flew it into Alaska said it wasn't very accurate, and it was defunct anyway when he landed. It hasn't been removed and we haven't installed a good one of our own, because the airplane has to look like what it is: a Soviet MiG-28D, in case they ever get a close look at it."

I saw Ferris move his head a fraction towards me, and folded my arms in acknowledgement. What Franzheim had just told me was that he didn't know this was a one-way trip for the plane: "in case they ever," so forth. Ferris just wanted to warn me to leave this subject blacked out.

"You can't use radio fixes," Franzheim went on, "because as you know you'd have to *transmit* a signal to get ranging information, and they'd pick it up. Also they'd pick up your radar pulses from the ground. So you'll be steering with visual fixes, compass and dead reckoning. I'm talking about the leg this side of the Zhmerinka field, where you'll start climbing and adopt your cover."

He picked up his coffee and finished it and dropped the cup into the disposal can and pulled another one off the stack and filled it at the dispenser. "I guess all you guys must be caffeine-shy. Omer, do you have those maps?"

Captain Baccari opened a briefcase and dropped three folders onto the table.

"Okay," Franzheim said, and pulled them open. "These are your three maps, colour-coded for the projected route, alternative legs, breakoff and escape routes. You'll see they're self-explanatory when you study them: We've made provisions for you to abort the mission and escape by air at calculated altitudes over the safest possible terrain, avoiding airfields, radar posts, missile sites and so on. You can take a look now: we're in no hurry."

They were printed by the USAF Cartographic Department and bore the NATO-designated COSMIC SECRET stamp. They were also marked KEEP FROM UNAUTHORIZED HANDS and DESTROY AT DISCRETION. The detail was elaborate and the contour relief was indicated to within twenty feet above sea-level. For the first time I saw the identities of the three points X, Y and Z.

"The first suspect village," Franzheim said as he leaned over the table, "is right here at Saratov, twelve miles north of the town. The second one is ten miles south-east of Dzhezkazgan, at this point. The third is ten miles from the town of Yelingrad not far from the Sinkiang border."

"I'll need special briefing on the camera runs."

"Right. Major Connors will see to that."

Franzheim asked for questions and I went over the whole route with him again, using the green-code map and spending most of the time on the low-level run through the Carpathians. The range was a mass of ridges and valleys, with a major road following the Latorica River for forty miles through the mountains.

"I shall be seen from the road, obviously, at a hundred feet."

"Okay, but we have to define the word 'seen.' At Mach .95 they won't see more than a streak in the sky and they won't be able to tell whether it was an airplane or a bat out of hell."

Major Connors said lazily: "The first time I saw a plane going over my head that fast and that low I just messed my pants."

Baccari squeezed out a laugh and went to get himself some more coffee. Franzheim said: "Where you *won't* be seen, if you follow the road and the river, is on the radar screens east of the range, and that's what we're really talking about."

I told him he'd sold me on that and we folded the maps and put them back into their waterproof pouches. This was at 7:31 and Ferris got up and stretched his legs and asked for flying instruction.

"Let's go see the airplane," Connors said.

The two guards were still at each end of the passage and they fell in behind us as we took the stairs. A Military Police sergeant and three men were standing in the main lobby and did a lot of circumspect saluting as we went through the doors into the rain. The wind-gusts were driving it against the buildings.

"What's my minimum take-off visibility?" I asked the major.

"A lot of things like that," he said close to my ear, "are going to be up to you. We can give you the standard safety rules, and you can push it from there if you want."

On the way to the hangars I counted twelve security men

dispersed at strategic points, seven of them in uniform. We were halted twice and one of the men came with us as far as the end hangar. There were now two MP sergeants and four dog-handlers outside the doors and we all had to go through the identity check. One of the sergeants telephoned our names through to his unit and waited for the okay before he used the intercom and ordered the door opened. Connors and Baccari hadn't brought their coats and by this time they were drenched and shivering.

We trooped inside and began leaving puddles all over the floor.

"She's still there," Franzheim said, and someone laughed.

Ferris was near me. "How are you feeling?"

"I'm all right. The briefing's first-class."

"They were hand-picked."

There were six Luftwaffe military policemen surrounding the plane and Ferris said something to Connors, then took him aside. In a minute Connors turned round and said we could take the covers off; then he and Ferris went back to the door and I heard Connors phoning someone.

We'd got the last cover off when an MP lieutenant came into the hangar and told the six guards to form up outside. Ferris said we could go ahead.

He was watching me carefully for nerves and so far I was all right but there was an awful lot about this job that was beginning to scare me: It was the first time in sixteen missions that I wasn't going in solo. I'd be on my own for the access phase and strictly speaking we weren't running yet, but the number of people we'd needed to bring in just to get me off the ground was increasing, and I wasn't reassured by all the security on show because you can deep-screen a man till you're black in the face and still make a mistake and that was why Ferris had got those guards out of the way: they'd had to see the MiG in here in order to guard it but they didn't have to see who was going to fly it and they didn't have to hear Connors telling him how to do it.

I looked at my watch without meaning to.

It was 7:56 and there were twelve hours to go.

"Let's get up there," Connors said, and we used the steps to the cockpit. "I'd like you to stop me if you've heard anything before, but a few points might bear repeating. Handling techniques have been dealt with in the simulator and I'm told you came out okay. I don't know how much you intend to use the mountain-range configuration and maybe you won't know yourself till you get there, but there's a couple of places where you could make a one hundred eighty degree turn, somewhere around 6 g's at the speed you'll be doing, Mach .95 or lower. For this airplane the radius of turn would be approximately 5,000 feet."

He draped his lean body across the edge of the cockpit and pushed his wet hair out of his eyes. "One of the most critical factors of course is fuel. It'd be nice if you could climb to peak altitude to conserve it but you'd have to come down to take those pictures and it might look a little strange to the radar teams on the ground. Now you can clip this chart to your log on take-off. We estimate that in winter conditions and with your prescribed altitudes you'll use 3,000 gallons per hour at Mach 1, which is military power. At maximum speed, using the after-burner, you'll use 17,500 gallons, or almost six times as much, and I suggest you reserve the after-burners for attack evasion of whatever kind; or of course for getting out along an escape route if you calculate you can reach home without pushing your bingo fuel. You don't—"

"Bingo."

"Right. Your bingo fuel is the calculated fuel for the distance. From Fürstenfeldbruck to plus five hundred miles escape distance is 3,815 miles and your internal and pod tanks will give you precisely the amount of fuel you'll need—which is your bingo. Okay?"

"Okay."

"You start pushing your bingo the minute you exceed the prescribed consumption rate. Any use of the after-burner or any unforeseen deviation will change our basic calculations, obviously. The ideal scenario is that you cross the border at Mach .95 with no after-burner, meet with no kind of attack from the ground or the air, and make your escape by the optimum route planned."

I put three questions and he got out a pocket calculator and made notes while we listened to the drumming of the rain on the big metal roof and the whimpering of the guard dogs outside. Ferris was pacing as far as the tail unit and back and I thought if he found a beetle I'd have to stop him somehow because I was getting sensitive about that: The closer we got to the jump-off point the less I wanted to hear a slight crunch and see a small mess on the floor. I'm not normally superstitious but I'm not normally forced into a crash-training operation with a high calculated risk and so much security coverage that one out of a score of people could set me up for killing in the access phase.

"These are the figures," Connors said. "I've put them on the chart." He turned round and looked down. "Bill, what's the difference in distance for those three alternate escape routes?"

"Route B is plus fifteen miles. C is plus thirty-four."

Connors checked his figures again and made one change. "Any more questions?"

"No."

"Okay. There isn't much more you need. The wing-pod tanks don't weigh more than five hundred pounds, but they create an awful lot of drag at the lower altitudes and higher speeds. They feed out together and empty at the same time, so you can get rid of them simultaneously and avoid asymmetric wing-loading problems. The centre-line tank feeds out next, leaving you with the internals. On this trip you'll have enough fuel leeway to wait for wooded ground or good cover before you jettison the tanks, though the drag factor governs this to some extent."

He was talking about the effect of the wing tanks on high-g turn characteristics when the phone rang and Baccari went over to the door and took the call and came back and told Ferris it was for him, something about "embassy," and for a couple of seconds I stopped listening to Connors and found myself hoping it was a signal from London calling the whole thing off on the grounds that the risk was too high for success or that someone had found a security leak in a vital-info area—I didn't care *what* grounds they had, as long as they cut the switch and let everything die down and leave me alive.

This wasn't very good because twelve hours before the jump you ought to be pulling the nerves tight and clearing the head of everything except the data you need to kick into the access phase and keep on going. You shouldn't be hoping for some bastard in London to revoke his decision and get you a reprieve: Because this is how you want to live, inching your way along the edge of the drop to find out how long you can stand it, hanging around that bloody place till they throw you the only thing that gives your life any meaning—another mission. It's all you live for, isn't it, the next mission?

It used to be.

Not now.

Not this one.

Ferris came back from the telephone and I wanted to shout at him—*This is a bit elaborate isn't it, all the bloody charade just to kill off one expendable executive? Why don't you get one of those discreet-action people to push me under a bus and save all this expense?*

"Of course it depends on the angle when you go into the turn," Connors was saying, "and also on the amount of fuel remaining in the outer pod tanks." He held his hand out flat and made a turning motion.

Ferris was standing at the bottom of the steps again, where he'd been standing before. He was looking up at us but not saying anything, not saying anything like I'm sorry to interrupt, Major Connors, but we're calling the whole thing off. I was waiting for him to say something like that, but he didn't.

"With the outer tanks empty, the wings are going to flip over with much less inertia. Am I getting across?"

"Yes," I said, "critical mass factor."

"Right. Now let's go through it again, from level flight characteristics through a loop and a turn, with only the outer tanks empty but unjettisoned."

So we went through it again, and I stopped thinking about the phone call because it wasn't going to save me so I ought to concentrate on the briefing data the major was feeding me: If anyone was going to get me to the other side of the Carpathian range still alive it was Connors.

He was taking me through the camera passes now: "At this point you should look for ground features such as railroad tracks or concrete roadways that could lead to and from the factories where the missiles are assembled."

Ten minutes on the photography procedures, then he started talking about seat-ejection.

"Now the technique for this ship is much the same as for the FM-30's you've been flying. With the anti-g suit you'll be wearing you don't have a lot of protection from wind force, and 350 knots would probably be the highest survivable speed. From there up to 500 knots and beyond, you'd have your arms and legs torn off. I'd say that if you eject at any speed from 250 knots down to stall zero you'll come out fine." He flattened one hand again. "An upward vector of 20 degrees is ideal for ejection and the procedure is the same as for all other planes: This one has an emergency release for the canopy and an emergency seat-detonator, and you shouldn't have any problems."

"Fair enough." I turned slightly and looked down at Ferris, pitching my voice higher. "Is it still on?"

He looked puzzled for a moment and then nodded.

"Yes," he called up.

The major waited till I'd turned back. "The procedure for ejecting in the event of total failure of the seat mechanism is about what you'd expect: You trim for nose *down* and hold the stick back, then let it go sharply. As the plane noses over you'll pop out like a cork because you're in a vector."

He went through this again and talked about harness release, chute deployment and angles of escape relative to the tail unit configuration at critical speeds while I brooded at the back of my mind about the sheer bloody stupidity of letting Ferris know precisely how frightened I was of this one. He'd got an awful lot on his plate and his responsibilities wouldn't end when Slingshot began running—they'd increase; and I shouldn't have let him know that all his executive was waiting for as the time slid down to zero was a phone call telling us it was cancelled.

Yes indeed, the gut-shrink syndrome produces the necessary adrenalin and triggers the organism for action and that's a valuable factor in the last hours before the jump, but it can get out of hand if you let it and then it's dangerous. The time to start praying for a reprieve is ten seconds after the red light's on the board and the mission's running because you're then in the access phase and too busy to get the twitch. I've proved it a dozen times and this time I'd have to prove it again.

But this time it's different.

Shuddup.

Connors blew his nose and rubbed his thin raw-looking hands together. "I'm ready for questions."

I didn't have many and we gave it five minutes more, then he went down the steps saying he'd fix up some cocoa before we all froze to death. The signals captain came up the steps and asked me to sit in the cockpit while he spoke over my shoulder; most of the radio panels were on the left side, below the throttle quadrants.

"It's routine stuff. Just as soon as you start climbing from near the airfield at Zhmerinka—which is your virtual frontier in terms of becoming radar-detectable—you can start squawking your codes and modes on the digital transponder." He moved the dial and began flipping switches as he talked. "Mode 4 is the classified super-secret squawk code for Soviet military airplanes. Mode 3 is for traffic control and nobody's going to ask you any questions when you hit that one. These are tactical frequencies, so if you went high you'd have to squawk on the Mode 4 and we don't have their code. As you'll be flying low at this point and across the camera-target areas at Saratov, Dzhezkazgan and Yelingrad you won't need to worry about that—but bear it in mind if for any reason you get forced high by missile or interceptor action. Okay so far?"

"Will they ask me to respond on Mode 4 in that situation?"

"You bet. And you don't know the code."

"So I use normal frequencies and tell them Mode 4 doesn't work. If they—"

"Okay, right, but do it this way: tell them you're sending and let them tell you they're not receiving. Then sound surprised, and you're into the act." He turned his sharp nose towards me and said: "And here's one buster who's glad he won't be there."

"My felicitations."

He blew out a short laugh and started prodding the radio panels again and we did some repeats and I told him I'd got it and he didn't believe it so we went over the whole thing again.

That was at 9:41.

"Okay," he said finally, "I'm satisfied. If you hit any problems it isn't going to be because you don't understand your codes and modes. Can anyone smell cocoa?"

He went down the steps and turned and looked up at me as I got out of the cockpit. "Just one little thing more you should know. We'll be code-alerting all NATO and Luftwaffe radar stations and air bases that a Soviet MiG-28D is going to be flying from Fürstenfeldbruck to the Hungarian frontier at dawn tomorrow, so you won't get shot down from *this* side."

They'd rigged up a camp-bed for me in one of the small offices in the basement where we'd begun the briefing, and I turned in soon after ten-thirty with four guards mounted in the corridor and six deployed at the top of the stairs to cover the main doors and the stairs to the upper floors.

I thought Böker was laying the security on a bit thick, but one of the guard sergeants woke me at 1 A.M. and took me along to the briefing office where Böker himself was on the telephone blasting at someone in German. Ferris was there and his face was white.

"I think we've been blown," he said.

7

Moth

The mountain was dead ahead and I began pulling the control column back without trying to turn because this was the middle of the range and there were peaks in every direction. The nose wasn't lifting so I dragged at the stick again and watched the line of rocks begin rising against the sky instead of dropping away and I remembered Connors had said *at Mach 3 you have to react very fast because everything takes more time.* I'd got Mach 3.4 on the dial and the after-burners were roaring but there was no point in bringing the speed down because the nose wasn't coming up and I heaved on the stick and watched the side of the mountain float right against the windscreen and burst and I could still remember shouting as I rolled over and felt the tubular metal of the camp-bed under my hand, sweat running on my face, still shouting inside my head, time—*what time.*

3:21 A.M.

Pitch dark.

Sat up and hit the wall because this thing hadn't got a head-board, *why wasn't I informed?* Böcker had kept asking into the telephone, his voice like a slowly traversing machine gun, its volume rising and falling as he tried to control his anger. It was the first time I'd seen him like that: no more silent laughter, no plump hand on my arm. He'd hardly recognized me when I'd come in.

Ferris had told me to go back to bed now that I knew what had happened, try to get some sleep in case there was anything to do in the morning. I'd had to go down consciously through the alpha waves with the mantra I always use . . . *karisma* . . . *karisma* . . . before I could reach delta and let go. I'd slept for two hours but it hadn't done me any good because the alarm had been in my mind when I'd gone under and the dreams had been violent and highly coloured, with vivid reds predominating.

There'd already been seven men in the briefing-room by the time I got there: five of Böcker's own security chiefs and two of the military. Others had been sent for, Ferris said. Counter-intelligence people are functionally paranoid and the security branches are the worst because they're geared to the risk of exposure from all quarters and especially from the inside, but I didn't think Böcker had over-reacted to this particular incident. The man's name was Corporal Behrendt and he was one of the close-security area guards in the Finback hangar and he'd been due to report for the midnight watch and he hadn't shown up. Böcker had worked on it for an hour before suggesting I ought to be informed.

"The situation is very simple," he told us. "This man was of course fully screened by the civilian and military branches and we have known him for more than three years. He is considered to be totally reliable, and that is why we are treating his disappearance as a priority alert."

The phone rang while he was talking and he answered it and spoke very slowly in High German, demolishing a subordinate with words that hit with the force of hammers while we listened. I hadn't seen this Hans Böcker before: There was suddenly a sinister aspect to him that made his fat blond amiable appearance look like a disguise. He rang off.

"Es wäre wahrscheinlich überflüssig zu sagen aber wir machen alle anstrengungen um den mann zu finden"—then he remembered the courtesies and switched back to English—"I don't need to tell you that we are making every conceivable effort to locate this man."

Some of the BfV people weren't catching some of this and

Ferris noticed it and said: "Nesbitt and I have German, so please use that."

Böcker accepted this with a polite gesture that made him even more sinister because of the contrast: Slingshot had run straight into the dark and we'd lost it and he knew that and he was going to be held responsible and he ought not to have time to consider good manners—unless he was some kind of machine. He went on talking, his short bursts of diction hitting the walls while we stood like men washed up on an unknown shore by a sudden storm. Ferris was still pale and I wasn't long out of sleep and I began thinking *Jesus Christ, Parkis isn't going to get this one started after all.*

Before I went back to the business of trying to sleep again Ferris told me he'd be in constant signals with London and I left him to it. Communication was fairly fast via the embassy phone and the Ministry radio at Crowborough and by this time Parkis and his team would be in Signals watching the board, but I thought Ferris would probably switch to the NATO channels and reach the Bureau through the War Office because this thing was the equivalent to a red alert and seconds would become important as the time ran out to the jump.

If, of course, there was one.

I don't remember feeling pleased at this thought, or feeling anything at all. The psyche was coming under a barrage of conflicting influences and the only thing to do was sleep.

Ferris woke me just before five o'clock, coming into the room without a sound and then sitting in the dark repeating my name until I woke.

"Ferris," he said quietly when he heard me stir.

There was a desk lamp and I switched it on. He was sitting on one of the wicker chairs they'd brought in here for me; he looked very held-in, and sat so still that I wished he'd get up and break something to get it over with.

"What's the score?" I asked him.

He was a long time answering. "We don't know. Böcker's still taking the place to pieces, with four interrogation officers called in from the BfV headquarters in Munich to grill the other security guards and anyone who might know what's happened to Corporal Behrendt." He began talking a bit faster now, taking some kind of courage. "All we know so far is that Behrendt was having trouble with his wife, who was threatening to leave him. This has been going on for the past few months and Böcker's blasting the people who knew this and failed to tell him: The man was obviously a security risk. The woman's being interviewed here—"

"Woman?"

"Behrendt's wife." He looked slightly surprised.

"I've only just woken up," I said through my teeth. I didn't like this, any of it. I could feel something big getting out of hand, far away in the background but rolling closer all the time, black and mountainous and unstoppable. I didn't think I was going to have enough time to get out of the way.

"The federal police are looking for Behrendt," Ferris said in a low monotone. "Everyone is."

I thought for a bit and said: "Böcker said he was considered reliable."

"Yes. That's why he's pulling the place apart."

Neither of us said anything for a minute. I would have liked to know where, precisely, they'd got the reliable Corporal Behrendt at this moment, and how far, precisely, he was forcing them to go before he broke. When he broke, the word would go out to the radar stations and anti-aircraft units along the border from the Baltic to the Black Sea, and if anyone tried to nip across in a MiG-28D they'd blow him out of the sky. Or of course, corporal Behrendt might be just drinking himself quietly under the table in his girlfriend's flat, with the security on the Finback still intact.

I was waiting for Ferris to tell me what he'd come in here to tell me, but he still held back. I suppose he hadn't the guts.

"Don't they know his girlfriends?" I asked him.

He looked up. "They're covering that." The light seemed too bright for him. "Do you want anything?"

"What like?"

He shrugged. "Something to eat, something to drink."

"Oh. No."

I got off the camp-bed and put some slacks on and sat in the other wicker chair between the desk lamp and Ferris so that the light didn't worry him. He's normally a very cool cat and it occurred to me that there could be something *else,* something *worse* on his mind; but I shied away from that one because the situation we'd already got was quite enough. It also occurred to me that the first man in the Slingshot team to break might be this one sitting here. It's usually the executive in the field, because it's his neck on the block, or the control in London, because he's got most of the responsibility. I'll tell you one thing: It wouldn't be Parkis. It was Parkis the *Titanic* hit, that time.

"Is it still raining?"

Ferris looked up again. I always seemed to be interrupting his thoughts, and that worried me too. He should have got all his thinking done before he came in here disturbing my sleep.

"I don't know," he said.

"Oh for Christ's sake, Ferris, when are you going to regain consciousness? You've got a mission on the board and the whole of the bloody North Atlantic Treaty Organisation standing at battle stations and you don't even know if it's *raining?*"

Just the excess adrenalin slopping over: I couldn't help it. This whole situation was new and it scared me stiff: I'd never been manoeuvered into the pre-jump phase under cover of *somebody else's* security organisation—we normally use our own and quite frankly the London personnel aren't the type who don't show up on guard duty because their marriage is on the blink: It's dangerous.

"I've made three calls," Ferris said. "Three so far."

"Big deal."

"It's all we can do."

The wicker creaked as he got out of the chair and looked at the map on the wall and turned away because it showed north-east Poland and we weren't interested in that.

He still wouldn't tell me but he'd left the opening so I got it over and asked him: "What's their decision?"

He looked relieved and said: "We've got to wait, of course."

Another turn on the gut.

"Until when?"

He made himself look at me. "Take-off."

Everything sounded very still, suddenly, in here. Because they were going to make me sweat it out with no options, right up to the time of the jump. No quarter, no concessions, nothing to bite on except the bullet.

"I want the whole directive," I said.

I knew he'd got it because he hadn't been in signals with London just to give them the situation: He'd asked for instructions.

"They'd like you to go ahead."

"That isn't a directive."

"I mean," he said awkwardly, "it's going to be up to you."

I looked at the clock on the desk and checked it with my watch and got 5:12. We'd arranged to have me woken at 5:30 for the final phase before the jump and I didn't think I could psych myself out for eighteen minutes without getting into a deep sleep-curve and waking up groggy. I might as well stay on my feet.

"We take everything right up to the off," I said slowly, wanting to get it right, "and then if nobody's found what happened to Corporal Behrendt we make the final decision whether to start running the thing or scrub it out. Is that it?"

"Yes."

I picked up my shaving-kit and the towel they'd given me. "Fair enough. I'll settle for that."

He moved to the door. "They'll be pleased."

"I'm happy for them." I put a new blade in, because there was going to be a lot of sweat under the face mask and stubble wouldn't help. "Ferris."

"Yes?"

"Before they put that directive together, did anyone actually want me to take off on orders?"

"On orders?" He knew bloody well what I meant.

"With no option. Even if they didn't find Behrendt."

He was on his way out and he didn't stop. "I wouldn't know, would I? I'm not in London."

"That's true enough."

But he knew what I was talking about. Parkis would have tried to get me airborne *whatever happened*.

Memo: Quiller is expendable, and if he can complete this operation before getting into terminal difficulties in the end phase, well and good. But if he fails to survive the access phase we shall have no real complaint. It would save us the unpleasant

task, later, of ensuring that the threat to security he would con-
tinue to present was nullified.

For your eyes only, destroy after reading, so forth. But someone
had said no. Possibly Egerton. Possibly Mildmay or one of their
lordships on the Admin. floor. It had been agreed that the executive should be given the final decision whether to take off or abort
the mission. It was, after all, his life. Or his death.

But I knew Parkis. And I knew that Ferris *did* have something
else, something worse, on his mind. There *was* something big getting out of hand, still in the distance but rolling closer, black and
mountainous and unstoppable. And I knew now that I wouldn't
have time to get out of its way.

"Ten thousand rubles. Fifty gold Napoleon francs. Four digital
watches and these six rough-cut diamonds."

I nodded and he put them into the leather bag and fastened the
straps. I'd seen him before, when Böcker had called those people
into the briefing-room: He was BfV with military cover, ranking
as captain.

Connors and Baccari were watching, looking a little tense.
They'd been told we were going ahead with the programme right
up to the point of take-off, when we would either proceed or abort
according to whether Corporal Behrendt had been found. Whenever the telephone rang they looked in its direction. We all did.

Ferris was sitting on the steps to the cockpit. Twenty minutes
ago he'd told me there had been a further signal from London
confirming the last directive.

The time was now 7:14.

There was no news of Behrendt yet. Not long ago Böcker had
called Ferris to say he had a lead from the mess sergeant, who had
seen the man talking to a civilian in a café in the town last evening. He would keep us closely in touch with any progress. We
didn't take much notice: Böcker had lost an awful lot of face over
this, and I thought the only thing that kept him going was our
decision to press on to the zero in the hope that security was still
intact.

"Hunting knife. Service revolver, officer's." He hesitated, glancing across at Ferris, who got off the steps and came up close to us, speaking quietly.

"We thought on this trip you might want a capsule."

They both waited.

But I couldn't see his reasoning, in terms of *this trip*. You need a capsule when you've been caught and they're going to take your mind to pieces and drive you mad in the process—but there'd been no mention of specific opposition in briefing: I wasn't going to penetrate a cell or filter through a screen or close in on any individual who might detonate if I touched him. You need a capsule in the wilds if you can't stand pain or thirst or privation, and if I ever reached Soviet airspace I might come down somewhere isolated—but Ferris knew me better than that: I'm an animal and the wilds are my home, whether they're forest-land or the jungle of the big-city streets.

So I just said no, because I couldn't ask him what he meant by *this trip* with so many people about and it wasn't worth our going off to talk in privacy: I know when to ask for one of those things —it'll be when I ask for a gun.

The man did some sleight of hand and the little red box disappeared. "The uniform, clothing and equipment were all manufactured in the Soviet Union or one of its satellites. Most of it was made in Tashkent." Close to the target area. This is the kind of meticulous attention to detail you get from Parkis, and I tried to feel reassured but it wasn't easy, because there's the other side to him: the inflexible slide-rule precision that doesn't give you any freedom of choice when a fuse blows.

I looked the stuff over as it was laid out for me: the only distinctive items were a peasant's fur coat and hunting gear, well worn, and a short collapsible fishing-rod bound with tape; the rest comprised the standard essentials: signal flares, matches, firelighting chemicals for use with damp wood, food concentrates, a small torch, a whistle and a compass. The first-aid kit included morphine and water-purification tablets, and there was a compact toilet bag. Almost every item was made in Russia, but the razor was Polish and the torch Czechoslovakian.

"Life jacket?"

"In the cockpit."

We began putting it all together and Baccari went up the steps with a testing kit and started checking the circuits. Franzheim was crouched over the landing gear with a tyre gauge and Connors went off on a tour of inspection of the airframe: They were doubling for the ground staff to keep down the number of people on secret commission. They worked without talking, and Baccari seemed especially subdued: it was now 7:27 and we were thirty-three minutes to zero.

Ferris went across to the small door and talked to the USAF MP sergeant on guard there; from this distance I couldn't hear what they were saying. The BfV man was stowing equipment in the cockpit and I started changing into the Soviet colonel's uniform. A few minutes later the telephone rang and Ferris took it. We had all looked in his direction for a couple of seconds, but he stood with his back to us.

I thought he was speaking German. He was on the phone for less than a minute and when he rang off he went on talking to the sergeant. It could have been London, through the embassy in Bonn or through NATO and the War Office, but I wasn't going over to ask him. He'd tell me what I needed to know, and if it was nothing then he'd tell me nothing.

The uniform fitted well: It would have been made by the Bureau tailor, the man with the artificial hand in the back room off Regent Street. The KYP are looking for him under the name of Zaphiropoulos and if they find him we won't see him again.

"Looks pretty neat," Connors said.

"What?"

"The uniform."

"Might get me a few girls. Are we fuelled up yet?"

"Sure. During the night."

I suppose that was why there were so many puddles in here: They'd brought the fuel-tanker in from the rain.

The telephone rang again and Ferris answered it, and there was an odd flash of understanding that passed between Connors and myself: We both wanted to look over there in case the call was important but we didn't want to show each other how edgy we felt, so we didn't turn our heads.

"Is it still raining?" I asked him.

There wasn't any sound on the hangar roof.

"Drizzling, I guess." He was peeling a piece of gum. "You use this stuff?"

"No. I'd probably choke on it."

He laughed unnecessarily: Things weren't so bad if we could make our little jokes while the time ran out and Böcker didn't call and we hit zero still not knowing.

"What's the visibility going to be like in the morning?" The morning was now fourteen minutes away.

"The last forecast was a mile and a half."

"What's the least I can work with?"

"I'd say twelve hundred feet, for this trip. That's the length of your take-off roll." He put the gum in his mouth and flicked the ball of paper into a puddle.

Ferris was still over there and the calls were coming through without a break now, all of them short, less than half a minute. He never raised his voice.

"How are you feeling?" Connors asked me.

"Fine."

Because they had another twelve minutes to find Corporal Behrendt and he might just have run away from his wife.

"You shouldn't have any problems." He gave a tight smile. "You're too well briefed."

"Correct."

Then some kind of vehicle pulled up outside the hangar and we could hear voices. One of the dogs started growling, deep in its throat, keeping it up until I could almost see the fangs and the stare of the trained-to-kill eyes.

"I wish that bloody thing would stop," I said.

"You wish what?"

He'd been half turned to the door, trying to hear what Ferris was saying on the phone.

"Nothing." I went up the steps to talk to Baccari in the cockpit, not pleased with myself, not pleased at all, ten minutes from the jump and showing my nerves to anyone who was around, dear Jesus, I'd have to do better than this, much better than this.

"We're all checked," Baccari said and climbed out. Then everyone was moving suddenly and I saw an NCO come through the door and go up to Connors. Ferris came off the phone and started across to the plane, walking a little quicker than he usually did. A nerve in my eyelid began flickering and I was aware of it and knew there was no way to stop it except by relaxing and I couldn't do that now.

"Everything's go," I heard Connors say, and the NCO went back to the door at a slow run. There were voices outside again and one of the dogs barked and a word of command silenced it.

Ferris was standing at the bottom of the steps looking up at me, his hands in the pockets of his mac and his pale head tilted under the lights.

"Böcker hasn't got anything definite for us," he said, "so far."

The eyelid went on flickering.

"How's London?"

"They're being kept informed."

Of nothing. Uninformation.

"The colonel's outfit looks good," Ferris said.

Then the hangar doors began rolling open, making a thin crack of dark that spread slowly with a noise like distant thunder. No stars, no trees, nothing but the dark. It wasn't morning yet, and I stared at the great black rectangle thinking that if morning never came it would be all right; and I've learned for a long time that the only thing to do about that kind of thought when you're within minutes of the crunch is to be aware of it, recognise the emotion behind it and remember that it's natural, perfectly natural.

Men were coming in from the rain, their camouflaged capes bright with it. They came towards the Finback.

Franzheim was waiting for me at the bottom of the steps.

"You want a final run-through with the maps?"

"No."

We'd covered it exhaustively and the day before the exams old Winthrop used to boot me out onto the rugger field. My God, that was a long time ago: Is he still alive? He used to smell of camphor.

Baccari was at the bottom of the steps, winding his instrument leads into a skein over his hand, turning to look across at the telephone: It had begun ringing again, and Connors took the call.

7:49 on my watch.

I looked at Ferris. "Have they pushed our zero forward?"

"It's not daylight yet," he said and walked off before I could ask him anything else. I suppose they were dragging their heels in

London, weighing up the chances and sending each other prissy little memos while these rain-caped men in here guided the tractor across to the Finback and dropped the lugs of the tow-bar into the holes and signalled the driver, sending each other memos for your eyes only, so forth, going through the required bureaucratic ritual, Parkis in Signals now, standing behind the man at the console for the Slingshot board with the red light not switched on yet, Egerton with him, possibly, or possibly not: Parkis might have kept him away at the last minute, clearing the place of everyone except the signals personnel. Parkis would be nervous now. Even Parkis.

The Finback began rolling, a man at each wingtip and one at the tail as the tractor gunned up a little and made for the middle of the doorway. Connors was coming over from the phone and I waited for him.

"We're cleared by the Met. along most of the course." Franzheim heard him and shook a map open. "You'll be running into cloud at two thousand feet this side of Zhmerinka but that's okay because you don't have to take any pictures there. Saratov is clear and the cloud floor over Dzhezkazgan is between four and five thousand, so you can go in below it with the camera. There's a cold front moving north across Sinkiang toward Yelingrad and they're looking for snow sometime before the afternoon, but you could make it and get pictures before it closes in, unless they offer you some kind of harassment that forces you off your course."

I asked him about wind strengths and we looked at the map again. Franzheim was folding it away when a short man in aircrew overalls joined us and Connors presented him to me as Colonel Lambach, the base commander. We exchanged courtesies and the telephone rang and the guard took the call but I was getting fed up with watching the thing and Ferris didn't seem interested so I went outside and saw the first flush of light coming into the sky behind the dark mass of the hangar.

7:58 with a light drizzle falling and the sharp angular form of the MiG-28D rolling through the haze, the tractor swinging it between ground markers to bring the tail at right-angles to a jet-stream barrier. There were no lights on, anywhere at all; even the tower was dark except for the directional beacon. The men followed the plane without calling to each other, two of them pulling the trolly-accumulators into position below the fuselage, making

no sound but for the hiss of the tyres over the wet concrete. I had
heard Conners saying that until daylight came the airfield would
be operating under war-time blackout conditions.

I went back into the hangar and got into my anti-g suit, with
Franzheim giving me a hand. The helmet felt too small and I took
it off again and we found part of the leather flap folded upwards,
and pulled it down.

"Feel good?"

"Yes," I told him. I took it off again.

We adjusted the wrist straps.

"You know something? I just wish they'd find that bastard."

"So does he," I said, "quite possibly."

Because we were almost ready and everyone had put a lot of
work into the project and we wanted to believe he was just a
young idiot in the throes of a domestic crisis, but we still didn't
know where he was and he could be holding out, even as late as
this, swaying in the chair in the cellar with the radio turned up
high to cover the noise, *why do they want a Soviet plane,* the
needle probing the urethra, *yes, you've told us that, but did they
bring it specially from the United States,* the radio very high
because he was losing control now, *but we want to know who is
going to fly it,* everything red around him, everything on fire with
what they were doing, until it didn't matter what they knew,
didn't matter what he told them, *very well, go on, we are listening, go on.*

Franzheim tucked the radio out of the way and checked the helmet again. "You think they've hijacked him?"

"How the hell should I know?" I said and went back to stand in
the doorway looking out at the drizzle. There was a taste of metal
in my mouth and it would have been good to have a drink of
water but I wasn't thirsty and the system had to remain as dry as I
could comfortably allow: It was one of the circumspect phrases
Connors had used in the briefing, *as dry as you can comfortably
allow.*

This too was natural. You remember meaningless things.

Then Ferris came up.

I'd been waiting for him.

The glow of dawn was increasing now, whitening over the seconds and touching highlights along the wings of the Finback over

there. I hadn't looked at my watch for a while because there wasn't any point: We'd overrun our zero for the jump and only Ferris would know why and when he was ready he'd tell me.

"They can't trace him yet."

He meant Behrendt.

Nobody was moving, now, over there by the Finback. The men stood like figures in a landscape, the light growing brighter on their wet capes, one standing upright near the tail unit, two others crouched on their haunches by the starter trolleys, their heads turned in this direction. Baccari was near the mobile steps, the test kit still in one hand, his eyes watching the hangar. I didn't know who would give the order to start up, if we decided to do that. Probably the base commander; he was talking quietly to Connors, somewhere behind us.

"All right," I said to Ferris, "so they can't trace him."

He was standing beside me, not facing me. He was watching the Finback, as we all were.

"I talked to London again, a few minutes ago."

A bird flew up, somewhere beyond the plane and the men who were standing there. Its call must have been an alarm cry, because the whole flock followed, darting from the ground at a sharp angle and wheeling away from us. I watched them till the haze blotted them out.

"What does London say?" I asked Ferris.

"Nothing's changed. They're leaving the decision to you."

One of the men near the Finback moved slightly, stamping his feet in the cold.

So nothing had changed. But it was academic now, whether I took off on orders or on my own decision: There was a substantial chance that a man so reliable as Corporal Behrendt had not simply run out on his wife while he was engaged in security duties, but had been taken by one of the Moscow-controlled cells in the area and held under duress and interrogated and finally broken. This likelihood made the idea of a take-off so dangerous that some of these people were waiting for the signal to abort.

But if he fails to survive the access phase we shall have no real complaint.

Parkis kept coming into my mind and this too was natural: In the last few seconds before a mission starts running there are only two people totally involved: Control and the executive in the field. I would be in Parkis' mind too for this brief time as he stood behind the man at the console, his hands tucked into the pockets of his impeccably tailored jacket and their thumbs hooked over the top. He would be waiting.

I hated Parkis because he was inhuman and he hated me because I wouldn't respect him and now he was daring me to do something dangerous and he was half counting on it to kill me and I knew that. He'd made certain I knew it: They tell you only what you need to know and he'd wanted me to understand that the only choice I had was to accept his dare or back down. And the thing that had been rolling towards me, black and mountainous and unstoppable, was the fact that I didn't really have a choice at all. That bastard knew there was one thing I could *not* do.

Signal, sir. The executive had decided not to take off. He feels the risk is too high.

The one thing I could *not* do.

Ferris was waiting.

"Tell him we're starting up," I said.

Because Parkis knows too much. He knows that all you have to do to kill a moth is light a candle.

8

Slingshot

I swung round as the van came up because they had the power ground-unit running now and the roar blanked out most of the other sounds.

"Franzheim! Have you seen my gloves?"

He threw open the door. "I got the whole bit!"

The time was 08:17 and we were late but it wasn't critical because the drizzle was steady and the daylight was only just getting through.

I put the gloves on and Franzheim gave me a hand with the parachute harness.

"So they found that guy?"

"What guy?"

"That goddamned guard."

"No."

I shrugged the harness comfortable.

"Oh Jesus," he said.

I wished he'd shut up.

Major Connors was in the cockpit of the Finback doing the preflight routine, doubling for the launch-control officer. His face was coloured by the glow of the panel lights and he sat crouched forward, concentrating.

"Got the helmet?"

Franzheim passed it down to me and climbed out of the van.

"Did you get your medical?" he asked me.

"Last night."

I noticed Lambach, the base commander, trotting steadily across to the hangar, the dogs watching him as he neared. I couldn't see Ferris anywhere.

Baccari was coming over from the mobile steps, looking up at the sky. It wasn't really the sky: It was a thousand-foot ceiling to the haze.

"Everything's go," he said and put a thumb up.

"Listen, has anyone told the people on our side of the border to leave me alone?"

"How's that again?" I had to repeat it because of the noise from the ground unit. He stood back and looked at me. "What the fuck d'you think we're running—Disneyland? You bet your ass they've been told!"

Franzheim gave a discordant laugh but it didn't help. Everyone knew that *bloody* corporal hadn't been found and they seemed to think they were setting me up for an execution.

"You want to put your hat on?" Franzheim asked me.

"Are we that close?"

"Sure."

"All right."

He helped me with it. We'd been handling it the right way up all the time to keep the rain out but the leather was ice cold and felt tighter than it was. The roar of the power unit was muffled now but I couldn't hear anything else. Someone came up and I saw it was Ferris. He said something, and I bent towards him and tapped the side of the helmet.

"Everything is under control." He gave me a small plain envelope and I wasn't surprised because I'd known all along that this thing stank of sealed orders. "Open on arrival. Feeling all right?"

"Yes," I said, and watched him as he walked away, feeling oddly reassured to think that if Slingshot was going to finish me there'd always be Ferris, a thin sandy man with untidy hair walking forever across the rainswept airports with his head down and his mac flapping and his mind on the access, the rendezvous, the courier route while his eye watched the ground for a beetle.

"Boots tight?"

"What?"

Franzheim.

I couldn't hear in this bloody helmet.

He said it again and I bent down and checked the laces. When I straightened up I heard the sound of the power unit dying away. Connors was climbing out of the cockpit and we began to see some of the F-15's standing in their dispersal bays, and the line of trees along the perimeter road at the far side of the airfield. The black Mercedes limousine wasn't there today: Böcker had moved it, *or they didn't need to watch anymore because they'd broken the corporal and he'd told them everything they*—oh balls, listen, the whole thing's a gamble and either you're going to get killed or you're going to beat that bastard Parkis at his own game and there's *nothing* you can do about it now because you're committed and that was what you wanted so *shuddup.*

There was a deep puddle and we splashed through it. "We're ready for strap-up," Connors said. He watched me for a moment and then looked away across the airfield. "Are you going to wait for some visibility?"

"They'll be giving me lights, won't they?"

"Sure thing."

"I'll use those."

I went up the steps and got into the cockpit and they began crowding around me, plugging in leads and making the man-machine connections, strapping me to the ejection seat and checking, double-checking, none of them talking. The pale green light of the gunsight reticle was making reflections along the cushioning rim of the visor and I moved my head slightly to face the front. Under my body I could feel the flexing of the hydraulic landing-gear as the men leaned across the edge of the cockpit.

One of them tapped my helmet and I looked up.

"Okay?" Conners asked me.

"Yes."

"Everything's go." He patted the helmet again. "Good luck."

I nodded. Someone else put his thumb up—Franzheim, I think: There were so many of them, a lot of faces and arms. I nodded again to reassure him; then they left me and I turned my head and saw the steps moving away. I reached up and slid the canopy shut.

The engines were rumbling and one of them fired, and thirty seconds later the other one came in. They began whining now, their sound rising slightly and then falling as they stabilized at idle with the exhaust gas temperature still cool at 380 degrees. Connors came through on the UHF and I adjusted the set and acknowledged; then we began bringing the systems on line and setting the configurations while I reported the oil, fuel and hydraulic pressures and the RPM.

Pressurise.

I flicked the switch.

Check trim.

I moved the controls, watching the mirror.

Okay. I turned my head and saw him holding his thumb up.

Wait for the green.

What about those lights?

You'll get them.

I began waiting for the tower to come through. They'd strapped the clip-board to my right knee and I took the pencil out: I couldn't crow-fly the first leg to the Carpathian range because it would take me twice across the Hungarian-Czechoslovakian border, so the initial magnetic course was 148 degrees and I filled it in. ETA for the turning-point was thirty-five minutes after take-off and I left it blank because I didn't have the data: The time was now 08:21 and the tower was still out.

Connors was standing where I could see him easily. He was looking up at me and then turning his head towards the control tower. I tried them again and they didn't respond.

"Shit," I said to anyone who was listening.

Connors heard me and went over to the flight van for a lamp. He was obviously trying to get the tower and couldn't.

I was beginning to sweat, and the cockpit pressure was uncomfortable.

When I looked down again Connors was pointing the lamp at the tower, pressing it on and off. I looked back at the main panel. The clock was out of synch with my watch by fifteen seconds and I adjusted it and began thinking that London must have come through with a fifty-ninth-second order to abort and that was why the tower was keeping us on ice like this, or they *had* found that corporal and seen the marks on his body and decided that if anyone slipped a Finback across the border he'd run smack into a duckshoot because—

Tower to SX-454.

Hear you, I said, *where the hell have you been?*

Stand by.

Sweat was itching.

Then Connors came on again.

Internal power.

I switched over.

I'm on internal.

They turned off the ground unit and the staff began moving clear.

Chocks gone. You can proceed to the runway.

I slipped the brakes.

There were no lights yet and I thought of asking for them again, but Connors had sounded a fraction curt the last time and I suppose they were going to wait for the last minute, to observe blackout orders.

The engines whined. The readings were satisfactory all over the panel but the cockpit heat was too high and I lowered it but didn't feel anything immediately. Sweat ran.

Birds flew up from behind one of the marker boards as I swung into line with the runway, their wings black against the glare of the haze in the east. Rivulets ran down the windscreen and I cleared it and sat waiting, watching the tower.

The tower was quiet.

Connors was off the air now: I tried him but all I got was my own dead voice. When I looked down and sideways I couldn't see anyone. Connors would be in the flight van: It had swung through the rain to line up parallel with me a hundred yards away. Ferris wouldn't be with him: He would have gone back to the hangar to wait by the telephone in case it rang and he had to get a signal to me to switch everything off. If he didn't get a call he would make one himself, the moment I was airborne.

I watched the tower again.

The set was still dead.

The birds that had flown up were circling now, lowering across the bright wet grass where—

Green light.

Tower to SX-454.

Hear you.

You're cleared for take-off.

Roger.

I pumped the brakes and pushed the throttles forward to military power.

Confirm canopy locked.

It was Connors again, from the van.

I checked the lever.

Confirm locked. All systems for climbout are now on.

Confirm ejection seat pin pulled.

Confirm.

I switched over to continuous ignition to prevent a flame-out and reported to Connors. The sound of the engines at eighty-five per cent of their power was a sustained scream and the aircraft was trembling as the thrust worked at it, straining against the tyres.

The tower came through again.

There's no traffic. There is no traffic.

I acknowledged and checked the engine dials and then looked up through the windscreen. Streaks of rain had formed again and I cleared them but it wasn't much better: I could see the control tower on my right with the green signal showing steadily but the view immediately ahead was a sheet of diffused grey light and I couldn't make out the runway beyond a hundred yards.

What the *hell* were they doing?

SX-454 to tower. Can you give me—

They must have had their hand on the button because the runway lights were suddenly glowing and I just told them I was rolling and took off the brakes and pushed the throttles forward to full power and heard the twin jets hitting up a scream that totally blanked out something that was coming through to me on the headset. I didn't ask them to repeat because this was the go and if someone had got it wrong they'd have to punch off a flare: The scream was filling my skull now and the set was drowned out. The amethyst light-path tapered ahead of the windscreen and the individual lamps were blurring into a continuous line as they slid past and out of sight. There was an awful lot of vibration at this speed and it was getting worse but Thompson had warned me about this and I ignored it and kept the throttles hard against the quadrant stop and sat watching the track of lights with the stick dead steady until I flicked a glance at the dials and pulled it back and waited.

By Christ this one was quick and they'd told me about that too: The lights fell away and the vibration eased off and I felt the tensions shifting in the airframe as the stress came off the undercarriage and the mass became cushioned and the aerodynamics came into play.

I hit the retract button.

Ten-tenths rain haze and the fierce push of the jets against my back and a microsecond image of Ferris at a telephone putting a red light on the board in London as Slingshot began running.

9

Access

They picked me up again between Budapest and Kecskemet.

¿Hava való?

I kept silent.

They'd got onto me twenty minutes ago when I'd slipped across the Austro-Hungarian frontier at Mach .95 and three hundred feet, and since then I'd been expecting interceptors. I couldn't tell if this second demand for identity was isolated or if they'd started signals from the frontier to get ahead of me on the ground. If they hadn't done it already they could start doing it now and I couldn't go fast enough to beat them.

Visibility had opened out since the frontier but the sky closed in now like a lid coming down and I was flying into a ten-tenths screen of rain.

¿Hava való?

Nothing I could tell them.

This was where I had to make a 118-degree turn to meet the east border near the Latorica, and the cement works that Franzheim had given me as a landmark were buried in the sludge so I used the compass and hoped for a break in the rain farther east to give me a visual fix.

¡Igazolja magát!

Oh for Christ's sake I'm a British intelligence agent up from a West German NATO base flying a MiG-28D into Soviet airspace with cover as a Red Army colonel and if you'll believe that you'll believe anything.

I checked instruments and noted the new course on the log card and took her up to four hundred feet because there were low hills on the map and I couldn't see them: I couldn't see *anything*.

The jets were rumbling like a freight-train and all systems were in good order but the cockpit air conditioning wasn't doing its job and I was sweating too much energy away. At 600 knots and close to the deck the air was bumpy and I went up another hundred.

They'd stopped calling.

That could mean anything. I didn't think they'd just give up but at this stage there wasn't much they could do because their interceptors wouldn't find me in this stuff and they wouldn't want to send up any flak because they weren't sure I wasn't one of their own pilots with a duff radio.

Some of the sweat wasn't due to the cockpit temperature: Flying blind at this speed put a lot of stress on the organism because if the altimeter developed a fault I could hit a hill or a grid or a radio mast at any next second and write the whole thing off. But I didn't want to go any higher because their radar would pick me up and I'd start running into the duckshoot before I'd even crossed the border.

Sit and sweat.

Parkis, you bastard.

Don't think about Parkis.

Check and recheck. RPM, EGT, fuel, warning lights, artificial horizon, altitude, airspeed.

Two minutes later there was a hellish bump and the top of my helmet touched the canopy and I took her up to six hundred as a reflex action because the hills were below and this degree of turbulence could drop me two hundred before I could do anything about it.

Parkis was on my—

Don't think about Parkis—

On my mind because Ferris had been so *bloody* shut-in while we were all waiting for that corporal to turn up and he'd been in constant signals with London while Connors was final-briefing me in the hangar before dawn this morning and a few minutes ago an idea had got into my head and it wasn't nice. Those bastards in London could have—

Bump and the whole of the airframe shuddered and I kept low on the seat and wished to *Christ* I could see something because there was an isolation factor getting into the psyche: I was flying into nothing and there was nothing behind me and the needle on the dial was losing its meaning—if this thing slowed down and stood still in the sky with the jets still running I wouldn't feel any difference.

Climb.

No. Radar.

Climb just a little bit.

I'm not scared enough. Not yet.

Those bastards in London could have ordered an execution during that last hour at Fürstenfeldbruck and that could have been why Ferris had been so shut-in at a time when it was his job as the director in the field to give me every possible reassurance and get me to the zero feeling I had a chance.

Noise like a freight-train, a freight-train going nowhere, standing still in a cold grey void: You can keep your bearings by looking at the dials in front of you but you can lose them inside your skull if you don't hang on.

That bastard Parkis could have given Ferris a final directive: *If that corporal is found to be in the hands of a Soviet cell or is considered to have been in their hands and under interrogation for a period long enough for him to have divulged the nature of Slingshot, the executive is not to be informed, and the operation is to proceed as planned.*

That would be logical because this was a new kind of mission and it had its own built-in destruct unit and there was a point we could reach where they would use it. The two components of Slingshot were a man and a machine and they were both expendable: This thing I was flying was a museum-piece and it'd be cheaper to junk it than take it all the way back to the States; and the pilot was due for throwing out if he ever got back alive and it'd be cheaper to let him go into the access phase and run into a certain barrage than take him back to London and debrief him. *It would save us the unpleasant task, later, so forth.*

Destruct. Destruct by neglect.

You're paranoiac.

No, I—

Ferris said so.

But they could have found Corporal Behrendt, or his body—

You surely don't believe—

Shuddup. They *could* have found Behrendt and that man Böcker *could* have called up Ferris with the news and Ferris *could* have told him to keep a blackout on it, a total blackout. Within the context of an expendable man and an expendable machine it's a perfectly logical premise, and I—

But even Parkis wouldn't do a thing—

He wouldn't what?

I was in his office with two other people the day Swanner came in half dead from fatigue after running the gauntlet from Prague to the border and losing two couriers. He'd blown the whole route wide open and Parkis had made the three of us stay in the room while he stood in front of Swanner and took a full ten minutes to break the man up while we had to listen to it. He never raised his voice, which made it worse. I was in his office a year later when Lazlö was brought in to plead for asylum. Parkis told him that for political reasons we were going to drop him back across the frontier where the KGB were hunting for him, and the poor little devil put a pill in his mouth and hit the floor before we could stop him.

Be advised: Parkis will do *anything.*

Drifting.

Wind gusts.

I corrected the attitude.

And there was another thing. One of our sleepers in Brussels had got himself into a Venus trap and one of the Moscow cells had turned him and he'd begun doubling and Parkis had sent a man out to deactivate him before he got dangerous, and the man was back within twenty-four hours and there weren't any questions asked but we passed the hat round in all departments for the sleeper's widow. The man who went out, and came back, was Ferris.

Drift. Correct.

And forget.

At this point I was thirteen minutes from the Hungarian-Soviet frontier and flying towards it at a steady six hundred knots and if Corporal Behrendt had been got at successfully I had these last thirteen minutes to live, so it was a good time to make a decision: go back or go on. But nothing had changed since I'd committed myself and put this thing into the air, except that the idea had come into my mind, about Parkis. But that could be paranoia and if I gave in to it I could make so many wrong decisions that I could wreck an awful lot more than the life and career of just one little shit-scared ferret on his way to a terminal explosion.

Twelve minutes now, not thirteen. Twelve.

I could for instance abort this mission and swing back to Fürstenfeldbruck and tell Ferris to get me to London, but they had a manhunt going on there and I was the man and it'd be no go because the Bureau wouldn't let me in: Once in the dock and with no defence I could bring down the Sacred Bull and they knew that. They'd order Ferris to hole me up on neutral ground and keep me there till they could debrief me and let me loose like a piece of junk with a pension, or save their money and rig a bang in a flight bag and put me in the records as *executive deceased between missions,* I wouldn't put it past them, I wouldn't put *anything* past those idolatrous bloody pagans if they had to choose between the Bull and a human being.

Bump, very bumpy. We dropped a hundred and fifty just then and I don't understand it because there ought to be flat land below us now without any turbulence.

I brought her to five hundred and stared through the windscreen at the blank grey wall and listened to the jets pushing me into it with the force of a hurricane and looked down at the clock again: eleven.

Or I could put this thing down on an airfield in Hungary or Romania or Bulgaria and blarney my way into the blue as a Soviet military overseer on a special mission: The slave-state security police would lick anyone's boots providing they were made in Moscow. But London would know where I went because they knew me and they knew my ways and they'd put a directive through the network and the moment I showed up above ground they'd make the snatch, *finis.*

Ten minutes and running into nothing and the isolation thing was creeping up on me again because I was strapped in an airtight pod with nothing distant for the eyes to focus on.

Check.

RPM, EGT, fuel gauges, artificial horizon, airspeed, all warning panels dark. Clock.

Nine minutes left.

Then something flashed and I looked down to the left and saw a break in the rain-haze and a long sinuous line running more or less parallel, its curved sections reflecting the steely light. The corner of the green-code map began fluttering in the airstream from a conditioner vent and I folded it back and checked the area from Budapest to the Carpathians. Fair enough: I was on course but three or four miles too far south, if that was the Tisza down there.

Over the next three minutes the turgid grey of the cloud-mass broke up gradually into landscape patterns that swung past me five hundred feet below. I kept the altimeter in view and went down three hundred feet, turning slightly and turning again to steady the course a mile to the north of the river. The cloud-base was lifting all the time now and the glare of the low sun filled the windscreen. I kept my head turned and began looking for landmarks but it was difficult because the terrain was streaming past at six hundred knots and becoming a blur as the sun's light strengthened and shone across fields and wooded areas still bright from the recent rains. There should be a tank-farm complex a mile to the north of the Tisza at this point if the dead-reckoning figures added up, but I couldn't see it yet; it could be five miles behind or five miles ahead of me and I began looking for the two adjacent landmarks: A highway intersection in the shape of an X and a village with two churches, one at each end.

Clock: six minutes.

There was no direct sunshine but the glare was blinding now and the streaming terrain immediately below had the glimmer of molten metal.

No farm.

No village.

Recalculate and note time: five minutes to the frontier, give or take the margin of error. I wasn't sure I would in fact be able to

distinguish the features of low-relief landmarks at this speed and
at a vertical angle, so I made a one-degree turn and held it for ten
seconds and came back one degree and brought the river across to
the other side, increasing the vertical angle and staring down again
until a visual-shift mechanism was set up and I had to look away.

Four minutes.

The most distinctive landmark to the north of the Tisza was a
bauxite minehead two miles east of a co-operative farm with
maize silos and I turned my head to the left again and looked
down.

¿Hova való? Hova való?

I didn't answer. Major Connors' reports from NATO Intelligence had been rather vague, since last year's attempt at insur-
gence had 'affected the disposition of Red Army units in this satellite state.' Nobody knew definitely whether a Soviet aircraft
moving flat out at low altitude through Hungarian airspace would
cause alarm, though I'd been warned to expect interceptors east of
the Austrian border if radio calls for identification became insist-
ent and went unanswered.

¡Igazolja magát!

I suppose they'd found me on the radar when I'd climbed
through the turbulence to give myself elbow room but I was now
skinning the deck at two hundred feet and ought to be off the
screens according to the map indications: the nearest radar stations to the Tisza within a hundred miles of the border were on
the northern side of a hill range and the terrain masking was noted
as *total for 17 m.*

¡Hova való? Igazolja magát!

At this speed and altitude I was producing a continuous roll of
thunder across the ground and it was probable that I was panick-
ing livestock and that agricultural workers and the garrisons of
isolated police stations were running to phone a report to the
nearest military airbase.

¡Hova való? Igazolja magát!

No comment.

I checked the instruments but had to do it in a series of
snatched glances because I could be miles out in my dead reckoning and the flat bright plains could break into low hills and I'd
need a lot of time to bring the nose up and clear them. The first

hills on the map began ten miles from the frontier and I'd have to start climbing in any case when—

Stubby tubular configuration low left: silos? Then angular super-structures ten or twelve seconds after: the bauxite minehead to the east of the farm.

Check map. Check time. The landmark was thirty miles from the frontier and the clock gave me three minutes to go. I waited thirty seconds and eased the control column back a degree and held it and flattened out again at four hundred feet and looked for the hills and saw their shadows this side of them in the lower half of the windscreen. They were sliding towards me in a soft green wave and I wanted to climb again to increase the margin of safety -but that was gut-think because the briefing sources were first-class and these hills were down at three hundred feet and the margin was as much as I could afford without starting to show up on someone's radar screen.

Two minutes.

I was now closing very fast on the frontier from twenty miles west and there was no reason to turn back but I switched on the set and made two clicks with an interval of one second. It was the only signal I'd been briefed to make and it meant that all was well and I was going in. I was to make it on the final approach to the Soviet frontier while I still had enough time to swing round and return to base if so ordered. The response would be one click as a signal to proceed as planned, three rapid clicks as a signal to turn round and head back to Fürstenfeldbruck.

I waited.

One click.

I switched off the set.

The hills streamed past the windscreen in a wash of undulating green and I estimated the visibility at five or six miles: a distance of thirty seconds in terms of time. Then I checked the whole panel and noted that all systems were functioning within their prescribed limits of efficiency and finally I tested the harness straps because the bumping had put a slight degree of stress on them and I wanted to know whether they'd broken.

One minute.

They hadn't broken. They couldn't have. They hadn't received one thousandth of the stress needed to do it. It was my nerve that was breaking and driving me into these final gestures of supplication: I couldn't pray and I couldn't cross myself and I didn't carry a rabbit's foot so I'd tested the straps because if they were all right then everything was going to be all right and to hell with your bone-rattling prophesies of doom.

Easy to say, because the primitive brain was aware that its organism was trapped inside a projectile and hurtling through the air towards the likelihood of death: *and not by accident.*

But if he fails to survive the access phase—

Get out of my mind.

Get out.

Concentrate. Thirty seconds: five miles. Check, recheck, recalculate, do anything, but give the consciousness some work.

Airspeed 640 knots, altitude 300 feet, steady on course, bearing 121 degrees.

Twenty seconds.

Ten.

Zero.

And ahead of me, spreading into the windscreen, the snows of the Carpathians. Despite all you have done, Parkis, and all you may do or try to do, you may write this much at least across the board: The executive in the field for Slingshot has penetrated Soviet airspace and is still alive.

10

Moira

"I don't give a damn who you are."

She meant what I was.

It was the first thing she ever said to me, and she didn't know it was important. She still doesn't.

"It's unusual," I said.

This was later.

"What is?"

"Not wanting to know."

"Oh." The head perfectly still, the long green eyes alone moving to look at me. "But then I'm a lot more than just sex, aren't I?"

She has rich auburn hair, clouds of it, but doesn't use it for effect: She uses her shoulders. They are slightly tanned and she likes them bare and knows how to move them, though she does it sparingly because it's an expression of foreplay and it can devastate. Somewhere along the line there's a car smash and a divorce and an autistic child she's slowly bringing to life, and other things.

"This business I'm in," she told me a year ago, "I don't know." We were looking down into the Thames, just before dawn. "It isn't doing anything for me. It's slowly beginning to hollow out my guts, but I can't stop." After a bit: "It's like that with you, isn't it?"

"No."

Too quick and she heard it, and laughed softly.

"You never turn your back, do you? Maybe I could learn from that: I've been letting things creep up on me."

She flew out to Taiwan a month ago with her director to do a remake of *Song of the Islands* and I couldn't see her off because this thing had started, but whenever she leaves, or I leave, I get the same feeling: That all she's going to see of me again is a dozen roses. I've been trying for a long time to break this insidious association of her name with death—my death—but it still comes in strongly when the odds are stacked and it looks like the end of the line, and I felt it now because the climb indicator was showing a ten-degree angle as I eased the control column back and watched the airspeed come down through 550 knots before I pushed the throttles forward and took her back to 640 and sat waiting.

This was the stage I'd been trying not to think about since we'd cleared the Carpathians without drawing fire; I'd grown used to being close to the ground where no one could see me but at Zhmerinka I had to shift out of the access phase and fly my image deliberately onto their radar screens and I was doing that now and it felt dangerous and in the microsecond intervals between practical observations I thought of Moira.

Altitude 500 feet.

600.

700.

What plane are you?

They were onto me very fast and I didn't like it because I was well beyond the Air Defence Identification Zone and only four miles west of the airfield at Zhmerinka and they shouldn't be so bloody surprised at seeing a MiG on the screen.

The briefing had been precise on this and I switched the transponder to the Mode 3 frequency and squawked.

800.

900.

What is your course?

I told them 104 degrees and went on climbing steadily.

One thousand feet.

It really was very hot in this bloody cockpit and I looked at the air-conditioning lever but it had been on full cool since I'd crossed the Austro-Hungarian border and the thing was obviously defunct.

1200.

They hadn't answered me.

I didn't like that either. I didn't like any of it because there was something in the back of my mind that was nagging all the time, something I'd missed.

There was still no answer. I was tempted to ask them for an acknowledgement and I resisted it because when in Rome you've got to do as the Romans do, and don't you forget it. That man down there was just not the talkative type: He'd popped a couple of questions and got a couple of answers and now he'd gone back to checking somebody's king, fair enough, it was the way they did things over here.

You're just cheering yourself up.

Wouldn't you?

Going through four thousand feet I checked instruments and brought the log up to date and changed course by five degrees to take me north of the missile site at Voliapin. They could reach me at a hundred miles' range and I wasn't trying to get out of their way: It's just that when you creep past the lion's den you take care not to tread on its tail.

Of course I was still on their screens and I was going to stay there now, wherever I went: This wasn't a sneak penetration anymore, it was a cover trip and everything was taking shape according to the briefing except that I couldn't get the thought out of my mind that I was missing something, some kind of factor that had started quietly developing like a slow burn fuse and would reach the point of detonation before I could do anything to stop it.

Something to do with time.

What plane are you?

MiG-28D No. SX454 from 36th Squadron, 3rd Air Command.

What course are you on?

101 degrees.

I didn't name my actual destination: Saratov.

There was no acknowledgement. It didn't worry me this time: Earlier I'd felt they were puzzled and had started checking on the information I'd give them. They were just untalkative.

And you're just trying to—
Shuddup.

Alter course four degrees south and maintain speed at Mach .95. This would bring me to bear directly on Saratov and I would be—

What course are you on?

I got back very fast with 105 degrees and started sweating hard because they didn't just have me on their screens: They were following me under a microscope.

I don't like cover trips. Sneak penetration is flexible and versatile and you can go flat out and break every rule in the book and out-think the opposition if you're quick enough and out-run them if you've got the speed: I could have done all that over Hungary and still got through because they didn't know where I was and they didn't know where I was going next. But these people knew precisely where I was and precisely where I was going next and I had to sit here and let them watch and if anything scared me I couldn't hit the controls and start scraping the deck to get off the screens because the instant they lost me they'd put up a flock of interceptors with radar and find me again.

They'd find me whatever I did.

Fly on a web.

ATA Saratov: 10:47.

I took photographs one minute later in level flight at three thousand feet without having to deviate and I don't think I could have done it in any other way because they started calling me up before I'd switched the camera off.

What plane are you?
MiG-28D No. SX454.
From what squadron?
36th Squadron, 3rd Air Command.

They asked me for repeats and I sent them.

What is your name?

The nerves went tight because this wasn't traffic-control material anymore.

Colonel Nikolai Voronov. I took a chance. *Listen, my set's out of order. I can't seem to get anything.*

Silence.

Sit and sweat.

I didn't know the frequency for the military Code 4 and I suspected they'd been trying to test me because *what is your name* is strictly not a traffic-control question.

They weren't answering.

Automatically I was easing the stick back to climb for the Saratov–Dzhezkazgan leg and save fuel, but I was also listening for any—

Have you been squawking on Code 4?

Yes.

Connors had said: "Tell them you're sending and let them tell you they're not receiving. Then sound surprised. And here's one buster who's glad he won't be there."

Signal on Code 4.

I waited 5 seconds and then span the thumbwheel against the ratchet and spoke slowly, this is Colonel Voronov calling you from MiG-28D SX454, so forth, repeating until the wheel came to a stop. At some point they must have picked up a few words and with any luck it had sounded as if the set was on the blink.

Silence.

This could of course be deliberate. They of all people know the effectiveness of keeping you guessing: They've used it as a tool in interrogation for centuries.

Watch what you're doing and get your RPM up for the climb and don't let those bastards work on your—

Did you squawk on Code 4?

Of course I did. I told you, nothing's not functioning properly.

I was safe up to a point because they couldn't ask me what frequency I'd selected: I'd been briefed that Military 4 was their top-secret code and they wouldn't want anyone in traffic control to know it.

Silence.

Ten thousand feet and still climbing. The optimum altitude for the thousand-mile leg in terms of fuel conservation was thirty-five thousand feet and the people down there weren't telling me to use a different level.

They still didn't answer but I knew now that it wasn't just because they were untalkative. They'd wanted to know my *name* because they'd been squawking on Code 4 and I hadn't answered and they'd wanted to find out why and I'd told them. That was all right. The thing that worried me was that they'd called me on the military frequency—they *must* have—for some specific reason and I couldn't ask what it was. It's one of the things the Soviets are very good at, these bland-faced silences that persuade you they're thinking of something else. They're not. They're waiting for your next question, because it's your questions, not your answers, that tell them what they want to know.

The set could have gone dead.

I fiddled with it and got static and some talk.

They were waiting for me to ask a question.

Bloody well wait.

I pushed her up through the last few thousand feet to thirty-five and levelled off and checked the panel and made out the log and tried to think what it was I was missing. I gave it a full ten minutes' concentration, going over the whole of the flight from take-off until now and looking for trouble and not finding any. The briefing patterns were intact and the schedule was on the line and you can forget the Hungarian phase because no one in Hungary is going to put a trace on a MiG-28D with Soviet markings seen going eastwards: If you want to defect in one of these things you've got to go the other way.

So there was nothing wrong. Except the missing factor.

Ignore.

ETA Dzhezkazgan was 12:16 and it was now 11:30 and I got fed up and pushed the levers all over the place on the air-conditioning control panel from full cold to full heat with zero to high on the fans and nothing happened except that I blew the map off my knee and had to get down there to pick it up and there wasn't a lot of room. The actual cockpit temperature wasn't too bad: It had dropped from 80 degrees to 63 since I'd started climbing from Saratov; it was the g-suit more than anything, and the increased heat of the organism due to stress.

At any given stage in any given mission you're not far from the crunch because you're usually working on alien ground and it's not long before an opposition cell picks up the action and starts coming in: I'm talking about the field executive in penetration work or in snatch jobs, where you've got to home in to the target and hit the objective or deactivate it or bring it all the way in, whether it's a document or a device or a flesh-and-blood defector. I'm not talking about the sleepers or the people in place or that sleazy crowd of pussy-footed pimps in the diplomatic infiltration set because the nearest they ever get to a crisis is when the paper runs out in the loo.

For the field executives the crunch is part of the trade and if it weren't there you wouldn't do it, but that doesn't mean you don't let it worry you, assuming you want to live. (Calthrop didn't want to: One of his contacts told him there was going to be a secret-police unit waiting for him at the airport but when he stepped out of the helicopter they weren't there after all because he stepped out ten minutes before it came in to land.)

With a thing like Slingshot the crunch was going to be fairly close the whole of the way: There was no specific opposition to initiate close combat but the *general* opposition—police, secret police and counter-intelligence forces—was there as a permanent background, because the alien-soil still applied and this was the sticky side of the Curtain: all they had to do was pull me in and there wouldn't be anything useful I could tell them that would get me back across the frontier with anything like a pulse. I'd got air-borne cover designed for getting me to Yelingrad through a reasonable degree of suspicion on the part of the traffic controllers responsible for the areas I was overflying, but if I ever let them get me down on the ground I wouldn't make any more progress because there wasn't any Finback SX454 on the roster for the 36th Squadron and if there was a pilot named Nikolai Voronov he wouldn't look like this man sitting here at the table under the five-hundred-watt bulb.

The stress to the organism was therefore normal but there was the missing factor on my mind and that was bringing out some of the excess adrenalin.

Something to do with time.

A time factor. An estimation of some sort. An assumption.

Never assume. Never assume *anything*. It can be lethal.

What plane are you?

I told them.

What is your destination?

I said Dzhezkazgan. If I said anything else they'd only start getting the twitters when I didn't alter course.

What is your present altitude?

Thirty-five thousand feet.

I waited for more.

There wasn't any more.

The headset was silent.

It was the first time they'd asked for my destination. That would be the military, putting the question through Code 3. They were getting warm now: I had to take photographs over Dzhezkazgan and there was still thirty-one minutes' flying time remaining on the log and that gave them plenty of room. They were already interested in me and I believed they were now checking on the information I'd given them, which meant it was a matter of time before they found I was putting out cover and ordered me down. This is what I meant when I said that on this operation we were going to work close to the crunch the whole time: If they decided to investigate me they only had to say a few final words into my headset and Slingshot would detonate. *You are ordered to land immediately.* Tick-tock-bang.

I sat listening to the long-drawn muted thunder of the jets. Through the windscreen the sky was bisected by a line of cloud reaching from somewhere near the ground fifty miles away to as high as I could see; one huge swathe of the darker half was almost black but there was no lightning: It was too cold for a storm, though it could be a mile-high drift of snow moving up from the south-east. It didn't worry me because my speed was consistent at Mach .95 and I would reach the camera target in twenty-five minutes from now and climb above the weather if I had to.

What worried me was the time factor: the thing I was missing. It had something to do with Fürstenfeldbruck and there was an image floating at the edge of consciousness that I still couldn't recognise. Ignore. Let it come in when I wasn't thinking of it: It's the only access to the subconscious.

Another thing that worried me was the shape of the airborne phase of Slingshot as seen on paper. It was wedge-shaped, in terms of increasing risk. I'd gone in at the wide end and I was now somewhere past the middle and I would soon be narrowing down to the point: Which was Yelingrad. But it was still open-ended, to a degree. I couldn't remain airborne over Soviet territory indefinitely because my fuel was limited and I couldn't cross a frontier because even at my peak ceiling I'd still be on their screens and they could shoot me down. Parkis had known this, and had framed a specific directive: At the moment when the wedge narrowed down to its point I was to disappear.

11

Duckshoot

ETA Dzhezkazgan was noon plus 15 and I began the run in from thirty-five thousand feet and made an ATA of 12:17 and took photographs and pulled out. From three thousand feet I couldn't see anything remarkable about the village, but the complex of farm silos might seem rather substantial and the long avenue of trees to the north could cover a transporter rail to the rectangular barns at the end: for rectangular barns read assembly plant.

Ten minutes later the centre-line tanks emptied and the light came on and I dropped them over the Golodnaya Steppe and felt the slight increase in airspeed as the drag came off.

Then I began running.

Yelingrad was five hundred miles and the fuselage tanks would give me that distance plus five hundred before we hit bingo and if nothing disturbed the pattern we could make it. But that was academic because an awful lot of things were going wrong: I was still on their screens and I'd overflown two suspect missile sites at low altitude and they hadn't asked any questions. To take those photographs I'd been prepared to fly a Mach 2 marathon on the afterburners and finish up with empty tanks a long way short of

Yelingrad. That hadn't happened and it should have and I didn't know why.

The Voronov cover wasn't *that* good. I was only a colonel flying a lone course, not a general with fighter escort. The planners in London would have spent a long time on this, working out *precisely* which rank would suit me best and having to choose between the authority vested in the higher ranks and the increasing availability of the lower: There could be a dozen Colonel Voronovs on the Soviet Air Force list and it would make rapid identification difficult.

Dzhezkazgan Traffic Control to Military SX454.

I told them I was listening.

Two minutes ago I had pushed the throttles forward and the Finback was climbing for thirty-five thousand feet at close to full power and I was not watching the three mirrors for contrails because I did not *believe* those people on the ground were letting me get away with it.

What is your course?

I told them 103 degrees.

What is your destination?

I told them Zaysan because Yelingrad was at the point of the wedge and I was heading in that precise direction. There was silence while they worked out that my course for Zaysan should be 101 degrees.

Repeat your course.

It had taken them five seconds.

I repeated.

Silence.

The jets were pushing me into the haze at a fifty-degree angle and the right side of the windscreen was filled with the dark cloud, its base line swinging gradually as I climbed.

Repeat your destination.

Told them Zaysan.

Use your Code 4.

Said I'd try. I didn't think much of my chances now because this wasn't Dzhezkazgan Traffic Control calling me: It was the Red Air Force.

I let sixty seconds go by and called them.

A different voice came on.

What is the purpose of your flight?

It was the Red Air Force and somewhere between Zhmerinka and this part of the sky above the wastelands of Golodnaya they'd started to investigate me on the computers and now they were going to give me the full treatment.

I refuse to divulge a military secret.

Thirty thousand feet and still climbing with the jets blowing out thunder and the windscreen darkening: there was no visual fix but the stuff I was going into looked like cloud-base.

The new voice began asking questions again: aircraft number, name of pilot, squadron, so forth.

Who the hell are you? I asked him.

Major-General Ivan Yashenko.

He didn't give his unit so the name should obviously be known to a colonel in the 36th Squadron of the 3rd Air Command. I put my left hand on the thumbwheel, turning it slightly back and forth while I was speaking.

The purp—my flight is—test the fuel-range—MiG-28D with— tanks of capacit—conditions of high—

Ten seconds.

You will repeat that.

So we were into the act and I moved the thumbwheel every time I anwered him and made sure to click back onto his frequency when he was speaking. There was a limited amount of smoke I could put out now and it wasn't going to cover me for more than a few minutes but it was worth doing because I was now levelling out at thirty-five thousand feet and sustaining Mach 1.8. At this velocity the sound inside the cockpit had taken on an orchestral quality as the ancillaries span at close to their peak revolutions, whining thinly above the bellow of the engines. The hollower roar of the exhaust was no longer audible because the machine was outstripping the sound of its passage by a factor of more than two, and this had brought a strange decrease in the overall volume: the ears, used to greater sound at greater speeds, felt deafened.

This is General Yashenko. Can you hear me?

Can—you intermitt—but—either channel. If—

I left it at that and stayed on the air and watched the contrails. They were about equidistant, one in each of the side mirrors, and had curved in from the left.

Yashenko had gone quiet and I span the thumbwheel, because it was possible he was now in touch with the two other aircraft. The contrails were expanding slowly and I could now see the machines themselves, small black shapes silhouetted against the white plumes they were leaving behind them across the sky.

I had to assume they were Foxbats, since according to NATO Intelligence reports that was the only aircraft capable of gaining on me so fast at my present airspeed of 1,200 knots.

I watched the mirrors.

—*Ko—can you hear—*

I waited.

This is General Yashenko. Can you hear me?

I can—times—but—

You are ordered to land your machine immediately.

One of the doors slammed in my mind: one of the doors to survival. I'd been expecting the order but not so early. Something had started travelling faster than the three of us up here, some new element of intelligence.

I didn't reply.

The two aircraft were now beginning to come up on me and their shapes were in each of the three mirrors, quite large configurations with rectangular sides and inclined tail fins, perfectly outlined against their white contrails.

Colonel Voronov: You are ordered to land immediately.

Sometimes a few seconds are worth saving and I moved the thumbwheel across and across a ten-degree arc as I spoke.

Suggest contact—base commander at—or—yevsk satellite field. My—to remain on—mission—

I set the wheel and concentrated on the two Foxbats as they drew gradually abreast, one on each side at a distance of something like a hundred yards. I could make out the pilots' heads: The one on the left had his face turned to watch me and I thought I saw his hand waving. I waved back. The one on the right was also waving, with a distinctive hand motion pointing over and down, over and down. I suppose they were calling me up and not getting any answer. I waved again to acknowledge and then checked instruments and made a calculation on the log. The city of Yelingrad was twelve minutes ahead if I remained on course, and the white ridges of the Khrebet Tarbagatay range were moving into the bottom right-hand corner of the windscreen.

General Yashenko to Colonel Voronov, aircraft SX454—

I took a quick look at the Foxbat on the right and saw the pilot signal again, his hand jerking impatiently. Below him was the glint of grey water as we flew parallel with Lake Balhash, and I checked the green-code map for the last time.

—I personally order you to land immediately.

Connors had told me to yell at them and show my authority but I was outranked and there wasn't any point in using the radio again because the two interceptors had been sent up here to signal me what I had to do. There was a fractional delay when I hit the throttle to the end of the quadrant and the Mach number swept up to 2.1 and held there while I pulled the stick back and watched the nose come up and the dark cloud swing across the windscreen.

Action is always faster than reaction and I had the Finback streaking over into a left-hand roll before the other two aircraft showed any change in their attitude. They were still in level flight as I met the wall of the cloud at an angle and ran into total obscurity.

The cloud-face had been ten or twelve miles away when I'd started the manoeuvre and it had taken upwards of twenty-five seconds to cover the distance but the interceptors must have lost something like a fifth of that period in total reaction time from the alert in the pilot's brain to the start of military power and for the moment they'd lost me.

The tight swing of the turns had sent the blood into my legs and the g-suit was swelling and compressing them but there was a tendency to black out and the bellow of the jets kept fading and coming back as I tried to keep my eyes open and couldn't manage it, too much singing, the head dropping on one side, it doesn't really matter because everything's—*it does matter*—singing softly and the light—*it does matter pull out of it pull yourself out of this* —the head coming up and the panel lights glowing below the blank windscreen and reflecting down from the canopy as the thunder of the jets came back and I shifted the controls and set the Finback into an inverted downward curve because I had to get out of this cloud and get out fast: I was still on their ground radar and they could reach me with a blind-flying missile if they decided to get one off.

White ice was forming on the outside of the canopy and I flipped the lever for defrost and began watching the altimeter: The cloud base had looked something like ten thousand feet high when I'd last seen it but at one thousand knots airspeed I was being taken down so fast that I could find cloud at zero feet at the point where I came out. There were voices in the headset but the cloud was putting out too much static and I couldn't hear what they were saying.

Assume they are ordering a kill.

Six thousand feet and going down like a stone.

Five thousand.

The city of Yelingrad should be somewhere east by south but the compass had been shaken up by the turns and the aircraft was still at an acute angle of descent and halfway through a curve designed to bring me out at two thousand feet in level flight but you don't take this big a chance on instruments alone and I was easing the stick forward at four thousand feet.

Three thousand and bright light burst against the screen and I saw low hills and the snows of a mountain range much higher and to the left. If the two interceptors had taken up pursuit I wouldn't see them from here: They'd have had to make a similar trajectory and by now they'd be thirty or forty thousand feet above me and possibly inside the cloud, but in a few seconds I ought to start watching the mirrors because they were faster than I was and if they came up behind me again they could float a missile at me without even taking aim.

The compass had steadied and gave a reading of 106 degrees but it didn't mean anything because the roll had taken me two or three thousand feet north of my original course and the blackout had lasted several seconds and I didn't know what the Finback had been doing while I was out. The weather had been moving in from the south and the only feature I could see clearly was the range of white peaks dead ahead of me and they had to be the Khrebet Tarbagatay, fifteen miles beyond Yelingrad. It was a fix and I continued level flight at close to Mach 1.2, still using a lot of the gravity I'd picked up from the thirty-thousand-foot dive. The ground features were streaming past the canopy when I looked down but I saw the missile because it was ahead of me and just lifting from the launcher two thousand feet below. It was long and thin and white and my instinct was to kick the controls and get out of its way but that would be fatal because it could home on me wherever I went.

I watched it.

At this airspeed forward and the speed of the missile upward the collision point was seven or eight seconds away and I decided to remain on course for four seconds and try to judge the closeness of the thing by noting its size. This wouldn't be easy because the combined speed at point of impact would be in the region of three thousand knots and the process of vision is not instantaneous: The brain has a mass of computing to do when the eye sees a moving object.

I sat waiting. *The idea,* Thompson had told me over his cup of tea, *is to leave it as late as you can.*

It was now very hot inside the cockpit because I'd left the defroster going and a trickle of sweat had reached a corner of my eye and there wasn't time to do anything about it. A stray thought was trying to come in but I blocked it and flicked a glance at the fuel gauges for the inboard tanks because at low altitude and military speed this Finback used three thousand gallons per hour and I couldn't sustain this speed for more than nine minutes longer.

Three seconds.

Stray thought: Resist, irrelevant.

The missile had canted over to the vertical and was well clear of the launcher and from this distance it looked like a white telegraph pole rising from the background of low hills. The warhead would not be nuclear because you can kill off any given aircraft with a prescribed minimal charge of conventional explosive but the result would be as effective and I became aware of my position here in the air and my relationship with the data streaming into the senses: the undulating hills and the idea of green grass and the summertimes of youth, kite-flying under the drifting cumulus; the sound of the engines that were driving me so tumultuously across the planet's surface toward the point of extinction; the feel of the pressure suit and the back of the seat connecting me to the mundane world of engineering while the psyche began its last long scream of terror inside the organism.

Two seconds.

Stray thought persisting: *Yes,* it *had* been the time factor I'd been overlooking since I'd breached the invisible frontier and entered Soviet airspace unmolested, because these people were now ordered to kill and they must therefore be certain who I was. They would deal with a rebellious pilot of their own forces less drastically, leading him down with their interceptors or simply waiting till he ran out of fuel: The quarter-master general of the Soviet air command would know better than anyone how much these aircraft cost, and they weren't to be thrown away. So now I knew this: The element of intelligence that had outpaced me from Fürstenfeldbruck had now been examined and assessed and was still in time to hurl a missile into the sky above Yelingrad.

Behrendt had broken.

One second.

Behrendt had broken and not long ago, holding out as far as the edge of lunacy and at the final moment saving enough of his mind for them to ravage.

When did this aircraft take off? Pain beyond comprehension, the body disintegrating. *What is its mission?* If I tell them, what will be left of me to go on living? *Is the pilot an American?* Stop just let them stop just let them stop just let them stop. *Throw water. Quickly—throw more water.*

So that was the time factor I'd got wrong. When I'd crossed the frontier without drawing their fire I'd assumed that security had never been breached, that Behrendt was no longer a threat. But at that time they were still working on him and he'd broken only an hour ago, or half an hour, in time for the information to be flashed through the priority-signals network and trigger the long white cylinder that was gliding upward and towards me now, curving slowly into the windscreen with the silence of a shark.

Zero seconds.

The idea is to leave it as late as you can, so when you go into the turn you're as close to the missile as you can get.

I watched it coming, through the clear glass of the windscreen. It was turning slowly at the command of the electronic guidance system, the pointed nose tilting to focus on the target and the fins swinging into line behind it. The trickle of sweat at the corner of my left eye had begun stinging but I had to ignore it because this was the time when an estimation had to be made about the size of the missile and its closeness: the delay of four seconds before starting to avoid it had been arbitrary, a desperate attempt to control the conditions by an educated guess. It could already be too late.

It was difficult to see, to judge. The thing was now lined up in a head-on attitude and looked like a white ball shining in the light and increasing rapidly in size as it floated toward the windscreen.

The organism was screaming.

Turn.

Shuddup and wait.

The distance has got to be so short that it can't make the turn when you do. You don't give it enough room to manoeuvre, okay?

Sipping his bloody tea.

Turn now.

Wait.

The whiteball came floating, its high-explosive content still inert in these last few seconds.

You're working on a very narrow margin, you see, between hit and miss.

Floating, dead centre in the windscreen, the fins revolving slowly in the light.

The left eye watering now, the vision blurring.

Somewhere along the invisible line that ran from the nose of the Finback to the nose of the missile there was the ideal point where the turn had to be initiated, before which the missile would have room to follow, after which the two objects would collide and explode. But there wasn't time to measure its position visually; nor had I had the weeks and months of simulator training and combat experience that would have allowed me even a reasonable guess. At a combined speed of three thousand knots the object in the windscreen was approaching my co-ordinated eye-and-brain system at a relative speed of zero: The ball was simply expanding, not moving, against a background of blank space that offered no reference. The most I could do was make sure that when I initiated the turn it was at the point where I thought it would be effective, not at the point where my nerve broke.

Don't forget to turn into the missile's trajectory.

It turned into mine. It's the same thing.

You just go into a very high g-turn at the last moment.

That's all I've got to do. It's easy.

Turn. If you don't turn now we'll—

Shuddup.

Wait.

The ball was quite large now, floating as if motionless but expanding at a rate my eye could measure against two lines of reference: the sides of the windscreen. It was expanding very fast now, like a visual explosion. The fins were becoming a windmill.

Allow for the risk of target attraction, the mesmeric influence that will sometimes take the pilot all the way home to extinction. Allow for the margin of error. Allow for luck.

Turn now.

Yes. Now.

The control column shivered in my hands and the rudder bar resisted as I kicked at it and hauled the column back and felt the long wave of vibration coming into the airframe as the jets thrust it into the new trajectory with the stubby delta wings cutting the air and the ailerons taking the overload of pressure against their upper surfaces. The spheroid configuration of the missile sank immediately below the windscreen but it was still there and still trying to home in to the target; it would already have started turning for me, upward and to the side as the Finback spiralled into the rolling climb and I waited, letting the mind go and the body instruct the machine. This was all I had to do. The organism would have striven to do a thousand other things, rather than be destroyed; but there was no need for them.

I realise you think you're going to break the wings off, but that won't happen.

I felt, though, that it was going to happen. The whole balance of this aerodynamic structure had been altered and by a factor so extreme that I could feel it reacting as if it were alive: It had become skeletal, animalistic, vibrant with nerves that quivered in the controls and the seat and the canopy above me. Even its voice had adopted new and undefinable tones as its shape was forced against the static air at its fullest angle, making a gigantic reed of its cowlings, curves and linear sections and sending them singing as finely as the song of the wind above the roar of the sea.

Information.

I would appreciate some information. Are the conditions such that within the next half second I shall be proved to have reacted too slowly, too late? If so, spare me the technical findings, the degree of heat engendered at the heart of the explosion from here inside this cockpit, the force exerted outward from the centre, the subtler effect upon blood pressure, heart rate and cranial activity in the miscrosecond before the body flowers into a surrealistic sunburst, its blood bright in the sky. Spare me that.

But I would like to know *where* that bloody thing is and how *close* it is. I would like just this much *information*.

Sweat running and the left eye streaming and the mouth like a husk and the air pumping into the g-suit and squeezing my legs and the pelvic area as the force of the turn pushed me against the seat and held me there so that I couldn't move. Trying to look into the mirrors but a lot of blood going down and away from the head because this is a *very*—

You just go into a very tight g-turn.

Yes. Exactly. Blackly, and the singing in the nerves. If it had missed the target, missed, it would have singing, nothing to see in the black, the roaring fading and coming back, would have gone ballistic and come down Christ knows where.

Look in the mirrors. Yes but it'd be too small by now. Has it missed me, then, *has it missed me?*

MISS.

Good old Thompson. What about a spot more tea.

Suit getting the pressure up and the blood going back and I eased the controls and brought her out of the roll and checked the altimeter: seven thousand feet.

They're got more than one.

What?

They've got dozens of those things.

Head went cold and I sat up and brought her level and looked down through the bottom panels of the canopy and saw another one lifting off a launcher a mile away and seven thousand feet down, long and thin and white with the winter sunshine making a highlight on the warhead, coming up very fast with a second one lifting off behind it, no bloody go.

They were out for a kill and they knew how to do it and it

didn't matter where I went: These things were medium-range and the gauges on the facia were reading out a six-minute deadline for me on the after-burners and I couldn't shut them off because I needed the speed.

Voices in the headset, and a lot of static.

The cockpit was an oven, baking a body alive.

Some kind of campaign necessary: a glorious ten-second campaign to prove we went down at least with banners flying and the head held high, so forth.

This is it. They're going to kill us, they—

Oh for Christ's sake shuddup.

Half roll and dive. There isn't time to think and then act: The thinking has got to be done while the action's running. And remember the mountains.

The *only* thing to do was dive because I had to turn into their trajectories and their trajectories were identical. And remember the altimeter because at Mach 1.2 everything looks farther away than it is: There's no optical illusion, it's just that every time you blink at this speed you're a thousand feet closer to what you're aiming at and I was now aiming at the ground, six thousand, five thousand, four.

Half roll to come back on them. The low hills span through 180 degrees in the windscreen and I saw the two missiles, one large, one small, both spherical and lined up and expanding. Remember the mountains and their direction from this new position: they would be due east when I came out of the dive and the snow cloud would be still moving across from the south and blotting out half the Khrebet Tarbagatay range but that wouldn't affect me unless I had to change course.

And remember your briefing.

Then they were coming, both of them, one very big and the other floating a little distance from it in visual terms. I didn't have to do anything complicated: I just had to wrench the Finback out of its trajectory at a speed approaching eight hundred fifty knots and against the force of gravity and hope that nothing would break.

Pull out. Pull out now before we—

Of course.

Blind in one eye because of the sweat but when I dragged at the stick the big metal sphere floated down past the bottom of the windscreen and out of sight and the smaller one followed, but more slowly. The stick was shuddering in my hands and the whole machine was coming alive as the airstream was forced against the ailerons. The high thin scream of the ancillaries overlaid the bellowing of the jets and the voices in the headset sounded unreal, their meaning lost in the tumult that was shaking the aircraft.

Blood pooling into the lower half of the body and the suit reacting, squeezing. The organism was in terror because somewhere below and behind it the two missiles were trying to turn or were already turning and moving into the target and there was no action, simply no action at all to be taken except to maintain the muscular strength necessary to hold the controls in their present attitude so that the Finback would eventually pull out of the dive before the ground came up and blotted it into a smudge.

One thousand.

The right eye had moved to look at something and snatch at an item of data for me and I examined it: We were flying in a diminishing curve at one thousand feet above the ground and my head was tilting upward to look through the windscreen because it wasn't going to be the first missile or the second missile it was going to be the surface of the earth that would provide the other component of the impact, so be it, go out cursing Parkis, I hope you rot in hell.

We must have cleared the missiles but it was academic because the needle was down to four hundred feet and colours were filling the windscreen and sliding downward, trees, building, gold on a dome, *Downward* as the nose began coming up and the buffeting, began and broke off and began again until the thing was shaking like a dog and we were flying level through ground pockets and shifts of air with the perspective of a townscape streaming across the windscreen—towers, rooftops, domes—and suddenly the trees again, spreading past and behind in a tangle of winter lacework against the frosted land.

You are too low.

Understood. Adjust altitude.

The blackout had fluttered at the brain and for a moment the windscreen had darkened but the light was back and cerebration started up again, avid for data and desperate to analyse.

Remember the mountains. And your briefing. I was now at the point of that wedge-shaped pattern and the risks had narrowed to the certainty that at any next second they would throw more missiles into the air unless I could keep low enough to use what terrain masking was available and get off their screens. Get off their screens and go for the Khrebet Tarbagatay and do what I had been briefed to do: disappear.

I assumed at this time that there were further missiles in launch or already airborne but we had two minutes left before we hit bingo fuel and it was long enough, would be long enough if I could stay this close to the ground without hitting a hill or a tower or a radio mast, and that was a matter of chance. The rest was a matter of following instructions.

The snow cloud was drawing across the range with its base on the ground, and its darkness began closing in as I held the Finback on its course while the buffeting started again and shook the ground and the sky and the blood inside my skull and then eased off gradually, leaving vision partially clear.

The terrain below was now rocky and desolate, with crags rising toward the mountain range in the first haze of the snow. There was nothing—

Mirrors.

The shape was in all three of the mirrors and steadily increasing in diameter as it floated in the wake of the Finback, the explosive warhead catching the light and the fins revolving slowly as it homed in on its target. The thing was coming at me faster than I could run and if I tried making turns it would follow wherever I went because I didn't have the speed to break away and send it ballistic so the *only* thing I could do was get out and the *only* way to get out was to slow down because at this speed my limbs would be torn off but if I slowed down that thing in the mirrors would close in for the kill.

My left hand dragged the throttles back. I didn't know it was going to do that but the organism was taking over and the brain went on recording, interpreting, as the senses fed in the data: eight hundred knots on the airspeed indicator, seven hundred, six.

Don't forget anything.

Signal barely understood.

Don't forget.

Five hundred.

Floating in the mirrors, the fins turning slowly and lazily against the cold grey sky, the warhead enormous, a great sphere.

Remember camera remember camera remember camera remem—

All right got it now but that bloody thing's going to blow us up and I can't—

Camera.

Pulled at the lever and snapped the release and put my hand through the strap and looked up and saw the needle at four hundred knots and looked higher and saw the three mirrors filled with the spinning shape.

At three hundred and fifty I blew the canopy off and triggered the seat and felt the cartridge fire and thought *Christ we're hit* and then the windblast sent me whirling in the sky and in the middle of a visual sequence I saw the Finback and the long thin missile closing on it in the final seconds before the detonation boomed and the shock wave kicked me away and fragments came fluting through the smoke of the sunburst that had been the aircraft, picking at my body and whining past and picking again until I felt the jerk of the harness as the main chute deployed, a sense of life after death and the reek of chemicals, a glimpse of a torn panel turning like a falling leaf, a numbness creeping and then cold, intense cold, embalming the consciousness.

12

Spotlight

The feathers fell.

"Now," he said.

"What was that?"

"You will open them now."

The feathers fell softly.

"All right," I told him.

"Then of course you will destroy them."

He sounded so bloody formal. What else did he expect me to do with them: post them to the KGB?

The feathers fell softly on my face.

My head was singing. The heat was underneath, not on top. It didn't worry me. But the blinding white was everywhere, and that worried me. I put my hand up and saw someone's glove.

"What the hell do you expect me to do with them," I asked him, "post them to—" but he had gone.

Look.

A flying glove. My own glove. My own *hand*.

Deduction: My eyes are open and I can see. But all I can see is my own hand in front of my face, big deal. The white blindness must be something else, an object, a sheet of some sort.

The feathers were cold as they fell on my face and I brushed them away and the flames leapt, the ones underneath, and the whole thing blanked out to nothing, like switching the set off.

The second time there was a lot more beta-wave cerebration going on and I felt for the release clips and pressed them and fell away from the seat and held my breath for a long time while the pain went on. It was underneath: the left hip, the rib cage and the shoulder. I was lying on that side with my face in the snow.

I could hear a throbbing sound.

The snow wasn't soft, for some reason. I put out my hand and swept some of it away and felt rock underneath. I suppose it hadn't been snowing for long: There was no retrograde amnesia that I could detect, and I remembered there'd been only a light haze when I'd jettisoned the canopy and ejected; the weather had been coming in from the south-east, and I'd flown into it just before leaving the aircraft.

The throbbing was duplicated, and I listened to it. Sometimes it went right out of synch and I didn't understand.

Time.

I moved enough to look round and that meant holding my breath again and then respirating slow and deep, slow and deep, drawing in enough oxygen to stay conscious. I could see the crags now, outlined by the snow, jutting against the white background in a faint pattern of shadows, rising above and behind me.

Time. You've been—

Moved again and sat up and waited till the worst of it died away. I didn't know how long it took. The throbbing was much louder and I listened to it and got the message and turned my wrist: 1:17.

Total memory came back like shoving a cassette in the slot and I started moving again and much faster now. There weren't any data for the periods of unconsciousness but that didn't matter: What mattered was whether they'd had time to put these helicopters into the air since the explosion.

They were quite loud now and the last thing I remember thinking about consciously was the time factor: They'd had something like thirty-five minutes from the moment when I'd ejected to the precise present and that was ample to get these things airborne. The logical thought process stopped just here because the snow was still light and they could move very slowly within a few feet of the ground and they'd see that bloody parachute if I didn't do something about it very *fast*. I didn't think I'd broken anything but the left side was heavily bruised from hip to shoulder and when I got up I just fell down again and had to lie there dragging a lot of breath in before I could crawl along the lines toward the canopy.

The light kept going on and off and the sound of the helicopters faded in and out because I suppose I was partially blacked out by the pain but the head was clear enough and I knew Slingshot was going to blow if I didn't get that spread of silk under some sort of cover: They were probably looking for the plane but they might conceivably have seen me eject on their radar screens and it's much easier to see a parachute if you're *looking* for one.

Their noise was heavy in the sky. Under me the rocks were slippery: The pressure of my hands and knees compacted the snow into ice and I couldn't make any headway until I learned to keep the pressure directly downward as I went on crawling with the lines on my right side; that was the side where the rocks sloped away to the edge of a shelf and I didn't know how big the drop was. *Any* drop would be too big if I went over because there wasn't time to flake out and start all over again when I came to: By the closeness of their sound I didn't need to know how many seconds I'd got left to do this job; I knew it had to be done in the fastest time the organism could manage.

The snow slipped under my hands. Even though I tried to keep the pressure *downward* the snow slipped sometimes and my head swung and the light flickered again and the noise softened away. The primitive brain was moving its creature along and there was no need to do anything about that: It was pushing me at a speed that was just this side of losing consciousness; but the term "consciousness" was relative because I wasn't capable of working anything out: There must have been choices and alternatives for me but I didn't think of any; I just kept crawling through the haze and over the ice toward the indeterminate point in the distance where I could start pulling at the canopy.

Think.

I can't think. Haze, rocks, the fall of the soft flakes, the enormous drumming in the sky. Those are my thoughts.

But there were vague periods of cerebration when the pain seemed less: Perhaps I ought to be crawling *away* from the canopy instead of *toward* it because they were going to see it at any second now and then they'd see me too. If I turned round and moved in the other direction I could find a cleft in the rocks, some kind of shelter.

Think snow.

Yes, it's snowing. And they're coming.

The whole sky thundered with them now and my skull was filled with the noise and I stopped crawling and looked upward and saw one of them, a darkness moving through the whiteness not far above the rocks ahead of me where the parachute canopy was lying. I kneeled there swaying as the air came in sudden gusts, whirling the snow against me and past me in a small blizzard, blinding me.

Think camouflage.

Kneeled with my head hanging. Basic thought process: too late, they must have seen it, so forth.

The sky hammered and the snow came blowing, darting against my face and sticking there. When I opened my eyes and looked down I couldn't see my hands because the snow had covered them, and the whole thing came together and I got the point, camouflage, yes, the stuff was covering that canopy too. Started shuffling along the other way, fast as I could, the thing was to get as far as possible from this area because they'd be searching along a narrow band in the direction of the Finback's final flight, and they'd see me even if they didn't see the canopy or the seat or the lines under the cover of snow.

There was another one coming. It was somewhere ahead of me again but I knew I was facing the opposite direction now so it was no good going that way. My hands slipped as I turned round and I got terribly annoyed and stood up and went forward with my shoulders leaning against the haze and no real sense of tilting over until the rock came up and I made a half roll to the right and finished on my hands and knees again you *bastards* will you go away you *bastards* with the whole sky swinging and the sound of them booming in my head, the last of the thoughts drowned out by the force of it, only a flicker of awareness now, the awareness that I was some kind of animal dodging and scrambling on the mountainside as the eagles came in for the kill.

Period of total unconsciousness.

Better, quite a lot better when I surfaced and looked round me. It could have been hours since I fell but it was obviously minutes because another one was coming in and I picked myself up and staggered across the rocks trying to get away from it but it was no go: The thing was heading straight toward me and it wouldn't matter which way I went because I couldn't go far enough to get out of sight. The visibility was about a hundred yards and I could make out a group of boulders, immense blobs in the haze, their outlines rounded by the juggernaut descent they'd made from higher in the range.

I would have to reach them.

Various objections: too far, too little time, so forth. Ignore.

The thing above me was so loud now that I couldn't understand why it was still invisible: There was just the wasteland of white, with the earth meeting the sky at no particular level, white upon white, and somewhere in it the relentless hammering din of that machine getting closer, louder, while I stood there for another second trying to see it before I moved again, lurching over the rocks with the body leading the mind, the feet finding their purchase by reflex alone and the hands spread against the haze to push it away and let me see as I ran on, let me see the boulders.

The sky had become a storm.

Run.

Run through the storm and keep running.

It's too far, and too slippery. They won't see me in all this snow.

That's dangerous thinking: They'll be using field-glasses and you're black against white, *don't stop.*

Feet skittering and the air freezing in the lungs, aching against the teeth, stinging the eyes. They won't see me now if I—

Don't stop.

The whole world white and without perspective, without definition, a wilderness without end. *Don't stop.*

The pace dizzying and the swirling snow mesmeric, I could run as easily with my eyes shut but that would send me off my balance and if I fell down again it would be for the last time because they'd seen me. The boulders were close now, great white shapes humped against the sky with only the grey of shadows to show where they were.

The thundering of the machine was a physical weight trying to push me down and I shouted at it but couldn't hear anything. I had to look upward now because I was afraid of something so enormous pouncing on me without my seeing it: In the final seconds I would have to take some kind of action, scratch at it, beat my hand against it before it blotted me out.

And here it came, a black mass taking shape in the whiteness, the snow beginning to whip into clouds under the storm of the rotors, the air screaming and the rocks trembling under the tumult coming from the machine. It was moving slowly and was low enough for me to see the numbers on it as I reached the boulders and pitched down and burrowed into the crevice below them and stayed there with my eyes shut and my lungs heaving while the sound drew down and over me, passing me by and leaving a vortex in the air that whipped and fluttered at the rocks before dying away, slowly dying away.

The silence was total.

8178716 38 198 18765413 17 1 829.

It was very cold. After the heated confines of the cockpit this degree of exposure was getting through to my bones. I hadn't changed out of the uniform yet: It was added protection under the hunting furs.

The falling snow accentuated the silence: It provided movement and with movement there is usually noise and there was no noise, and the silence seemed more intense. There had been no further aerial activity: The helicopters had made three more runs along their line of search, spreading out each time they came back and flying slowly up the mountainside, following its contours. Now they had gone. I didn't know whether they'd located the wreckage.

8 1876 23 489873890 38 782 1 0109.

In the final briefing my instructions had been to disappear at the end of the airborne phase by ejecting at very low altitude and letting the Finback fly into the Khrebet Tarbagatay range and destruct. The missile had taken care of this requirement and the only thing I had failed to do was to photograph the suspect village near Yelingrad, because the surface-to-air crews had opened fire too soon; but Yelingrad was the target area and I might dig up some material on the village later, possibly something better than low-level photographs.

19 28889198614 15 1555 166 1887.

Ferris hadn't given me a gamma: I would have needed the matrix and co-ordinates and this way was much faster once I'd plugged in the introductory 8178716. There were ten variations and this was the sixth, indicated by the final numeral, and all I had to do was transpose, reverse, and remove blind numbers.

Kirinski. Alexei Kirinski.

I went through them again. The films were to be removed from the camera, and the camera destroyed. A courier would take the films from me at a pretended time, when—re-read: 9198761846, using the *sixth* variation, not the seventh—at a *prescribed* time, when I could give him any material I might then have for transmission. The main subject of the orders was the man Kirinski. I was to investigate him and send a report, again by courier. He was a forty-two-year-old engineer and at present lived in apartment 4B of the Union Building in Gromyko Prospekt, Yelingrad. And that was *all*.

I thought at first that it looked like a screening for entrapment, but they wouldn't have mounted an operation the size of Slingshot, involving the USAF and NATO, just for three aerial pictures and a screening job: An agent-in-place could do that with his eyes shut. It could be that London was preparing to bring Kirinski across and wanted to make sure he was clean, or that he'd requested screening as a potential a-i-p, but the same objection applied: Slingshot was a mainline project and the target had to be something bigger than one isolated Russian.

Just before three o'clock I read the orders a fourth time and committed the essentials to memory and burned them, burying the ash. It was now below freezing and I got back into my niche and opened some more food concentrate and nibbled at it slowly: It was the same bloody protein amalgamate they'd given me the last time out and it tasted of fish. I munched some snow for dessert and then struck camp, getting out of the uniform and putting on the polo sweater and slacks. The hunting jacket and hat were some kind of ancient astrakhan and smelt of moth-balls, but the fit was perfect and the feeling of chill eased off within a few minutes. The pain in the hip and shoulder was still a nuisance but I could move around well enough; the rib cage only hurt when I took too deep a breath.

I left only the fishing-rod behind, buried deep in a cleft among the boulders. The snow was now driving hard across the mountainside and visibility was down to less than fifty feet. My tracks would be well covered but that was all; there was no horizon now, and no visual reference for size or distance—a sheer drop a few feet in front of me could look like a ledge much farther below, and a smooth area of snow could conceal loose stones and an incipient avalanche.

It took me nearly twenty minutes to find that fishing-rod again and screw it together; then I began moving down the mountain with it, tapping my way like a blind man.

The target area is always a trap.

I went into the railway station at nine o'clock in the morning, waiting until there was a train in and a certain amount of activity going on. The descent from the mountain had taken most of the night and I'd spent an hour on the horse-drawn wagon from the farmstead to the town: They'd found me walking with my bundle and had given me a lift after the woman had insisted on giving me some broth and watching me drink it; she had been very concerned and I'd promised to write when I arrived safely back in Moscow.

The target area is always a trap because your work is clandestine, and by definition you are doing something illegal and will have the whole strength of the local police department against you the moment you make a mistake. Once the police have got control of you the problem escalates and involves counter-intelligence, interrogation and the inevitable consignment to the labour camps or the firing squad. The thing is, of course, not to make that mistake.

This leads you to take precautions from the moment you enter the area, as a matter of routine: precautions even against dangers that can't possibly exist. That was why, when I pushed my bundle into the parcel lockups at the left side of the booking office, I went across to the far side of the hall and bought a copy of *Sovietskaya Kazakh* and took up a secure position behind a crate of drilling-bits to watch the consigne from a distance of a hundred feet or so from the big plate-glass window I was using for the mirror. I gave it ten minutes and then left. The station-master had the keys to those things but there was absolutely no chance of anyone's taking an interest in me at this stage: I was merely instilling red-area routine into my movements so that they would become automatic.

I began working as soon as I left the station, checking for tags as an exercise and watching the people on the street, noting their dress, listening to their speech as I queued up in the government store and bought a cheap suitcase and a map of the city: They'd been out of stock at the station. Gromyko Prospekt was two miles away and I made a detour to get me to the only car-hire office marked on the map. Papers galore, of course, and I spread them out on the counter, noting that Credentials had used two different photographs for the Social Security card and the driver's licence, and made them as dissimilar as they could. The personal-identity *propusk* had the same photograph as the driver's licence and their dates were within six months of each other, though I was stated to have been a journalist with the *Sovietskaya Rossia* for the past four years, covering the southern provinces.

The best vehicle they had was a six-year-old Mercedes 220, which I suppose had filtered down from one of the East German consulates. It had an automatic shift, which the man demonstrated at some length, pointing out its advantages: You could lean one arm out of the window, light a cigarette in safety, or put your arm round your girlfriend while you were driving along.

"That's fantastic," I said. "Where are the wiper blades?"

"In the glove compartment." He showed me. "You want them fitted?"

"I'll put them on when it starts snowing again." The spare-parts situation was obviously no better than the last time I'd been in Russia: You'd still lose your wipers if you didn't watch out.

I paid the deposit and took the car three times round the block to make sure it wasn't going to break down right away, then checked the map again and drove to Gromyko Prospekt. They'd put some sand down along the main streets but the ice had begun to pack and quite a few Volgas and Zhigulis were cocked against the kerb with their bodywork bent in various places. A black Moskwicz came into the mirror three blocks after I'd started out and stayed there for another mile before it turned off at an intersection. Soon afterwards a Chaika limousine came hounding along in the center lane, slewing from side to side and pulling up outside a red-brick building near the main square. There was no indication of what went on inside, which was typical, and I put it down as the Communist Party headquarters or the local KBG, because of the guards.

By the time I reached the Union Building it had started to snow again, and I drove past the block and made two left turns and got out to fit the wiper blades. I then drove off and made an expanding box search of the streets in the vicinity until I found a hotel. It was a tall narrow building wedged between a market produce exchange and an employment bureau, and I left the Mercedes and walked round to the rear of the place and checked it out for access, exposure and geometry: single iron fire-escape from the fifth floor to the ground, high double gates to the yard with their hinges rusty and one of them broken away, a parked van with two of the tyres flat and the spare wheel missing, and a row of dustbins below the three barred windows on the left side looking out from the building. The exposure looked all right except for the place on the far side of the street at an angle of thirty degrees and I went across at the first intersection and walked back on the other side and read the official-looking board over the main doors: It was a home for unmarried mothers. I walked back round the block and went up the steps and into the hotel.

Papers, papers.

For two nights; perhaps for three, but that would depend on the snow. Andreyev Rashidov, an ex-captain of the Red Army, now a journalist. Yelingrad is a fine town, and its people are welcoming. I am sure I shall be very comfortable here.

One narrow staircase. No lift. Two doors to the rear, three to the side of the entrance hall, the front door being fitted with dead bolts top and bottom, the panels being glass but too narrow to let an average human body through in an emergency.

My baggage is in the car. I will bring it in myself.

It was a room on the fifth floor, which I had asked for. I like a good view and it isn't necessary to go down the steps of a fire-escape if you're in a hurry: Using the series of swings they've worked out at Norfolk you can reach the ground within three seconds per floor of any given building with ceilings eight feet high.

Roman-style central heating with grilled vents in the floor, two narrow windows overlooking the rear, a drain-pipe running down past the left-hand window but with one of the U-clamps broken away from the brickwork, discount. No telephone.

There is a bell to summon you to the hall, should you receive a caller or a message. You may order simple meals from the state restaurant across the street and eat them in the parlour on the ground floor, with vodka if you wish. To close the heating you merely slide this shutter, so. The bed is comfortable, as you can observe.

He was a tired stooping man with a habit of holding his head on one side as if he were listening to you with one ear and to something else with the other. The badge in his lapel showed him to be a Party member of the Yelingrad district headquarters, as he explained with an air of faded fervour. I was permitted male guests in my room.

When he had gone I checked for bugs and of course found nothing: This wasn't Moscow, but a small agricultural-industrial city with a garrison of the military installed on its outskirts at the end of the road that ran seventy miles to the frontier of Sinkiang. Beets, zinc and soldiery—and somewhere not far away a helicopter base I would have to locate—they had been short-range WSK Swidniks and I wanted to know more about them; it was conceivable that London would finally insist on that third photograph.

A little before ten o'clock I left the hotel and drove to the post office near the huge Museum of Folklore and Minerals and telephoned Chechevitsin. The number was reported as being out of order but in Russia this normally means the operator is in the middle of a conversation or didn't hear the number correctly, and I insisted and finally got a connection.

There was nothing I could tell from Chechevitsin's voice, which reassured me. He repeated after me that the twelve tungsten drilling-bits had arrived at the freight station and were in order. The consignment number was 3079. I thanked him and hung up. On a scale of one to twelve I was in good physical condition;

tungsten indicated that I had read, understood and was following
sealed orders; drilling-bits meant that I now had a car and was
therefore fully mobile; freight indicated that I was at present totally clear of surveillance; and station referred to the films. The
consignment number was of course that of the telephone at my
hotel. There's a diminutive ginger-haired clerk in London Cyphers
who sits on her thin little bottom all day working out one-time
speech codes for specific operations, and although we twig her a
lot she does a good enough job and searches out the local scene
very thoroughly; as I'd noted this morning at the railway station.
When we twig her too much she says she's going to give us a
birds'-egg collection in the code, which would of course mean
we'd been blown.

Ten minutes later I left the post office and took the Mercedes to
the junction of Gromyko Prospekt and Union Square and parked
it under the bare winter trees. There was no kind of surveillance
on the Union Building from the front, unless use was being made
of a window somewhere within sight of the main entrance; I had
no way of finding out. When I drove through the square and
round to the rear of the building I again saw no evidence of a
watcher. It took me forty minutes to satisfy myself about this because the man on the corner had been walking up and down and
blowing into his bare hands until a taxi picked him up. The other
man, in charge of the hot chestnut stand on the south side of the
square, had also interested me until I noted that he had been
standing with his back to the main entrance while seven people
had left the building and three had gone in.

At 10:45 I left the car in the square and walked across at the
intersection, going up the steps to the double doors.

There is a specific time during any mission when the executive
moves into prescribed hazard. The access phase for Slingshot had
been dangerous but only in a general sense: The Soviet security
services had become aware that one of their own military aircraft
with a foreign pilot aboard was penetrating their domestic airspace with a view to photographing ground installations, and had
shot it down. All that Corporal Behrendt could have told them
was that it was probably a photo-recco mission. That general dan-
ger was now past and at this moment no one in the U.S.S.R. knew

that I was on Soviet soil and engaged in the capacity of an intelligence agent. *No one.*

I could live, if I had to, in the city of Yelingrad for weeks or longer, walking the streets and sharing the life of the people here and getting in nobody's way until the time came when I made a mistake. The Finback had disintegrated and the snow had covered the parachute and it was unlikely that any search could be made until the spring. So I was in the clear and my status was neutral— the condition we apply to an executive during the first stages of his mission until the specific instant arrives when he becomes exposed.

That instant was now. I'd checked for surveillance on the Kirinski apartment and found none; but there could well be a permanent watch mounted at any one of the hundred windows overlooking the entrance to the Union Building, and as I climbed the steps to the double doors I had the familiar nerve-tightening sensation of walking into a spotlight.

13

Liova

I clumped the snow off my shoes as I walked into the hall and crossed to the iron staircase. The *dezhurnaya* poked her head out of the closet immediately.

"Look at my floor, comrade. I have to clean it!"

"There is no doormat," I told her.

She took me in with a quick movement of her head, noting my shoes especially. They were good ones.

"There is a mat on the steps," she said, more in sadness than in anger. To have good shoes like mine you must have either money, power or *blat*.

"It's covered in snow." I began climbing the stairs.

"Whom do you wish to see, comrade?"

I thought this was particularly blatant. It's the unofficial function of the *dezhurnayas* of all the Russias to observe and inform, should anyone demand the information; but they work under the accepted cover of a concierge and they don't often poke their noses out of it because they're unpopular enough as it is.

"What is your name?" I asked her deliberately.

She stiffened at once. "I wished to be of assistance, comrade."

"That is appreciated. I have official business with a resident."

She watched me as far as the second floor, through the railings.

The fourth floor was at the top of the building and I went along the passage and stopped at the door marked B and listened for voices. The fanlight was closed and I heard nothing. There was a bell and a visiting card in a bent brass frame: *Alexei R. Kirinski, Geological Engineer*. This was appropriate cover in a town where there were drilling bits stacked all over the station but of course it might not be cover alone: We've got an agent-in-place in Stockholm with an international reputation as an ornithologist and a man in Cadiz who charges five hundred pesetas an hour for teaching musical voice.

The door opened and a woman stood there.

"Yes?"

The smell of borscht and a wave of heat from the wood-stove.

"I would like to see Comrade Kirinski."

She studied me with large limpid eyes, taking her time and remaining perfectly still, finally throwing the dark curve of hair back from her face and asking:

"Who is it?"

"My name—"

"Excuse me," she broke in and turned away quickly: There were sounds of the borscht boiling over. In a moment she called from the kitchen that I should come in.

Good furniture, Chinese rugs and heavy curtains: The couch didn't come from the state store, nor did the inlaid cabinet. Of course they might have been left to them by someone, possibly a grandparent.

"What name was it?"

She came back, shaking her hair away from her high cheekbones. The camel-hair sweater wasn't from the GUM either, nor the soft suede boots. She too had money, or power, or *blat*. Or perhaps just Alexei R. Kirinski, Geological Engineer.

"My name is Andreyev Rashidov."

She waited for me to produce my card, in the manner of the bourgeoisie; but I wasn't going to do that. Now that I'd seen the jade I wanted to convey an air of discretion.

"Kirinski is not here."

"I know." I waited for her to take that in. "But I'd like to see him. Can you make an appointment for me?"

She went on looking at me with this stillness of hers. Her eyes were deep and her mouth was sensual, a down of dark hair shadowing the curved Slav lips; my awareness of her as a female of the species was getting in my way and I'd have to forget it because this place could be a death-trap.

"Is it an official matter?"

That didn't mean very much: In this country almost every aspect of life is official.

"No."

There were a dozen pieces, some of them a foot high, one of them a blue-green slab lying below the window, where it caught the light. Beyond it, through the window and through the black boughs of the trees in Union Square I could see the glitter of a headlamp reflector against the snow, and the blurred outline of the car itself. I shouldn't have left it there, in that particular spot; but there had been no way of knowing which side of the building the apartment was situated.

"Have you already met my husband?"

"No. I'm interested in minerals."

Her eyes moved slightly to the block of jade on the massive sideboard near where we stood. "How did you come to hear of my husband?"

I turned away, noting other things while my eyes were out of sight: the number on the telephone dial, the brass-framed photograph of the woman in nurse's uniform—*From Liova, with love*—and the two bolts on this side of the door where I'd come in.

"I was crossing the border," I said and turned back in time to get her reaction, "at Zaysan, and Kirinski's name came up in a conversation I had with some engineers who were coming through."

This was strictly groundbait—there was jade within forty miles of the frontier in Sinkiang and the Russians had mining concessions, Kirinski was a geological engineer, his apartment was full of roughcuts, so forth—but there was a lot of info coming through because she didn't seem surprised at what I'd told her.

"Who were you talking to?"

That was an easy one.

"We didn't exchange names—there was a holdup while they

were searching some vehicles." A throwaway with a lot of top-spin: "You know what the border's like in winter."

She was really very good. I couldn't tell whether she knew or not: She just went on watching me, perfectly still, while the borscht vibrated the saucepan lid in the kitchen.

"He won't be here until tomorrow."

"Has the snow held him up?"

That didn't work either. She moved for the first time, going over to the mirror and reaching up, pushing her dark hair back and showing me how hard her breasts were, under the camel-hair sweater. I hadn't expected that.

"The snow didn't start again," she said, "until yesterday." She was watching me in the mirror.

"You'll be glad to see him again."

Not groundbait this time. She knew what we were talking about and I knew what we were talking about, because of the way she'd reached up like that, and the way she was watching me now.

"It's lonely," she said, "when he's away."

The whiteness coming in from the window, lighting half her face; the heat of the wood-stove filling the air; the brass glow of the samovar in the mirror; the stillness.

"I can well imagine," I said. "But of course you've got friends." The quiet bubbling of the saucepan out there, with its sound of comfortable domesticity; the heaviness of the curtains; the weight of the minutes.

"Not many," she said, and moved again, this time towards the samovar. "Would you like some tea, Comrade Rashidov?"

"I wish I had time." I touched the piece on the table, outlining the jade with one finger. "Perhaps I could come again, before tomorrow, to discuss the proposal I have for Alexei."

She considered this, as she considered everything before she spoke. We stood within three feet of each other, across the low table; her back was to the windows now and her body was in silhouette.

"If you wish."

"Thank you."

"I shall be here this evening."

"Very well."

I bowed slightly and turned away, and she came with me to the door, opening it for me and waiting, perfectly still. This would have been the moment but I let it go and went into the passage and walked to the staircase without looking back. The door didn't close until I was going down past the third floor.

The old *dezhurnaya* called something to me as I went out through the hall but I didn't stop: There was a minimal risk I had to take care of as a matter of routine and time was running out.

The Mercedes started on the first go and I put the lever into drive and pulled out as the Wolga swung into the mirror and then slowed, giving me room.

Time check: It was four minutes fifteen seconds since I'd turned away and walked down the passage to the staircase because I'd looked at the time then: the minimal-risk phase had begun running at that point.

The Wolga didn't have a transmitter aerial of the conventional sort but it might have something more sophisticated slung underneath or built into the bodywork and I assumed it could send and receive at short range. There wasn't anything stuck on top of the Union Building but it had a flat roof and there could be a deep enough parapet to conceal a whole array of antennae. Or of course she could simply have picked up the phone.

Traffic was light: They'd thrown sand along the main streets but everywhere else I was driving on snow and the snow was becoming ice as the traffic packed it down. The automatic gears were going to be a nuisance on this kind of surface because I wouldn't have any control over the back end but I couldn't just let them sit there because they'd got my license number already and they could bring in a mobile police net as soon as they wanted to push the button. I started by using the truck just ahead of me and went into the first intersection with enough acceleration to give me steerage but they knew what they were doing and the Wolga was still in the mirror when I slewed out of the camber and straightened up along the street to the right of the square.

There wasn't any point in pretending I hadn't seen them or didn't mind being followed about because I minded very much indeed: I'd only just got into the target area and it was going to waste a lot of time if I let them do a snatch and put me into the KGB headquarters for grilling, strictly no go because there was also the risk that I might not be able to get out again.

Two trucks and I got between them by swinging deliberately wide and hitting some piled snow at the roadside and bouncing off and getting enough traction across the ruts to put on a little speed before I had to start slowing in time to stay clear of the truck still in front. At this point there weren't any brakes because on this stuff you could go just as fast with the wheels locked and I had to keep turning across and across the ruts in a series of zigzags to break down the speed. One of the trucks had started hooting because I wasn't making the conditions any easier for them and I saw their point but hoped to Christ they didn't decide to take a swing at me.

Two skid turns and I hit something, part of a street island, but nothing burst.

I don't think London had known I was going to walk straight into a trap when I called to see Kirinski, or if they'd known they'd had a good enough reason to let me do it my way: When you start investigating an unknown man on Cold War soil you take a lot of care and the only risk had been that the Union Building might be under permanent surveillance from one of those windows and that the observer cell had instructions to report on strangers. Apart from that consideration there'd been no hazard in calling at the flat because the woman Liova couldn't make a move while I was with her: I'd watched her through the doorway to the kitchen when she'd gone in there and in any case she couldn't have timed that stuff to boil over at any given effective moment—you can get terribly paranoiac about this kind of thing in the first few hours of work in the target area because everything's new to you and you haven't got any friends.

Crump.

I think the Wolga had crumped a wing on one of the trucks because it was hooting again and I could see the black saloon going into a slow spin across the street with some bare metal flapping up and down on the left front corner. I kicked at the throttle but there wasn't any traction: The 220 was keeping a reasonably straight course at just below forty miles per hour but we were on ice and there wasn't any useful degree of control. I was looking out for patrol cars now because it was essential to assume this was going to finish up in a concerted snatch with every department brought in to make sure they got it right. At any next second they could start coming in from somewhere ahead of me and then I'd have to do something different.

Much too fast and I took my foot off and touched the brakes and didn't get anything. There were some deep ruts in the middle of the roadway and I managed to bring the 220 over there by turning the wheel a few degrees and waiting for some grip; then I did the zigzag thing again and got down to below twenty miles an hour and found some sand and made an immediate left turn into a side street because on principle you can get an advantage by changing the pattern though of course there's the calculated risk of running into terrain you can't handle, I mean a truck across the road or a cul-de-sac, so forth. This one was all right and I thought I'd lost them because in Russia you never make a left turn: You're meant to go past the side street and do a U at the prescribed place and come back the other way, so they hadn't been ready for it and it could have given me a couple of seconds or a couple of yards while they shifted their planning but it wasn't a big success because the Wolga came into the mirror again and I said shit and sped up as best I could and started using the kerb as a cush to keep me off the crown of the road: You could hit something head on without even trying and London is terribly fussy about that sort of thing, *You will remember that on foreign soil you are a guest and your status is civilian,* so forth, reference to the rights of citizens and the sanctity of private property and all very fine, we really do see the point about leaving innocent people alone and not scraping their paintwork but when it comes to the crunch and you're running straight into your very own little private Armageddon with sirens and flashing lights all round you it's not quite so easy to remember the *Active Executive General Rules and Procedures* thing and last year Fairchild dropped a grenade down a sewer outside the British consulate in Costa Rica because some silly clown had pulled the pin out and he couldn't see anywhere else to put it. There weren't any casualties but Tewson said they'd had a signal through the Foreign Office complaining that someone had blown the ambassador off the pot, but Tewson's always saying things like that.

Very nasty slide and the front end caught the post at the corner and the 220 swung right round and lost most of its speed and I had to throttle up in a series of jerks until the rear wheels found some rubbish in the gutter and pushed the whole thing forward to the point where I regained some of the steering. The Wolga was filling half the mirror now and I didn't like it because we'd got into phase two a long time ago—it works like this: You can just drive off as if you haven't noticed them and try to lose them somewhere in the traffic without it looking deliberate or you can let them tag along and stay with you long enough for them to know where you're going, that's all right, they won't give you any trouble because all they want to do is get a fix on your travel pattern and find out where you're based and you haven't shown your hand.

Or you can decide to get rid of them as fast as you can and that's what I'd done and we'd gone straight into phase two and the next decision was up to them: They could bring in the traffic police to set up a block or put out a stop-and-arrest call and that would be that because the odds were stacked and in this particular case they could simply wait for me to hit a wall or another car and come and get me while I was picking the glass out of my hair.

It was a T-section and I turned right, looking for phase three. There was a tramway on this street and they'd thrown a lot of sand down and the moment I saw it I gave her the gun and whipped up to forty again and slid wide to get past a horse-drawn wagon and got it right and saw the police car coming across the intersection and touched the brakes and got some friction out of the sand but not nearly enough: We were still going too fast and the lights were at red and if I did anything wrong they'd want to pull me in for it.

Wolga close now. Close in the mirror.

They could have called for that patrol car. I didn't know.

No sirens yet.

A lot of slewing because I was trying to bring the speed down and the surface as a mixture of sand and ice where the traffic had packed it down on the approach to the lights. Speed now below twenty, nothing like slow enough to be able to stop. Traffic going across at right angles: pickup truck, two Moskwicz saloons, *a man on a bicycle* so I span the wheel hard over and got into a slow spin that smashed the rear end across a parked van and sent pieces of glass and chrome scattering across the snow. Facing the wrong way and I put my right foot down on the floor-

boards and waited for traction while the black Wolga saloon came
skating towards me, two men in it, I hadn't been able to make out
the details in the mirror but now I was facing them and there was
a siren starting to wail but the thing was I'd missed the man on the
bike and the rear tires were getting through to the rough stuff underneath the ice and the front came round in a slow waltz and we
got going again, snaking into the side street, two sirens, the other
one fainter but nearing.

Phase three is when you get out and run but it won't work unless you can get into some kind of cover and there wasn't any here
or at least I couldn't see any because the 220 was pulling straight
now and I had to concentrate and put on *all* the speed I could
with this *bloody* surface like a skating rink and sirens all over the
place and the Wolga close suddenly and the shriek of metal on
metal as it clouted a lamp standard and heeled half over, rocking
a lot until I lost sight of it, klaxons beginning and a voice on a
loudhailer, no go, there isn't a phase three because there's no hope
of any cover in a street like—

Hit something again, a parked truck, oblique-angle front impact
with the seat belt biting across the shoulder and a cloud of steam
as the rad took the crunch and I hit the buckle and kept low and
waited for the sickening force of the swing to lose its momentum,
side to side, the sirens closing in and the klaxons barking, side to
side and still slowing, watch it, watch it and wait, slowing, try
now.

Hit the door open and got out very fast and went for the nearest
oblong shadow, dark green gate *but it was locked* and I swung up
and over, dropping and hitting a stack of crates with one foot
smashing through the slats and having to *tear it out,* the whole
stack lurching as I tugged the foot and fell back and flung a hand
out in time, dogs somewhere *I can't stand the bloody things* and
someone shouting and hitting the gate you'd better *run* you'd better *run like hell,* a man's face surprised with his mouth open run
very hard with my shoes slipping on the snow where it had drifted
into the corners of the yard, *stop,* they were shouting, *stop.*

There was some kind of basement and I went through it and
out again, nobody in it, a stink of resin or some kind of industrial
chemical *keep running.* Wide street with nobody near me, several
doorways, a window grey with steam and some peeled lettering so

I stopped dead and opened the door at the side and walked into the restaurant, taking my time, going through to the back and finding the lavatories, three small windows, two of them jammed by the ice, the third one swinging upwards and out.

It took me fifteen minutes to get clear, walking just fast enough to keep warm, the way everyone else was walking, head down against the light fall of the snow, eyes on the ground to avoid slipping. Two police cars went past me with their chains clinking over the snow and their lights flashing, and another siren started up somewhere north near the area they were still searching.

I used the map and worked my way east to the post office near the Museum of Folklore and Minerals and called up the hire firm and told them in a shaky voice that the Mercedes had been stolen from Union Square while I was in the reading room of the Civic Library in Gromyko Prospekt. Then I called Chechevitsin and asked if he'd got anything for me and he said yes there was a courier coming through from Tashkent on the evening train arriving at 10:25, central station, Yelingrad. Name, description, rendezvous instructions, so forth. I said I'd be there.

4:56.

The snow had stopped.

I watched the Union Building.

I'd been here two hours and I was frozen stiff.

Every five minutes I had to wipe the inside of the windscreen because it kept misting up; there was ice on the outside and the wipers had seized up on the way here so I'd scraped the last of the snow away and left it like that. It was a fourteen horse-power Trabant with a stick shift and a defunct heater and a body like a foreshortened turd but Chechevitsin had said it was all he could get for me. It had been no good my trying another car-hire firm because the police would be on to that one: My call reporting the stolen Mercedes was just a routine action. On the principle that your survival in the target area can often depend on the narrowest margins of error you always take every possible step you can to cover yourself—it was highly unlikely that the civil and secret police would miss the obvious but I couldn't be certain. I only had the two sets of papers and I couldn't use the Voronov cover because the whole of the Red Air Force knew by this time that his MiG-28D had been shot down within fifty miles of this city and that he might have got out alive.

There was another risk factor coming into phase and it was the same wedge shape as the first one had been: Comrade Andreyev Rashidov and Colonel Nikolai Voronov were now the subjects of a search from two directions and the more the opposition found out about them the nearer those two lines would get, until they came to a point. When it did, I wouldn't have to be there.

4:59.

I'd counted more than thirty people entering or leaving the Union Building in the last two hours but she hadn't been among them. She could be away from the place now, in which case I was wasting my time, but the train didn't have to be met until 10:25 this evening and I could work on the target centre for the next five hours and maybe pick up some extra material for the courier to take away with the film.

This area was clean, at this moment. I'd checked it thoroughly and dangled my image three times round the square and twice past the Union Building in case any one of the hundred or so windows had an observer posted. There wasn't one. They'd picked up the Mercedes in this immediate area and I'd pulled a phase three on them and if they were going to set traps anywhere it would be here.

At 5:12 the first street lamps came on and I started up and took the Trabant closer, parking it in fair cover between a military Jeep and a small black Syrena at the corner of the square. It had meant taking my eyes off the field for a few seconds at a time and I nearly missed her as she came down the steps and started walking towards the corner. The engine was still running and I switched off and got out and waited two minutes and took up the tag.

She was crossing the intersection at Prospekt and Station Street when she saw the queue of people. I think she was on her way to a different place because there was a kind of double take in her attitude and she stopped to talk to a woman outside the store. She then joined the queue herself and I made a close detour and saw that a consignment of kitchenware had just come in: A truck with a Tashkent number plate was still unloading. There were approximately forty people already in the queue but that wasn't too long

for a Russian provincial city store in the middle of winter when
transport problems were added to the general lack of supply. If
Liova Kirinski stayed the course she'd be here for more than an
hour because she'd have to reach the head of this queue, choose
the merchandise, join the next queue with her order form for pay-
ment at the cashier's booth and then join this one again to collect
her purchases.

I gave it ten minutes. She was then off the street and inside the
store, with exactly thirty-two people still in front of her. Assuming
she'd been on her way somewhere else and might still go there
when she left this store I assessed the risk as low and calculated
and walked back to the Union Building and made one circuit on
foot to check for ticks and then went round to the rear. The last
of the daylight had gone but there was a three-quarter moon
hanging across the eastern skyline and the street lamps were
throwing down an ash-grey diffusion of light that picked up the
iron fire escape. On my first visit here I'd noted that the traditional custom was in force: On a lot of apartment buildings they
remove the lowest section of the fire escape so that it's still easy
for people to come down and drop to the ground if the place is on
fire but difficult for them to climb it. The official reason is to dis-
courage burglars but everyone knows that it's to oblige people to
go past the *dezhurnaya* every time they leave and return home:
The Party, police and military factions are particularly interested
in strangers visiting any given residential area and in Yelingrad
this interest is increased by the city's proximity to the Chinese
frontier.

There was snow on the windowsill below the first platform and
I threw dirt on it and got the necessary purchase without making
any noise. The rest of the climb was slippery but I was in shadow
the whole way up and the back door of the Kirinski apartment
was in good visual cover because the three buildings standing
nearby were blank-walled on this side and five storeys higher. The
door had a glazed panel but I didn't want to break it unless I had
to. The lock was a standard tumbler bit and I started work on it.

At intervals I listened to the sound background: a line of trucks
crossing the bridge over the canal half a mile away, presumably a
military convoy; men's voices on the far side of the nearest build-

ing, and the scrape of snow shovels; a radio programme, much closer, coming from the apartment below and on the left side.

The tension bar went into the keyway and I felt for the notch on the underside of the bolt, then gave it enough pressure to push the racking stump against the tumblers; I didn't know how many there were but the standard number was three. My hands were freezing and I was clumsy, getting the pick into the keyway but having a lot of trouble finding the tumbler and raising it. I had to try three times before I could feel the gate lining up with the stump, and I made a time check at 5:43 to establish temporal orientation because you can fiddle with a lock for half an hour and think you've only been at it ten minutes: It's concentrated work and you tend to forget the environment and that can be dangerous. Even with these small tools I was making a degree of noise and Liova could have left someone in the apartment: sister, neighbour, so forth.

I had two of the tumblers raised and felt the third one lining up with the racking stump. My fingers were now partially numbed and I wasn't sure whether it was the gate coming into alignment or the other tumblers moving laterally because of wear. Below the fire escape a car had begun moving, accelerating into second gear and going slowly past the corner and into the square. I'd allowed for various contingencies as a matter of routine: the merchandise running out before Liova was at the head of the queue, her original errand becoming abortive, a neighbour giving her a lift back in his car and shortening the time element. At this stage I'd hear her coming in through the front door and the risk was minimal.

I eased the pick away and increased the force of the tension tool and felt for movement and got it and steadied my right hand as the racking stump went through the gates of all three tumblers and the bolt slid back.

5:47.

Once I was inside I put the lights on because I could work faster and that was essential because the risk of being disturbed was greater than the risk of the light's being noticed and bringing some kind of enquiry.

Living room, one bedroom, kitchen, small dining room, bathroom, large closet, skylight, fanlight, four minutes to make certain there was *no* radio transmitter and *no* short-wave receiver, then

steady work, every cupboard, every drawer, every contained
space, and every visual cover material—rugs, curtains, pictures—
and every disguise feature—radio, lamp-bases, bookshelves, the
big leaved table. Forty-five minutes and no go, a blank, try again.
The deadline I'd estimated was one hour from the unlocking of
the door but that was arbitrary and she could be back here at any
next minute and I hadn't worked out a cover story because I
didn't yet know her personal relationship with Kirinski and that
was the key to what I could do here.

Box mattress, clock-case, Chinese vase, sink-cupboard, cistern,
gas geyser—the telephone rang and persisted and I waited and the
room was quiet again and I went on working—pelmets, toolbox,
sideboard base, cutlery cabinet—blank, every time a blank—and
the deadline one minute away and I began sweating.

Something had changed in the background sound and I went
into the kitchen again and cracked the door open and listened and
tried to fit this aural pattern against the one I'd heard before and
finally got it: The radio was still going but I couldn't hear it in the
living room because the walls were thick. I shut the door and went
back and began working on surfaces—walls, wainscoting, panels,
doors, cupboards—tapping and listening for hardness, softness,
diaphragm tones, reverberation, echo effect, dissimilarities in tex-
ture sounds, inconsistencies in surface structures, drawing blank,
drawing blank wherever I went.

7:29 and an overrun on the deadline of forty-two minutes, it
was no bloody go but this was the target centre and London had
worked for three months on *just getting me here* and if Alexei
Kirinski was clandestine in *any* way he'd have to conceal material
where he lived.

Sounds: clock, creak of the wood-stove, a door shutting a long
way off, *she didn't have to come through a door,* otherwise total
silence. I would hear her footsteps first. Listen for those.

Air vents, ledges, the skylight, the plumbing access panel at the
end of the bath, blank, all of them blank. I began measuring,
using the wooden spoon from the tray in the kitchen, comparing
widths and thicknesses: the wall over the kitchen doorway, the
side of the big closet, the depth of the sink recess, the base of the
sideboard, the rear wall of the closet again where I'd tapped before, with nearly four inches unaccounted for, warmer, measure

again, four inches, represented by seven spoon's-lengths from the master wall *outside* the closet and six and a half lengths *inside,* try tapping again, higher this time, all the way up to the ceiling, a slight echo effect in this section two feet between the beams and the beams *don't go all the way down* so it must be a frame of some kind and this knot-hole is in a separate panel and it—

Slides.

They don't tell you everything, in London. The principle is that if you know the overall background to any specific mission you'll tend to over-think and over-react to the point of actual purpose-tremor when you're at the target centre picking a lock or laying a fuse or setting a trap: If you're aware of the responsibility you'll shy at an action you'd otherwise take in your stride. When Gary Powers was shot out of the sky in Soviet airspace the imminent East-West summit conference was cancelled and the Cold War broke out again in Cuba, Laos and the Congo, and this was the direct consequence of one failed mission. It wasn't his fault because the U-2 didn't destruct: The point is that if he had *known* what the consequences would be he might have turned down the mission at the outset because he was only an executive in the field and he carried the built-in responsibilities of a five-star general in a hot war and that's loading the dice in any language.

I didn't know the background to Slingshot and I couldn't have turned down the mission in any case because those bastards had me over a barrel and indirectly this was a help as I slid the panel back and found the spring release and swung the flat zinc box away from the wall and lifted the lid.

Two compartments, each of them a foot square and with separate serial numbers: Z-A23V2/S and S-1289, the suffixes presumably belonging to one file and the main-body reference belonging to two different systems. A lot of material: photostats, diagrammatic printouts, two sets of holocryptic gammas with red and black pages printed on nitrated cellulose, KGB/GRU Monome-Dinome tables with complete matrices and side and top co-ordinates, and so forth.

Local military deployments and facilities.

Airfields, underground communication channels, silos.

Names, file references, variable cypher drafts.

One code-word heading: *Opal Light*. The first and last pages

were slashed across with a graphite pencil and the whole sheaf
was stapled top and bottom.

I didn't begin hurrying because there was no point: The deadline had burned out and all I had time to do was swing the zinc
box back and slide the panel across before she said:

"How did you get in here?"

14

Fusillade

She stood there watching me for two or three seconds with that total stillness of hers, her large eyes intent on me. The brown paper package she was holding looked heavy, and I said:

"Let me take that."

"No," she said and put it down on the desk near the door and picked up the telephone and pulled a short 9mm automatic from inside her astrakhan coat. There wasn't time to reach her but I was close enough to the low table and didn't move.

"Operator," she said into the phone without looking away from me.

"You've got the safety catch on," I said, "so you can't—"

She looked down and I went for the big piece of jade on the table and swung it in a curving vector and pulled the table upwards against me and the shot sent splinters whining across my face an instant before the jade hit the gun and she cried out in pain and I got across to her before she could try it a second time.

The gun had slid across one of the Chinese rugs and she wrenched herself free and got halfway there before I caught her again and threw her against the settee and went for the gun myself and got it and hit the magazine out and slipped it into my pocket and kicked the gun hard and sent it spinning across the floor-boards into the kitchen as she came at me with her nails and got close before I caught her wrists and crossed them and put some pressure on, twisting her round so that she had her back to me, snow on her astrakhan coat and her neck cold against my face as I whispered to her.

"If you make any noise I'm going to kill you." It was the closest I'd been to a woman since that stupid bitch in Fürstenfeldbruck and she smelt of woodsmoke and damp hair and the oils in her skin.

A door had opened. I only just heard it.

She leaned her back against me and took deep breaths, moving her arms slightly to find out how much strength she'd need to free herself. I didn't have to warn her about this; the pressure I was using was already cutting off the circulation.

They were outside now.

I whispered again, close to her ear. "When is Kirinski coming back?"

She didn't answer. They were knocking at the door. Kirinski wouldn't do that. I brought more pressure on her wrists until a sound came from her throat; then I stopped because I didn't want any noise. They began calling through the door.

"Liova! What happened?"

"It was nothing," I whispered. "You broke a light bulb."

I gave a quick twist to inflict pain as a warning and then let her arms free because she had to get her voice steady and I wasn't sure she could do it.

"Liova Kirinski? Are you all right?"

Then she called back to them, doing it well, even getting the hint of a laugh in her voice as she told the woman it was a light bulb, that was all, she'd dropped it and frightened herself with the noise.

We listened together and in a moment heard them moving away along the passage; then she swung her head to look up at me and lifted her hands and I parried them with a wedge lock because I thought she was going to try for my eyes with her nails but she cried out softly, *don't,* and put her arms round me and kissed me through the wing of dark hair that lay half across her face, bring-ing her thighs against me and moving them from side to side as she went on kissing, drawing her hair away and using her tongue, using her pelvis against me until my body began responding and my mind warned me that she'd tried to kill me once and would try again the instant I was off my guard.

But there was nothing she could do without a weapon and if she broke free and reached the gun it wouldn't do any good and if she began screaming and managed to throw something and smash glass I could be clear of the building fast enough for total security so I let her go on and began using my own hands to open her coat and bring her against me as she asked on a breath *who are you,* again and again, as the girl had done in the snows of Prague, *who are you?*

We were on the floor now and she was already in orgasm as she pulled me in with her nails burning across my thighs and her dark head rolling from side to side as she moaned softly, from side to side in a rhythm she couldn't stop. Part of my mind became occupied with impressions as twilight cerebration went on: the curved head of a dragon on a Chinese rug, an empty gun lying on a kitchen floor, a telephone dangling on its cable with a faint continuous whine coming from its black plastic, the glow of a huge iron stove and above it a bright copper samovar, and her name, Liova, and her sweat slipping on me, her breath against my face and her sharp hands everywhere, wanting to hurt and draw blood. And the smell of cordite still in the room.

In a moment she was lifting me with her thighs, faster and faster, her breath coming desperately as if she were drowning; so I hurt her as I knew she wanted me to and her second orgasm came at once like an explosion and she cried out and I put my hand over her mouth and she bit the palm with the sharpness of a snake but I kept it there because she was supposed to be alone here.

After the third time she let go and went limp against the floorboards with her arms flung out and her hands open, and I watched her face, bright with sweat and as if sleeping, the dark lashes throwing soft crescent shadows in the light of the stove's embers, her hair spread like a wing across the edge of the rug, her mouth quiet and her breath inaudible.

I wondered what her fantasy had been. I didn't think it was Kirinski.

The swing of headlights passed across the ceiling, faint in the room's illumination, and I came away from her.

"Stay with me," she said. Her eyes were open, watching me.

I said: "You don't know who I am."

My body was too relaxed, the nerves too quiet.

"Don't go," she said.

I went over and put the phone back on the hook.

"Why do you carry that thing?" I asked her.

"What thing?" She got up from the floor, tousled and drowsy.

"The gun."

"He makes me."

"Why?"

"To protect myself."

"Against what?"

"I don't know," and she was suddenly angry, either because I wouldn't stay or because I'd reminded her of something. "How should I know?"

"You know him, don't you?"

"Nobody does." Her face was white, some kind of reaction, the shock of the gun going off and then the animal need and now the real world still going on, something like that or of course I could be wrong, she could be the head of the local KGB for all I knew.

"When is he coming back?"

"Tomorrow."

I didn't think she meant to answer: She did it without thinking, her head swinging to look at me, as if caught out.

"Who did you call, when I left here this morning?"

Her eyes went down. No, she wasn't working for anyone: She was unsuited and untrained. "I didn't call anyone," she said.

"Don't call them again, when I leave here." I went up to her and waited until she looked at me. "Kirinski wouldn't like it." That was a direct hit: She looked frightened.

"Who *are* you?"

"Andreyev Rashidov." I turned away. "The telephone rang about an hour ago. Would that have been Kirinski?"

"I don't know."

"Who were you going to call just now, when you came in?"

She hesitated. She couldn't get anything right.

"The police."

"Why?"

"I was afraid of you. I didn't know how you'd got in."

"It's not important." She was an amateur and they're unpredictable and therefore dangerous and I didn't want to know any more, not from her. "What time do you expect him here? Kirinski?"

She hesitated again and I said—"Come on, what *time?*"

I saw her flinch: The tensions were coming back in her faster than in me. I went up to her again and said: "You're in too deep, Liova. For God's sake get out while there's time. Go away, where he can't find you. There's no future in this game, even for the professionals."

She didn't say anything. She didn't know whether to trust me, and I knew I couldn't trust her. Living things only bite when they're frightened and she was frightened sick.

"What time," I asked her quietly, "is he coming back?"

In a moment she said: "In the morning."

"All right." I went across to the kitchen and picked up the gun and snapped the magazine back into it and gave it to her. "Tell him to meet me on the north side of the Lenin Memorial tomorrow at noon."

She looked down at the gun as if she'd never seen it before, then dropped it onto the settee.

"Tell him to be there alone." I picked up the telephone and tore the cable away. "Tell him I can get him a life sentence at a forced-labour camp if he makes a mistake." I went out and down the stairs and into the snow.

His name was Gorodok.

This must be one of the military roads: It had been cleared after the last snow and I'd only seen three private cars and a produce truck; the rest of the stuff had the red star on it—Jeeps, transports, armoured cars, a mobile gun with a full crew muffled up to their ears in their greatcoats. There was a camp somewhere; these weren't convoys.

I drove steadily, not too fast. I didn't want any attention.

It was 9:32.

Of course, he could be from London—some bright spark from

the reserve pool on his first Russian assignment or one of the agents-in-place working the area south of the Omsk-Novosibirsk line, it could be anyone, cover name Gorodok, it didn't mean anything.

I wanted to drive fast because my mind was racing but this had to be done with care and there was quite a bit of traffic on this stretch and if I hit anything I'd have to argue the point with the military and that could screw the whole thing up if someone hadn't done that already. It was freezing cold in the Trabant but I was sweating because Chechevitsin had only given me the action signal and *nothing* else, no explanation.

He'd got pretty desperate because there were three messages for me at the hotel when I'd got back there and all of them were for me to call him. I did it from the pay phone round the corner at the household store because this one obviously wasn't for the hotel connection.

Three military trucks in a line and I felt their wind-blast as they went by and left the night black again after the glare of their lights. The road was tricky along this bit because there were hedgerows and the traffic had blown the loose snow across the surface and it had got packed down over the sand.

I wished to *Christ* I knew what had happened. All Chechevitsin had said was that I had to stop the 10:25 express from Tashkent twelve miles north-west of Yelingrad and rendezvous with Gorodok at the south end of the Litsky Bridge. I had to fill in the gaps for myself and that wasn't difficult but I didn't like the message because if I had to get the courier off the train in open country it meant he'd already been blown at this end and if he got off at Yelingrad Central they'd snatch him cold.

So I'd been moving into a trap before I'd got the signal from Chechevitsin and I hadn't known it, but London had. It's not my favourite feeling: It's like when you're going across on the green and someone takes it on the red and it's a question of inches and you think Jesus, *what if*. The labour camps were there in Murmansk and Chita Province for me too, as well as Kirinski.

9:41 and two miles to go and I took the left fork and found the dirt road that ran alongside the railway. There were clinkers and broken asphalt and bits of timber the whole way along it because it was a service road for the maintenance crews when they had a problem on the line: I'd talked to a switchman for half an hour at the station when I'd gone there to pick up the films.

The moon was in the south-east and I tried shutting the head-lights down at intervals and found I could keep up the speed if I watched the left-hand side below the embankment. The switch-man had said the signal box was a mile this side of the bridge and the express was due at the bridge at 10:09 unless the snow had delayed it. He'd asked me why my department was surveying the line in mid-winter and I'd said there were some embankment faults showing up on the far side of the bridge and he didn't seem inclined to argue.

I passed the signal box at 9:45 with my lights full on and kept going for two minutes and then slowed and doused them and turned round and stopped and waited. The timing had to be cut fine because the man in the box would put a call out for emergency crews and I would only have as long as they took to get here.

The snowscape was bluish-white under the three-quarter moon and the stars were huge; the line of telegraph poles alongside the railway cut the dome of night in half, their stark outlines diminishing to a vanishing-point where the squat black rectangle of the signal box made a blot against the snow. Over to my right, to the east, a small cluster of lights drifted, red and green and white, as an aircraft went into the circuit above the field six miles away: The maps had it down as a civilian aerodrome. With the window down I listened in the silence and picked up the sound of its engines: It was a turbo-prop. Nearer and much louder a night bird called across the desolate countryside.

At 9:53 I started up and put the headlights full on and reached forty miles per hour over the rough surface before I hit the brakes and began using the horn in short warning blasts as the yellow-lit windows of the signal box loomed above me on the right. I was already running with the cinders crunching under my feet and the Trabant sliding to a halt with the door open and the handbrake on and the engine still running. The steps to the box were free of snow and dark with sand as I went up them two at a time and hit the door open.

"There's a plane down across the line!"

One man, thin, greying, startled, dropping long-legged from the stool and standing uncertainly, staring at me.

"It's blocking the down line—give me some flares!" I was looking around for them but the light was bad in here: a couple of enamel-shaded bulbs hanging low above the plotting desk that threw awkward shadows.

"Are there people?"

"What?"

"The pilot. Does he—"

"Yes. Have you got a first-aid box too?"

He went on staring at me for another two seconds, was I a drunk, was I a joker, was I a psychopath, so forth, then he moved steadily and threw one of the big metal levers and ducked below the plotting desk and dragged out a bucket with a wooden cover and swung it towards me. I caught it and he pulled a cupboard door open and slid a box down, white-painted with a red cross, using his fist to make sure the lid was secure.

"You have a lamp?" he asked me.

"Yes." I made for the door.

"Where is the machine down?"

"Just this side of the bridge—"

"The Litsky Bridge?"

"Right."

I left the door open and dropped down the steps and ran to the Trabant, gunning up and slinging a wave of snow and cinders into the moonlight as I skid-turned and hit the lights on and got going. At this point the time pattern became critical because the train had to reach the bridge before the emergency crews got there and in snow conditions it could be half an hour late, an hour, it was totally unpredictable and therefore characteristic of what happens when a wheel comes off: You can keep going but you're always just this side of a smash till you make a mistake and then the whole lot goes.

I wouldn't have to make a mistake but Gorodok could make one and so could Chechevitsin and so could London because they were running this thing by remote control with no director in the field and the courier line beginning to blow. We could go down on luck alone because tonight's action was strictly shut-ended. If the Tashkent express arrived any time after the deadline I'd have to get out, and the deadline was the precise moment when the emergency crews would start asking questions. If they got here before the train came they'd want to know where the aircraft had come down and I could expand the timing quite a bit by telling them it was between here and the signal box, hadn't they seen it, so forth: the embankment was forty feet high along this stretch and they could easily miss any wreckage because it'd be above them and unlit. But then they'd come back because they hadn't found anything and at that point they'd start asking me questions and that would be when I'd have to get out of here and there was no guarantee they wouldn't use the phone in the signal box and report a hoax and get me stopped by a police patrol on my way back to the city, strictly shut-ended if I pushed the deadline to that particular point and just as bad if I decided to get out before they suspected a hoax because they'd douse the flares and change the signal and let the train go through and Gorodok would get off at Yelingrad and walk straight into a snatch, no bloody go: The classic mortality rate of a courier line after the first courier gets blown is a hundred per cent and that's perfectly logical because they're a chain and a chain is as strong as the first link to break, *finis*.

By 9:59 I was near the bridge and saw that the signal for the down line was still at red. It was a dead straight stretch and I left the Trabant on rough ground, kicking the throttle and holding the wheel hard over and burning the snow off the surface to leave me with a reliable take-off pad for use in an emergency. The flares were a foot long, red-paper-wrapped pitch with an iron spike at one end and a friction-ignition cap at the other. The moonlight was good enough to use as background and I staked them out at fifty-foot intervals on both sides of the track but left them unlit because on the wrapping paper their duration was given as fifteen minutes and they could burn out before the train got here if it was late.

I began waiting.

From where I was standing, at the top of the embankment, the night had two components: a disk and a dome, the gigantic disk of the earth's surface spreading blue-white under the moon and the gigantic dome of the sky, pricked and glittering with stars. Only the bridge made a connection between the two, breaking the skyline a quarter of a mile away with its dark skeletonic girders curving across the snows like the bones of a dead rainbow. In the opposite direction, to the north-east, I thought I could glimpse the windows of the signal box a mile distant, a yellow point of light that I could see only when I looked slightly away from it, and not always then. That was where the headlights would begin showing along the service road, a little while from now.

Eastwards a small plane was taking off from the airfield; its navigation lights were still invisible but I could hear the distant snarl of its engine as the power came on. Moments later the red-and-green motes of light began rising and floating across the stars, turning and drifting towards the south as the engine's note died, over the minutes, leaving the night soundless. To the south-west, beyond the Litsky Bridge, there was nothing. The whiteness of the land, lit from overhead, had lost all definition: I could only tell where it ended by noting where the stars began. Somewhere in that direction was the train and Gorodok.

10:10 and from this moment my nerves began tightening: When the ETA is reached you start thinking that a minute late is going to mean an hour late, and the situation seems critically changed.

Gorodok. Who was Gorodok?

Smith, Jones, Robinson, Brown, nothing in a name, but he was certainly English because a courier can be any nationality providing he's not in a *line,* and the Bureau has a strict ruling on the point. Too many operations have come a mucker because of a blown courier line, and apart from all the other considerations it can be deadly when it goes up. Two years ago we crashed a mission in Scandinavia like that and the ruling was established immediately afterwards.

The air was freezing and I had to keep on the move, going down the embankment and along the road and up again fifty yards on to make channels in the snow: If I had to get out of here fast I didn't want to waste any time doing pratfalls. In one place there was a lump of rock about halfway down and I pulled it out of the frozen earth and threw it farther away and filled in the hole with gravel and looked at my watch again and saw we were going to cut this fine, too fine for comfort, 10:21 and the night quiet with no sound from the south-west, nothing to break that silence out there.

This time I was certain I could see the yellow light of the signal box, low on the horizon. He had seemed an efficient, steady-handed man, the type who would think of telephoning the airfield while he was waiting for the train, asking them if they knew there was a plane down across the line not far to the west of them: in which case there would be a helicopter over with a searchlight and as soon as it had made its first run I'd have to get out because they could scan the track for five miles in five minutes and report it clear.

10:24.

Silence across the night.

Whoever he was he knew what he'd got to do because we had a definite rendezvous and he'd be expecting the train to stop and he'd be ready. God knew when the alert had gone through but they must have warned him before he boarded the thing at Tashkent: They couldn't have got a message to him after that. The network was in a big hurry—he could've been simply sent to ground and someone else could have come in his place to take over the films but that hadn't happened and the obvious answer was that they hadn't got anyone else to replace him, but I don't like obvious answers and I would have said that London wanted to give me a direct contact and I wished them luck because some-one had blown Gorodok and they'd have his description out and he was going to have a bad time getting clear.

Who had blown him?

I stood listening to the night. My hands were now numb and I blew into my gloves but my breath was cold before it reached the skin. The stars had the glitter of broken icicles and the snow was an ocean, stilled and frozen, capping the curve of the planet and reaching to infinity, making it seem absurd to wait here for a thou-sand tons of metal to come steaming out of the void with the force of a fallen comet. There was a degree of sensory deprivation in this vast silence as I stood here, small as a molecule, between earth and sky.

Of course it didn't strictly matter who had blown him. What mattered was that the whole of the line was now vulnerable and would become exposed if he was caught and interrogated: It wasn't certain that the network could alert the rest of them before Gorodok was broken and the KGB went to work on what he'd given them. A courier is a mobile entity and not always at the end of a phone.

10:32 so there was snow on the line or the points were frozen or there'd been a derailment because we were now running twenty-two minutes late.

Or they'd stopped the train at Alma Ata and taken Gorodok off and he was sitting there now under the bright lights and they were starting with a cosh. They might have to work all night on him but in the end—

Sounds north-east, vehicles, and I turned round with a jerk and listened, cupping my ears. Lights. The sounds were intermittent, a series of low rumbles, and the lights flickered up and down. They were coming from the direction of the signal box and I watched them. The distance was a mile and over this road they'd keep up a good speed and be here within three minutes.

I turned and looked the other way but there was nothing.

Four and a half miles south-west of the Litsky Bridge there was a tunnel marked on the map and the express would use its whistle on the far side of it, assuming standard procedure; and in this stillness I'd hear it over that distance unless the emergency crews were too close by then. Their headlights were bright now, already throwing shadows over the scrubland and silvering the telephone wires along the track.

I gave it ten seconds and stooped and lit the first flare and then the next, moving back from side to side until there were ten of them going, their short stiff flames reddening the snow. The Trabant was directly below me now and I slithered down the embankment through one of the channels I'd made and got in and started up and gunned into a half turn with the lights off and headed for the bridge.

The flares would burn for fifteen minutes and in that time the crews would be here asking questions and if I told them the plane had come down halfway between here and the signal box they'd take less than ten minutes to look for it and come back and at that point I'd have to get out and if they'd left one of their vehicles in the way I'd be blocked and it'd be no go.

The light was tricky and I hit something with a front wheel and the Trabant lurched and half span and dug into the snow at the side of the road until I banged the shift into first gear and put the power on and burned the snow down to solid ground and took off again with the back end snaking across the surface until we got traction. On the far side of the bridge I slung it in a U turn and stopped under the first outrigger girder from the south end and got out and stood listening.

The only sound was from the north-east and I watched the lights moving in line and slowing as they saw the flares, the first vehicle halting below the embankment and dropping its crew off. These were *not* railway emergency units: Their lights were shining on the next truck ahead as they stopped in convoy and I could see the red-star insignia on their sides. The closest place to find help must have been the Army camp and that's where the signalman had phoned.

Soldiers were climbing the embankment near the flares, the blood-red light spreading over their uniforms and glinting on their rifles as they stood together, uncertain what to do. I could hear an officer shouting.

The flares had seven minutes to burn and I turned and walked to the other end of the bridge, watching the snows to the south-west and seeing nothing. The deadline had shifted to a new phase: It would now depend on how long the officers in that unit took to decide there was no plane down and go back to the signal box and report the line clear. The journey would take them two minutes and the night was freezing; they wouldn't stay here very long.

I heard shouting again and saw that a party of men had been formed up and was off on a jog-trot down the track: It had obviously been decided that the service road didn't offer a good enough view and that a search by foot parties was indicated. A second one was starting off, with an NCO running beside it. The leading transport got into motion, turning and going slowly back along the foot of the embankment.

Whistle.

Or my imagination. I turned and looked to the south-west again, cupping my hands behind my ears and hearing nothing. The snows were infinite beneath an infinite sky, and the track's perspective was lost to sight within a hundred yards of the bridge where I was standing. Somewhere to my right an owl called again and I cursed it because I wanted to bring the vastness of that silence out there to my ears and pick it over, searching for the one sound that sooner or later must break it. All I could hear was the tramp of the soldiers' boots along the track behind me and the rumbling of the transport on the move, and I had to shut them out of my consciousness, keeping my ears and my whole body oriented towards the south-west. And then it came again, a far note vibrant on the winter air, from this distance as faint as the piping of a flute among the snows. It sounded a third time and died abruptly as the train entered the tunnel four miles away.

Behind me the whole convoy of trucks had begun moving off, their lights swinging across the slope of the embankment in a sparkling wash as they accelerated nose to tail, their rear lamps forming a ruby chain that lost size and definition as they rolled towards the signal box. Nearer and half concealed by the structure of the bridge the flares were burning low. The deadline was close but there was nothing I could do so I turned again to face the south-west and for the first time saw a gleam of light below the horizon and heard the constant tremble of sound that was coming into the land.

The signal was behind me, a hundred yards down the track, and I didn't need to watch it because I'd hear the levers if they moved, and the weight of the arm coming down. The rumbling of the Army transports had died away, with the tramp of the soldiers' boots along the track. Time was taking over and the last few minutes were running out: The flares were burning low and when they finally guttered there would be only the signal left to stop the train. But if the military reported the line clear then the signal would change and the train would go through and I'd stand here watching it as it carried Gorodok to the trap.

Over the minutes the earth began shaking under my feet and I saw the great length of the train cutting into the snowscape, its lights brightening until I could make out the separate carriages. When I turned round I saw that two of the flares had burned out and a third was guttering, but the signal was still at red and for a moment I watched it, and then looked back at the train as it began slowing.

It was already nearing the bridge and I heard the steam shutting down and the brake-shoes clamping against the wheels as a short blast came from the whistle. Ten seconds later the locomotive passed me and I turned my back on the wave of air and smoke as it swept the surface snow from the bridge and whirled it away in clouds. I couldn't see the signal anymore but the brakes were still on and the carriages, passing so slowly now that I could see people's faces in the dim yellowish light. The guard's van was across the bridge and I stayed in cover, seeing one of the Army trucks coming back along the service road, its headlamps dipping and lifting over the bumps. The signal was still at red and a minute later the train rolled to a stop, with faces coming to the windows to peer at the flares.

A guard swung down from the rear van, bringing a lantern, and from farther along the train a man called to him. In the headlights of an Army truck I could see one of the locomotive crew coming down from the footplate. He went forward along the track, looking around him and then turning back as an officer shouted to him. I couldn't hear what was said.

I began looking for Gorodok.

Two more transports were moving back in this direction, their headlights making a glare below the embankment, and I moved deeper into the cover of the bridge. Two people were dropping from the train about halfway along, to stand looking around them. There were only three flares still burning now, and the signal was still at red. More passengers were getting down to see what was happening: From Tashkent to Yelingrad is a thousand miles and there are only two stops, at Frunze and Alma Ata; passengers are glad enough to get out and stretch their legs, even at the risk of freezing. A score of people were wandering along the edge of the track, clumping their feet in the snow and pointing to the military convoy below them.

I moved to the other side of the bridge: Gorodok would have a better chance to break for cover there, unless he decided to mingle with the passengers and soldiers before melting into the half dark. I could see a dozen people on this side, two of them walking at a distance from the train before a guard called them back.

There was nothing I could do for the courier: I couldn't recognize him and I couldn't break cover to go and meet him. The rdv was for the south end of the Litsky Bridge and this was where he had to come. A group of passengers had started walking alongside the train, three or four of them stooping to make snowballs and throwing them at the others: They looked like a party of young people, and a guard was going along to bring them back. Two soldiers were on this side now, with an officer, and the guard went up and spoke to him, gesturing at the passengers who were wandering about.

I watched for Gorodok, for one man on the move by himself.

There was no one.

It was the guard at the rear who saw the signal change to green, and he at once blew his whistle, climbing to the step of the van and swinging his lantern. Shouting started along the train and another whistle blew. Some of the groups broke up and began hurrying in a single line alongside the carriages and it was then that I saw a man move away from the people on the service-road side of the train and duck below it, coming out on the other side and beginning to hurry. Someone shouted—one of the soldiers, I thought at first—but he didn't stop or turn round. A transport still had its lights on and there was a glare below the train, with silhouettes and shadows intermingling, so that I couldn't see clearly what was going on.

Farther to the right of the bridge was a mass of low scrub, humped under the snow, and the man seemed to be heading for it now as he passed a group of passengers and veered to his left, breaking into a trot. There was another shout but I couldn't tell where it came from: the guards were trying to get everyone back on board and their whistles were still blowing. The last flare had gone out and the signal was still at green.

The man broke away now and began running harder, stumbling through the snow and falling once, then getting up and going on until the first shot cracked and the whole scene froze, with people standing perfectly still, their heads turned to watch the running man. The shot had only checked him and he was going hard now with his legs splaying out as he tried to keep his footing on the snow, his coat open and flapping and his hands out in case he went down. When the second shot came I saw who was firing: a man in a dark coat hanging onto a rail at the side of the train, aiming his pistol high and shouting to Gorodok before he fired again.

Two other men were breaking away from the train and going in pursuit, shouting for the fugitive to stop, but they hadn't gone very far before I saw a rifle swing up and bang out a shot aimed low at

Gorodok——and now I could see what was happening, and what was going to happen: The civilian in the dark coat was either an escort or a surveillance agent and he knew who the running man was. The soldier was some peasant trained to handle firearms and he'd decided to get himself a tin medal and feel the thrill of taking a life, and when a second soldier brought his rifle up and loosed off a round it was because he was excited: There were officials shouting and the hunt was up and they couldn't get their prey and the military was here and must not be found unequal to its proud duty, so forth, and there was nothing anyone could do about it now because it was like a fire taking hold as three more soldiers jostled into line and went down on one knee and brought their rifles to the aim and put out a fusillade of shots and reloaded, taking their time.

Smith, Jones, Robinson, Brown, his name didn't matter: He was a man running in the night, one of the countless men who must one day, for their own reasons, run from what they have done or from what they have been or from the life they have made for themselves, and made badly, so that eventually it will turn on them and hound them to their death.

Another fusillade and he pitched over with his coat flapping like a wing and one hand going up as if he wanted to signal something to us all as he fell and the snow covered him.

15

Kirinski

The little man stood at the top of the monument with snow on his head and his mouth in a shout and his fist raised, for a moment bearing aloft the great red disk of the sun as it travelled through the noon, low in the south. The early fog still lay across the city, half covering the nearer buildings and making them look insubstantial, as if the little man were shouting that the show was over and the scenery must go.

There was nobody else in the park.

Ten minutes ago a dog had come racing through the lean dark trunks of the trees, following some scent and then losing it and looking around in frustration before it pissed against a tree and trotted along the soot-black railings and disappeared, a clown too late for an audience. A clock chimed, then another, their notes muffled in the chill. The scene was a steel engraving, snow-white and frost-grey and silvered by the light in the sky, with only the deep red sun for colour. Everything was frozen: The trees were made of ice and looked as if they'd snap off if you shook them.

He came punctually and I moved my head to watch the three entrances to the park where the open gates made gaps in the railings and the hedge. The streets were hidden except in these three places; I couldn't see any vehicles out there, or anyone walking. Twice in the past half hour I'd heard a bus go past on the other side of the long north fence, the second one stopping not far from where I was standing now. This was a few minutes before he'd come into the park, his black fur hat set straight on his head and his hands dug into the pockets of his short paramilitary jacket. He walked fast, leaning backwards slightly with his black knee-boots kicking up the snow, his thin pointed face turning to left and right as if, like the dog, he'd lost his way.

Nearing the monument he stopped to look up at Lenin for a moment and then marched on again, taking a paper bag from his pocket and tossing crumbs around him, stopping again to watch the birds as they came down, dipping and wheeling from the stark black boughs. I'd seen quite a few dead sparrows on the snow when I'd come here; it was below freezing again today and there was no food for them.

I was standing between the hedge and the dark green hut where the gardeners kept their tools, and I'd come here from cover to cover and with great care, because there were windows overlooking the place. It had taken me nearly an hour and I was satisfied, having covered the last fifty yards through a tunnel formed between the hedge and the north fence. For the man to see me he must come quite close; for me to see him I only had to look through the leaves. He might not, of course, be Kirinski.

Just before midnight I had telephoned Chechevitsin, telling him that the inspector of mines had met with a fatal accident on his way to the engineers' symposium, and unfortunately had not been able to study the material. This morning I had gone to the library to photocopy the Kirinski material and then to the consigne at Central Station and left the films there, taking thirty minutes to survey and effect security. The whole place had become a red-alert area and I could *not* live peaceably among the good citizens of Yelingrad for weeks or longer if I had to: The opposition had been on to Gorodok and I'd come close to walking straight into a trap at the station and I could walk into one now when I left cover unless I was *very* careful. The only bit of luck we'd had was last night out there in the snow: The KGB people would have brought that courier in alive for interrogation if it hadn't been for those young clods in the Army; it was typical soldier mentality—

they'd poop off at a bloody mouse if they saw one, just to feel that sexy hairspring flexing under the trigger, bang and you're dead. But they'd stopped the rot because no one would get a word out of Gorodok now.

Two girls came into the park from the opposite end and walked arm in arm along the curving path with their heads down and their hands tucked into their sleeves. As they came along the railings I could hear their voices in the still winter air: One of them had been reprimanded by the factory manager for not reporting a jammed lathe a week ago . . . *the same as Misha when she . . . but a serious matter if . . . her father to intercede . . . managers take them . . .* fading away and I checked the man feeding the birds and then went a short distance along the fence and used a crack in the boards and saw them crossing the street and going into a café just past the first corner, fair enough, the park was a shortcut for them.

When I came back I saw that he'd crumpled the paper bag into a ball and dropped it into the wire basket that sagged from its rusted support near the monument. Some of the birds flew up as he passed close to them, then settled again to squabble murderously over the crumbs. He was walking quickly round the frozen surface of the pond with that odd backward-leaning gait of his, and soon he passed the monument again and came towards the hut, keeping to the path between the wire hoops and for the first time looking at his watch. His face was raw with the cold and his eyes were watering as they glanced restlessly across the hedgerow and the open gates. His thin jutting nose moved like a pointer, and several times he seemed about to leave the park, but each time decided to stay. Even his smallest movements had an intensity that gave them a false significance: When he pulled his raw red hand from its pocket to blow his nose I could have believed he was bringing out a gun instead of a handkerchief. He was so close now that I went into deeper cover, losing sight of him; but I could hear him moving, his boots kicking at the snow and his breath coming sharply, as if the cold air was painful to inhale. He had stopped now, and there was a short silence until he began stamping his feet and letting out his breath in brief little puffs, until I had the feeling I was listening to an animal in the wilds of the countryside. I thought I heard a sound coming from his throat, a kind of low tuneless humming, but wasn't sure; it could have been just that he found breathing painful at this temperature.

The first clock chimed the quarter and he moved off again at once, his boots thudding along the path; and I went back to the gap in the hedge to watch him. He was impatient now, but stayed close to the monument, standing for a time underneath it and moving away to a distant point and looking back at it. It was nearly an hour before he gave up and left the park.

By this time my feet were numb and I slipped twice on the snow as I left cover and took up the tag at long distance. He walked quickly, passing two bars where he could have used a phone. Five people passed him and he spoke to none of them. Soon after leaving the park he crossed the street and made north for one block, walking past the Trabant that I'd left parked between an Army staff car and a van with plain sides. A minute later he turned suddenly and went into a small restaurant with steamy windows and a chipped sign picturing a pig hanging above the doorway.

The heat hit me as I followed him in and took the stool next to him at the counter.

"A bowl of *solyanka*," he told the woman.

"The same for me," I said, and waited until she'd gone to the hatchway before I spoke again. "I suppose you thought I wasn't coming."

His whole body jerked as he swung his head to look at me.

"She *told* you I'd be alone," he said softly and fiercely, his boot scraping on the rung of the stool as he twisted farther round to study me. His teeth were chattering as he blew into his hands but his eyes locked their gaze on me, angry and apprehensive.

"No," I said, "she didn't. And if she had, d'you think I'd believe her?"

He took a long breath and sagged suddenly, as if the anxiety of the past hour had been too much. But even now the tension in him remained, an inner shaking of nerves that he couldn't stop.

"Tell me your name," he said suddenly, looking down. God knows why he asked me that; perhaps it occurred to him that this was just a crazy coincidence and I wasn't the man he was meant to meet.

"Rashidov," I told him.

Another breath went out of him. "Kirinski."

"Turned out rather cold today," I said because the fat woman was back with our bowls of soup, putting them down and brushing her wispy hair away from her face where it was sticking to the sweat: This place was more like a sauna bath than an eating-house.

We spooned our soup without talking. There was a phone at the end of the counter and I pushed my bowl away before he did and excused myself and went through the curtains at the rear and into the first cubicle, standing on the seat and finding a gap between the curtain rail and the bedraggled Christmas decorations that gave me a narrow field of vision that took in the top of his head. I let him have three minutes but he didn't leave the stool so I went back and got some money out and put it onto the counter and said we were going.

After the heat of the restaurant the air was like cold water thrown in our faces and his teeth began chattering again as I took him halfway down the block and opened up the Trabant and got started, driving north and parallel with the Gromyko Prospekt for half a mile and turning across the wasteground alongside the railway lines with the mirror perfectly clear the whole way. There was a rubbish dump in the far corner and I turned the car and backed up and stopped with the rear against the fence and a good view through the windscreen.

"This stuff," I said and reached under the seat, "ought to be kept somewhere safe. Where the hell did they train you?"

He swung his sharp head at me. "Who do you work for?"

"That's none of your bloody business." I was sorting it out, putting some of it back into the envelope: I was going to hang onto the gammas and the Monome-Dinome tables because I might conceivably pick up some kind of signal in somebody else's hands before he could warn his base. The cypher drafts were no use but everything else looked interesting, even some of the airfield dispositions with the Chinese hieroglyphs because those bastards in London weren't going to spring me and I'd have to try anything that came along.

"Have you got a pencil?" I asked him and he felt for one in his jacket and I hit the end of the barrel so fast that it almost broke his wrist because he cried out and went dead white and had to

double up so as not to be sick while I opened the Walther and
dropped the magazine out and threw it under the seat and lobbed
the gun into the back of the car and spread out the top map in the
Russian material and got out my felt pen.

"These airfields," I said. "What's their strength?"

He was trying to sit up straight but his wrist was still painful
and all he wanted to do was nurse it and I got fed up because he
was wasting time.

"It's your own fault," I said, "you shouldn't be so bloody un-
civilised. These are the only three airfields in the whole of this
area without squadron designation and combat strength and I
want to know about them, come on."

His face was still white but he was making an effort now and
looking down at the map. I think it was more shock than anything: They're the cock o' the north all the time they've got those
piddling little toys in their pockets but as soon as you take them
away they go to pieces; it's always the same.

"Come on Kirinski for Christ's sake I'm waiting."

"Decoy airfields," he said on a breath, "they're decoys."

"What the hell for, if they—" then I got it: The whole of the
Sino-Soviet border was an armed camp and they were keeping a
hot war on ice and that meant a permanent state of military intelligence preparedness and that was why Kirinski was so busy working for both sides like this. "What are these planes," I asked him,
"dummies?" It was one of the aerial photographs presumably
taken by covert reconnaissance from the Chinese side and the two
aircraft were standing in dispersal bays some distance from the
hangars.

"We fly two planes from each field," he said and got out his
handkerchief while I watched him carefully. "Can you read Chinese?"

I didn't answer. You never admit to knowledge of a foreign language and he ought to know that. Most of the sheets detailing Soviet installations and military strengths carried Mandarin hieroglyphs, and the Sinkiang-Mongolian-Chinese defences were
annotated in Russian.

"Where do you cross the border, Kirinski?"

"At Zaysan."

"What's your cover?"

"You *know* what my—"

"*Answer my question.*"

He hissed something through his teeth and took a breath and said: "Geological engineer."

He didn't like this a bit: he was doubling for two camps across the border and had a nice comfortable apartment with a girlfriend installed and a protection agreement with the KGB and this bastard Rashidov had come along and rifled his safe and threatened to blow him if he didn't behave. I could see his point but I wasn't going to let him waste my time because as soon as London heard the courier was dead they'd belt out another signal through Chechevitsin and throw me into a new phase and it might not give me any leeway.

"How difficult is it for people to cross the border from this side?"

"It's impossible," he said.

"Why?"

"The situation is sensitive."

"Listen Kirinski, when I ask you a question I want you to go on talking till you've told me all you know, you understand? I don't want any more of your bloody monosyllables. *What* situation is sensitive and what does *sensitive* mean?"

He made that hissing noise again. I think he was still frozen stiff and of course his nerves were hitting an all-time high and there was something else: He was a proud man and he didn't like people treading on him.

"The total strength of the Red Army," he said with careful articulation, "is one hundred and fifty divisions. Forty of those are deployed along the Chinese frontier. That is the situation and it is sensitive in terms of unpredictable flareups. Six months ago there was a battle on the Sinkiang border involving fifteen thousand troops who were carrying out field exercises. Two thousand were killed. Since that time the frontier crossings have come under very strict control, especially at Zaysan. I trust I have answered your question."

"You're getting the idea." I checked through the rest of the Soviet stuff and slid it into the envelope because there wasn't time now to ask him for translation from the Mandarin: I was going to freeze everything until I got a signal from Chechevitsin. "What was Opal Light?"

He looked down at the batch of sheets stapled together top and bottom, and I thought he wasn't going to answer; then he looked away and said: "It was a Chinese operation."

"What sort? Come on, Kirinski."

"It was directed at the Lop Nor missile installations security services, last November. Intelligence was obtained."

I let it go at that because it looked like a closed file and London wouldn't be interested in a Sino-Soviet mission: Most of this stuff would probably go to the CIA and I didn't expect them to find anything new because the Americans were far more concerned than the British with the Sino-Soviet confrontation and its potential for world war, and they had the field well covered.

I put the batch away and looked at the photographs again and put those away too and asked him: "Did you start working for the KGB first?"

Another fractional pause: This was an assault on his innermost privacy and he was feeling the exposure.

"Yes."

"How long had you worked for them before you started working for Peking as well?"

Pause.

"Two years."

"Is it the money?"

I didn't think it could be anything else: There was no kind of motherland ideology involved because this man wasn't a double agent for *one* organisation—he was doubling for *two*. The amount of material I'd found in his apartment was equally secret and equally substantial for each side, and if either side found out what he was doing he'd go sky-high and that was why I could control him like this, as long as I had the material.

"Yes," he said. Yes it was the money.

I didn't believe him but I didn't think he was lying to deceive. He wasn't the type to go for the money: There was too much tension, too much pride, and too much resistance to my attempts at dominance. The reasons why we go into this trade are varied and we never talk about it because it's always personal—we do it for money or out of some buried loyalty to a flag or to express an ingrained sense of duplicity or simply because of the razor's-edge syndrome: the inability to live too far from the brink without getting bored or drunk or going round the bend for the want of a starting-point to distant horizons we hope never to reach. It's convolute and involute and we don't question even ourselves, *especially* ourselves, because we don't want to come up with an answer we can't live with.

I'd put Kirinski down as a psychopath. That is the type I know best, and for good reason.

"Does Liova work with you?"

He jerked his narrow head to look at me. "No."

"Does she work for the KGB?"

"No. She is my wife, and that is all."

"Your legal wife?"

A slight hesitation. "Yes."

I didn't go into it. The art of interrogation is a paradox: You learn more from the questions than the answers, if you know how to bring out those questions by your silences; you also learn more from the way the answers come than from what they purport to tell you. Most of them are deliberate lies and this is accepted by both parties, but lies will protect you only up to a point: the point where you produce so many of them that you get lost in the confusion of your own making; the truth is easily remembered because it exists, but lies demand a trained memory and the stress can become overwhelming. This again is paradoxical: The more you lie, the more you reveal the truth.

She wasn't, for instance, his legal wife. Because of the hesitation.

"Does she have any connection with the KGB?"

"No. I've told you, she—"

"Or any other police or intelligence or security organisation?"

"No. None."

"Is she afraid of anyone?"

"Of course not!"

"So she doesn't need protection."

"No."

"Even the protection of a gun?"

His hesitations lasted only a fraction of a second but they were beautifully consistent.

"No."

"All right. Now I want a general preliminary picture: Your contacts with the KGB, your contacts with Peking, then liaison, couriers, communications and security background. Take your time."

He hissed in his breath again and began pointing with that long nose of his like a parrot trapped in a cage and I watched his hands because they'd be the first sign of movement and at some stage in the interrogation he was going to try making a break for it.

I could feel the tension in him and it was communicable: I was getting on edge. There was something about this man that I couldn't place, some extra dimension that explained the inner shaking of his nerves. All right, he knew I could blow him and he knew what they'd do to him as a result; but I've been in the company of men in the final stages of stress and I've been there myself and all I knew as I sat in the cramped confines of the Trabant with Alexei Kirinski beside me was that his tension was a part of him and not wholly induced.

"I have no regular contacts," he said, shivering.

"Names," I said, "come on."

"But I tell you I—"

"I want their names."

He began making them up and I let him because their names wouldn't mean a thing to me and he didn't seem to know that: He wasn't KGB himself because even those people are put through a modicum of training and he wasn't even a beginner—you don't just walk away from a missed rendezvous and settle for a bowl of soup without even looking behind you.

We worked at it for fifteen minutes and I didn't interrupt except to goad him on, and after a time he picked up the tricks and started hesitating deliberately to make me believe I'd asked a sensitive question.

"There is no direct contact with Peking. I use couriers for material, through Yümen."

"What about signals?"

He hesitated and for *no* reason: There was no equipment in his apartment and he could throw me another bunch of phony names and get away with it.

"I signal through a frontier post."

"Both ways?"

"No."

"Come on then—*which* way?"

"From here to Sinkiang."

"What about the other way—look, I want you to go on talking."

"The other way I use a contact in Yelingrad."

With a transmitter and cyphers and onward transmission to his contacts in the KGB, so forth. I let him go on talking while I listened for the right lie in the wrong place and watched the scene through the windscreen. Only a dozen people had crossed the wasteground since we'd got here and only a few vehicles had come past the corner, all of them with chains on. The cold was coming into the car and slowly cancelling out the heat of our bodies and Kirinski began rubbing his hands together but his teeth went on chattering as he talked.

"How much money do they pay you?"

"Not very much—"

"How much?"

"Five hundred rubles a month."

"Plus bonuses?"

"Bonuses? What kind?"

"For a special assignment, or special information. There must be bonuses." It's a major part of Russian economic thinking.

"I received an extra hundred rubles for the decoy airfield photographs on the Chinese side of the frontier."

"What about Peking? How much do they pay?"

He was tremendously fast and caught my throat with a curving ridge-hand before I could block it and followed with his elbow rising as my head came forward on the reflex but I avoided it and formed a four-finger eye-shot with my left hand but it wasn't any good because all that tension was coming out of him and he was like a wildcat and I stopped trying to do anything formal because any kind of reaction would have to be instinctive if I were going to get out of this alive.

The first thing he'd go for was the gun but the magazine was under the seat and he knew that. The second thing he'd go for was the envelope because without that stuff I couldn't blow him and he knew that too. At present there wasn't time for him to go for either the gun or the envelope because I was catching up on the initiative and had his left arm in a clamp while I went for his face again. He was trying to get leverage against the dashboard with his foot and I saw the heel of his black leather boot gouge into the speedometer as he straightened his leg and got the pressure he needed and started to use it, his shoulder braced against my throat and his right hand darting for the eyes and missing and darting free again as I blocked him every time until he used a wedge-hand against the throat and half succeeded: I began choking and brought my knee up and smashed it into his ribs and forced some of the pressure off.

The horn had sounded three or four times because we were milling inside the confines of the car and whatever we hit we smashed: the windscreen went and I saw his boot rip from the heel to the top because this stuff wasn't safety glass. The envelope had slipped down between the driving-seat and the door and I freed my left hand and tried to push it under the seat but he saw what I was doing because if he couldn't get the gun he'd settle for the envelope: It was all he really needed. The horn was sounding again and I realised I had my knee against it as he wrenched his arm free and drove a palm-hand downwards and connected with a shoulder-blade.

I tried three consecutive eye-darts and they fell short because my arm was half locked but they worried him and he span sideways and got purchase again on the dashboard and kicked away from it and broke the seat frame and sent me on my back with the effect of a rabbit chop as my neck hit the edge of the rear seat: bright flashing lights and momentary paralysis, dangerous and I rolled over to miss his boot as it crashed down and ripped some of the seat fabric away, sensation of losing touch, sounds muted, felt him lurch across to the driver's side as someone began shouting, which I didn't understand unless it was the noise the horn had been making, face at the window and a gloved hand shooting out and trying to stop Kirinski as he hit the door open and pitched through and began running, knocking one of them down——there were more people here and I got up and heard someone asking what had happened, was it a thief, so forth, down on my knees so I made a *lot* of effort and got *up* again, still choking because of the wedge-hand strike, still seeing flashes.

Men running and calling out *stop thief stop thief* and I told them *no*, it was just a quarrel that was all and someone said *hospital* and I made another effort and said no, I didn't want a hospital. That would mean the police and statements and what I had to do was get away from here as soon as I could because he'd taken the envelope and that was going to change the whole situation: He'd let the KGB loose on me now because there was nothing to stop him.

16

Courier

The TU-154 came out of the haze like an image taking shape on a negative, breaking through the low ceiling a mile from the end of the runway and flopping down only ten minutes late despite the weather: They said there was more snow coming in from the south-west.

People began leaving the observation deck, their faces pinched with the cold. I waited until the plane had turned at the end of its run and started rolling in this direction; I was frozen from the drive in the Trabant but there were other things to consider. I was getting to know Chechevitsin: His signals were brief and security-conscious to the point of being uninformative. This wasn't typically Russian and I suppose he was probably someone out from London and worried about making mistakes. This time the rdv was for 3:05 at the airport, courier arriving Flight 96 from Moscow, recognisable on sight. No precise point of rendezvous: I was expected to pick him out of a hundred and fifty passengers. No specific instructions: I was to assume that he was to receive the films.

I'd say the problem had been the Trabant. It was the driving-seat that had broken away and I'd had to take the other one off its runners and use it as a prop, wedging it between the rear seat and the driver's squab. But there'd been nothing I could do about the smashed windscreen except clear the rest of the glass away and drive with my eyes half shut against the freezing blast of air. I'd told the man at the hotel there'd been an accident on the snow and he'd let me put the car into the yard at the rear and I'd left it there, walking around to the household store to call Kirinski and then Chechevitsin: I wanted it out of sight as much as possible because there couldn't be too many dark-blue Trabants driving around the city without a windscreen and I might just as well put my name on the bloody thing. I'd asked Chechevitsin to get me another one but he'd said it would take time and I couldn't put any pressure on him because even a used car would cost the earth and he'd be lucky to find one.

Only a few of the people were left on the observation deck now: The 154 was swinging into the reception bay and the service vehicles were going out to it. I waited another two minutes and went through the swing-door and down the steps, moving a little faster than normal but not running. He was still behind me at the end of the passage and I turned sharply, using cover and going into the open again to watch him react when he saw me. He'd lost me for only a few seconds but it had worried him and he shrugged himself deeper into his coat as he walked on past the information desk.

There'd been nothing in the mirror when I'd driven here but the Trabant had a unique image because of the windscreen and I'd left it parked between a big Chaika and a wall and I'd walked into the main hall through the freight entrance and taken a lot of trouble with mirrors and mirror substitutes and drawn blank everywhere. That had been at 2:40 and I'd come up to the observation deck through a clean field but at 2:53 the man with the sloping shoulder had come through the swing-door and stood there for a couple of minutes making a lot of fuss about the cold, stamping his feet and blowing into his bare hands and going out again. A lot of people were doing that: It was the first big freeze of the winter and they were feeling it; but this man had kept his back to me and faced the line of windows at the right angle and I'd noted it but hadn't been sure until I'd checked on him. So it had been the Trabant and he'd picked me up at some time after I'd turned into the car park and kept station on me and held back too long and lost me and looked for me and found me on the observation deck, going out again and waiting for me at one end of the passage, not a first-class tag but he wasn't running any risk because the other one had closed in and was watching me now from light cover near the main entrance.

"Excuse me, comrade."

A man with a bunch of faded carnations, God knew what they'd cost him but he had the eyes of a romantic and he was past the age when he could afford to lose a good woman even if he couldn't afford the flowers either.

"Yes?" I answered.

"Is that the Moscow plane, just in?"

"That's right, comrade. Flight 96. She's a lucky girl."

"They were all they had left," he shrugged wistfully and walked off across the hall with both tags watching him and a man coming away from the newspaper stall on the far side, a *third* man, waiting to question him when the time was right.

Three.

It didn't look good. There were things I wanted to know and there wasn't time to think about it because the courier would now be coming through Gate 1 and I'd have to make a decision within the next minute and then act on it. But the same pattern was here: The second courier was moving straight into a trap and this time London hadn't been on to it. Either that or Kirinski had thrown the whole thing at the fan: I'd called his apartment as soon as I'd got the Trabant stowed away in the hotel yard, but Liova had answered the phone and said he wasn't there so I gave her the message: I'd taken copies of the material so if he thought he could blow me now he'd better think twice. But he must have triggered the KGB on his way home and when he'd got there it had been too late to do anything about it, and the Trabant must have become red hot within half an hour of my driving away from the wasteground: He thought he'd got nothing to lose if the KGB put me through interrogation because I had no *evidence* and they wouldn't take any notice of what I said: a man under interrogation will say whatever might save him.

The first of the passengers were coming through, all of them muffled against the cold and hurrying from habit, many of them with the slightly Mongol faces of the region, a group of children in red jackets, three youths with long hair and jeans getting attention from the provincials here, a man waddling alone with a cello case, no one recognisable on sight.

Alternatives: Keep back and let the courier go by without seeing me and put it down as a missed rendezvous; let them trap him if that was what they'd come here to do. Or let him see me and let him go by and try to make a rendezvous later; this would depend on his degree of training and if he wasn't any better than Gorodok he'd foul it up and blow both of us and therefore Slingshot. Or tag him and get him alone in a clear field and make the rendezvous then; this would call for miracles and I hadn't got any because Kirinski had been very strong and my right bicep was still numb from one of his strikes and the neck-blow from the edge of the back seat had left me with nerve shock and I'd never had to tag a contact and throw my own tags, *three of them,* except in training at Norfolk—and a lot of the stuff they give us at Norfolk is too sophisticated to work in practice: It's on the curriculum as a mental exercise.

Five Red Army officers in shiny boots and enormous greatcoats, one of them a general with his jowls overflowing his collar; three Tadzhik women in traditional costume; another man with a musical instrument and now a plump woman smiling over her bouquet of faded carnations while the man explained to her that they were all he could find.

Decision: I wouldn't let the courier go by without seeing me. I would make eye contact and take it from there.

A group of men came past in black coats and homburgs, most of them with beards and gold-rimmed spectacles, their Muscovite accents chipping at the air as they herded together towards the main doors. I glanced at their faces: I glanced at *every* face and looked away to the next, forming the habit. At this moment I was under close scrutiny and had to take the utmost care because my eyes, staying too long on one face among all the others, could condemn a man to death.

It had happened in Oslo and it had happened in Singapore: An opposition-surveyed eye-contact situation can be the same as an identity parade and in Oslo the executive had taken the slightest step forward when he'd seen his cutout coming down the gangway and in Singapore a courier had glanced down quickly when his man came through the gate at the airport and we'd lost two good operatives because of it. For this reason it's a situation we don't get into if we can help it but today I'd arrived here shortly before a plane was due in and I'd left the observation deck shortly after it had landed and the first tag was already on to me and the only thing to do was to conform to the pattern: I was obviously here to meet someone off the Moscow flight and so I must stand here looking for him.

Five young girls in red woollen scarves and pom-pom hats, their arms interlinked as they came past me, singing and giggling.

A woman in a wheelchair, her face grey and her eyes already dead; a young man pushing her, watching the girls.

An Air Force captain, eating the last of an apple down to the core.

Ferris.

He was looking vaguely around him and our glances met for a half second and passed on and *this* was when we could have blown Slingshot if we hadn't worked together long enough to know each other's style.

I went on waiting, watching the rest of the passengers as they came through and wishing to *Christ* that Chechevitsin had put a little more information into his last signal: I was in the target area with the KGB moving in and the *last* thing I wanted was a top field director dropping out of the sky to make a rendezvous. The signal had said courier and if it had been a courier I could have left him to fend for himself and take the risk that Gorodok had taken and I could have handled these tags on my own. If I'd known London was sending Ferris here I would have made damned sure of getting a different car and I would have waited *outside* this bloody place and watched from cover without even showing myself because Ferris is a veteran and knows precisely what to do.

He was doing it now, walking straight through the hall and out by the main doors, no hat, a light gabardine coat, a tan brown overnight case. I was watching his reflection in the three glass panels along the wall beyond the stream of passengers and now he had gone.

When the last of them came through I gave it another minute, going up to the gate and looking along the passage and coming away disappointed, checking my watch and then going out through the main doors at a steady pace. This was when they would have made the snatch if they'd received the instructions and I was sweating because I had the films on me to give to the "courier" and they were enough to get me a life sentence and those places aren't easy to get away from because of the barbed wire and gun towers and guard dogs: Cosgrove had tried it six months ago at the Potma Complex in Chita Province and he was badly savaged because they couldn't control one of the dogs, I hate those bloody things.

Ferris had got it right: He'd had a rough idea of how many more passengers there'd been behind him and he'd known I'd have to wait till they were through and he'd used time outside the building and was now walking steadily north along the airport boulevard, his fuzz of thin hair blowing round his head. Most of the passengers were getting into the terminal bus or sharing cabs but a dozen or so were walking along the boulevard and Ferris was keeping pace with them, swinging his case and not looking round him any more. He couldn't be feeling very happy: A rendezvous is normally secure and I hadn't had time to warn him and he'd seen immediately that we had a problem when I let him go by.

I wasn't very happy myself. Parkis had put an executive and a director into the field in Central Asia and at this precise moment they were in a KGB trap and I didn't know if we could get out of it because this was the third alternative I'd begun working on and it was the one that needed miracles.

Ferris hadn't been sent down here personally for *nothing*. I didn't need a director in the field because the operation was close focus and London knew that: The target was one man, Kirinski. So Ferris was here to slam something new on the board for me to handle and I wasn't ready for it but I had to know what it was and that meant I had to bring him to some kind of rendezvous in a safe place and there weren't any safe places in this city now that the KGB were into the action: They'd hold off until the point came when they could see they'd never drive us to ground and then they'd pull us in, *finis*.

I didn't know how good his cover was but in a sense it was only as good as I could make it: At the moment there was no connection between us and technically he was in a clear field but as soon as I went too close to him they'd get the point and put the drop on us and start interrogating.

A black Moskwicz saloon went slowly past from the airport, chains biting on the snow and scattering it across the ruts, a face at a steamy window, featureless, the acrid scent of exhaust gas as the car gathered speed and turned the corner. Shoes crunched faintly behind me and on the other side of the boulevard a short dark figure walked insubstantially through the reflections on the Intourist windows, a man with a sloping shoulder. Far ahead of me, Ferris.

He could only go on walking, or stop: He hadn't got the training or the experience to take any kind of initiative and we both knew that. The one move he could make would be to hole up in public cover and wait for me there but it wouldn't be easy and it might be impossible because this operation was based on geometry and involved angles, distances and vectors: We would be moving, he and I and these other men, across a chessboard as the light of the day began lowering across the streets.

He turned left and I stayed on this side of the boulevard and began looking for cover. This too might be impossible to find in time but it was my main concern. Without Ferris on the scene I could have flushed these tags within minutes because a city is a warren and I am a ferret who knows its way and who knows how close to go and how far: I've done it before, a hundred times, and I could have done it again today but there was Ferris and I mustn't lose him.

I crossed at the intersection and for the first time turned my head to watch for the traffic and saw *five* of them among the people who were walking from the airport, five or conceivably more because I couldn't see farther than the second group who were crossing farther down, hurrying before the bus came, one of them slipping and finding his balance again. They were men with coats and hats and gloves and they didn't look any different from the others in actual appearance: I knew who they were because I'd seen them before, hundreds of them, Russian and Czechoslovakian and Polish and French and Italian and Turkish, average and undistinguished men in respectable suits and worn shoes, their movements casual and their faces noncommittal as they worked their daily round like pilot fish. Of course they vary in their temperaments: The subtlest are the French and they'll hang on whatever you try to do; the Italians will do well until they see a girl and then they'll go off with her and leave you flat; the Turks will hound you to the ends of the earth and then drive you into the ground; and the Russians will keep their distance but never lose you unless you can pull something totally unexpected, because they are logical and trained to move in straight lines as these were doing now.

A hundred yards after I'd crossed at the intersection and started west along this street the black Moskwicz came past again, but faster this time: It had turned left along the side street parallel to the boulevard and come up and turned left again and found me crossing from the first to the second block and it would now make a series of right turns and come back and look for me two blocks ahead and that was all right, providing it went on doing the same thing and didn't stop. I liked the pattern as it was, because at this stage I knew where people were and what they were doing.

I suppose London had waited until I was down on Soviet soil and still alive before they'd pulled Ferris out of Fürstenfeldbruck and shot him into Moscow with instructions to come down here; it's relatively easy for the field directors to cross frontiers because they're never in action and their cover is conservative: Most of them double as cultural attachés or commercial first secretaries at the major embassies and at least half of them are permanently down on the Intourist waiting lists for educational travel-group tours through Russia and the slave states: It's infinitely easier to get out of a country if you can prove how you came in.

The Moskwicz was turning right.

Ferris was a good fifty yards ahead of me and I lost him sometimes because he was using the environment and doing it well, staying with a chance group of people and finding another before they split up, keeping to the right-hand side of the pavement and pacing his way steadily, sometimes looking at his watch to express purpose and a sense of destination: It was a model performance and it kept my nerves off the limit as we hauled the five men and the Moskwicz westwards along Lenin Prospekt and past the square.

It was now twelve minutes since we'd left the airport and there had been no chance of shaking off these people and I was getting worried because the longer Ferris and I remained in the same street within sight of each other the sooner they'd see the connection and start working on him too. At the moment he was perfectly clear and they weren't taking the slightest interest in him, any more than they were taking an interest in the other twenty or thirty people moving with us along the Prospekt.

Moskwicz.

Its number was half covered in slush but there was a small triangular dent on the rear wing and that was good enough. It went past at the same pace as the traffic; it wasn't observing me: It was standing by in case I decided to find a taxi or get on a bus. If that happened they—

Ferris had gone.

I kept walking.

Clothing store. Warehouse. Three unidentified offices in a row. Bus station.

The Inter-Kazakh State Lines, a vast roofed area with water puddling below the mudflaps of three long-distance buses that had just come in, one of them still discharging passengers in the blue-grey artificial light. No sign of Ferris: He was too good for that.

I walked steadily for three blocks and checked everything twice: every doorway, every parked vehicle, every wall, basement and side entrance to every building, and drew blank all the time. I didn't want to alter the basic pattern but the time factor was now taking over: Ferris couldn't wait for me indefinitely at the bus station and I had to get back there and locate him as soon as I could. His own timing might be critical: He was in this city to rendezvous with the executive but there could be other things he had to do here, involving Chechevitsin or a mobile Bureau cell or Kirinski himself through any one of a dozen Central Asian channels. I didn't know the background and I wasn't going to assume anything at this stage. The *one* thing I had to do was to get back to that bus station and if I couldn't find a chance then I'd have to make one and risk blowing Slingshot.

This was normal. In any given mission you're operating right on the very edge.

Three doorways: two deep, one shallow.

A line of Red Army vehicles, one of them an armoured car with a gunner perched on the roof struggling with the antenna. I stopped and called up to him.

"Comrade! Is this the way to Central Station?"

He looked down, his eyes dark with frustration: It looked as if they'd hit the antenna on something hard enough to bend it at the base, and his hands were too cold to straighten it.

"Where?"

"The station. The main station."

"Straight on."

I nodded and walked away, checking my watch and looking around for a taxi. The station was three miles from here and the first of the street lights were coming on and it was logical for me to hurry. They knew I'd abandoned the Trabant because of the windscreen, and the railway station was a plausible destination, and in any case they wouldn't question it because they would go wherever I took them.

The nearest tag would now be questioning the soldier: what had I asked him, so forth. I'd done it to reassure them, and if I'd only succeeded by one degree my chances were by that one degree improved.

Doors, windows, railings, a parked truck, blank, drawing blank.

Three blocks and I was walking through the night, with the street lamps taking over the evening sky. Three taxis had gone past and I'd tried to stop them because sharing was an established custom but they were obviously full.

Moskwicz.

This time it turned at one of the prescribed U junctions and went back the other way, a blurred face checking me before it turned right and began working its way back to Lenin Prospekt.

One of the tags was quite close behind me: I'd seen his reflection twice in the past few minutes. The light was less reliable now and they were tightening their distances. I was getting a better look at them now because whenever I heard a car I turned round to see if it was a taxi and they knew what I was doing because I'd shown them.

Two more went past but I got the third and it was empty.

"Where to?"

"Central Station."

One of them had broken into a short run but the Moskwicz had made its circuit and come back into the Prospekt and he left it for them to take up the tag in its mobile phase and we moved off with the black saloon a reasonable distance behind and with one small Syrena between us.

It was no use relying on the traffic lights: The Moskwicz would cross on the red if it had to, even in snow conditions. Unless I did something to change the pattern we'd head slowly for the station and with every yard we'd be heading *away* from the bus depot where Ferris was waiting and I couldn't let it go on for too long because the Moskwicz had a radio and they'd bring in mobile support: they'd have to.

I didn't want to wait for them to do that.

"Are we going to get more snow?" I asked the driver.

"What was that, comrade?"

There was a glass division, grimed and cracked and repaired with adhesive tape, and he cocked his head towards the opening.

"Is there more snow on the way?"

"It says so, on the radio. From the south-west. But I can tell you, we don't need it!"

Checking, checking. Blank.

Of course if you wait for a chance you may never get it but if you decide to make one for yourself you can often use the environment even if it presents only one positive feature. The alley was on the right as he braked for the lights and when I looked round I saw there was still another car between the taxi and the Moskwicz so I waited another two seconds for the speed to go down to a crawl and then I hit the door open and got out and swung it shut and the driver didn't start shouting before I was across the pavement and into the alley, running some of the way and sliding the rest. A flare of headlights came and my own shadow flew ahead of me: They'd slung the Moskwicz across the pavement and lit up the scene and I heard a door snap open and then another one and there were three shadows now, two of them enormous and flitting like giant bats across the face of the building as I got halfway and tripped on something frozen under the snow and went headlong, sliding headfirst and hitting the wall with my hands and bouncing away, *get up,* sliding across to the other side while the bats hovered in the dazzle of the lamps and I hit out with one hand to stop the momentum, *get up they're coming,* another door banging and a shadow bigger than the others and the sound of running feet.

Got up and got going and found sand near the end of the alley but the shadows were smaller now and therefore closer and I knew I'd blown it because the terrain was the biggest hazard and there wasn't anything I could do about it, their footsteps very close in the confines, thudding behind me, no go, it was no go.

Ferris. They didn't get Ferris. I'd kept him clean.

Feet flying and the street empty when I got to the corner and turned to the right, slithering and fetching up against a lamp standard and using it to change direction, empty except for a car moving towards the intersection and a bus starting off within a few yards of the alley, its doors shut against the cold and its windows steaming and not a hope in *hell* of jumping on, but the rear wheels were spinning on the snow in spite of the chains and I let my own momentum take me across the kerb and then I had to be careful because if I got it wrong it was going to be nasty: The rear end of the bus was sliding into the gutter and the wheels were churning for grip in the piled snow and I had to throw myself flat on my back and kick at the kerb and slide underneath the thing before it got under way, hooking my hands upwards and hitting the muffler and burning them, hooking again and finding a strut running sideways across the chassis, a strut and a brake rod that flexed under my weight but held me until I could find a purchase on one of the cross-members, my feet dragging now as the wheels got a grip and the bus moved faster, swinging out from the kerb and getting into second gear and accelerating again, the heat of the exhaust pipe against my face and its sound throbbing, beginning to deafen me.

I didn't know what the chances were: Either they'd seen me or they hadn't. They might have shouted to the driver but I wouldn't have heard them because of the exhaust and the driver wouldn't have heard them because the doors were shut and his window would be up; in any case it was academic: If they'd seen me they'd go back to the Moskwicz and head off the bus and I couldn't drop off now because I could hear traffic coming up from the rear and it sounded like a truck or an army transport with heavy-duty tyres and no chains, keeping pace and sending a flush of light reflecting upwards from the snow against the mud-caked chassis just above my head.

It was a strictly shut-ended situation because I didn't know how much traffic there was behind the bus and it was going to depend on how long I could hang on like this: Given a run of three or four green lights I'd have to drop and if I dropped I might just miss the wheels of the truck behind but there might be a whole line of traffic and sooner or later there'd be a blood-red smear on the snow, *finito*.

My heels were dragging on sand now and I kicked upwards with one foot and hooked it sideways and felt nothing and kicked again and got it lodged across a brake rod but it slipped off and I tried the other foot, feeling for a cross-member and not finding one, trying again and hitting the open propeller-shaft and letting it drop back to the roadway. Technically my heels were taking some of the weight and relieving the strain on my fingers but there was sand along this stretch and my shoes could wear through and I didn't know what was going to happen in the next fifteen minutes: I might have to run for my life and I could lose it if a shoe came off.

Tried with my hands next, feeling for a girder where I could hook one arm through and hold the wrist to lock it in position, but I was too far forward and my face was just to the rear of the gearbox with one of the universal joints spinning within an inch of my head and if I moved too much the bolts would cut into the skull like a circular rasp: It wasn't worth risking so I let my body hang limp and began waiting out the time, it was all I could do.

Oil was dripping against my face and I turned it slightly to let it run downwards, clear of my eye. There was a leak in the exhaust pipe and the fumes were acrid and sickly, setting up an irritation in my throat that I tried to control by swallowing. The deep-cut tyres of the truck behind us were sending out a moan as they ran across the hard-packed snow and I could see other lights now, showing beneath its silhouette: There was a line of traffic, possibly a military convoy, and somewhere in the din of the exhaust-pipe I could hear their chains jingling on the snow.

My fingers were burning now with the strain of hanging on.

Ignore.

The oil dripped again and I turned my face away, feeling it

creep down to the lobe of my ear. I was taking shallow breaths to keep the carbon monoxide out of my lungs but the muscles were working hard from the fingers to the shoulders and demanding oxygen and I began breathing more deeply because I couldn't help it: There was no equation possible and at some distant point my hands would lose their grip because the gas had swamped the brain or because the muscles ran out of oxygen, one way or the other. If I could—

Slowing, we were slowing.

No brakes yet: The rod against my shoulder hadn't moved. Just a gradual deceleration with the exhaust note snarling lower on the overrun as the cylinders went dead.

Assume traffic lights.

Fingers burning but hanging on. If I dropped too soon there'd be nothing to save me: The truck couldn't pull up on this kind of surface even if the driver saw me and if I tried rolling to the kerb I could get it wrong and his front wheel would—

The exhaust was throbbing again and the whine of the universals rose to their normal pitch and I saw the faint green spread of light on the snow along the gutter as the bus got up speed and the traffic behind followed suit: The lights had been at red and the driver had started slowing and they'd changed to green and I'd have to keep hanging on and I didn't think I could do it now because a muscle is electro-chemical and the will can push its limits but not to infinity.

My fingers are steel hooks.

Nothing can break them.

We were going faster than before and the gas began fluttering against the side of my head and I turned it the other way and felt the heat on my hair but that was all right, I could stand that, I could stand anything that didn't increase the strain on the fingers because they'd got to hang on.

They are steel hooks.

Nothing can break them.

But the throb of the exhaust was vibrating inside my head and the stink of the gas was sharp and sweet and permeating, stinging my eyes and making them water, making them close, making my thoughts drift, *steel hooks,* until my body sagged lower and the heels of my shoes began skating from side to side as the thigh muscles loosened, *nothing*, from side to side on the sand and the snow, *nothing can break them*, side to side, *wake up or you'll—*

Tighten the fingers: *Tighten*.

And be aware of the gas because it's lethal. Christ's sake cerebrate: necessary to stay conscious, *essential* to review the situation and get it into normal perspective because it was simply a question of *time*. Soon the bus would stop and I could drop and roll clear and all I had to do until then was maintain the tension in the finger muscles and concern my mind with nothing else, *nothing at all*.

My fingers are steel hooks.

Nothing can break them.

Sweat pouring over me and cooling in the freezing air, my hands burning, my arms burning, my shoulders burning, *steel hooks*, and the sound of the drumming in my head and the sweet tang of the gas swirling inside and my body swimming, slowing, we were—

Slowing again.

Hooks.

Slowing.

The truck was still behind. I could hear it and see its lights. Its lights were yellow on the snow. Slowing. My feet dragged on the sand, from side to side, side to side, slowing.

Hooks.

The traffic shunting behind us, a bumper banging: They couldn't pull up on the snow.

Slow.

A flush of red somewhere below me, coming from a light.

I watched the light on the snow, holding my breath because of the gas. My head was full of it.

Slowing.

Stop.

Drop and roll clear.

17

Objective

"These are copies," I said.

"Of everything?"

"Of everything I could find."

He looked at them in the light coming through the window.

"This is all you found?"

"Christ, I've just told you."

He looked at me and away.

"What happened to you?" he asked me.

"When?"

"I mean what sort of condition are you in?"

"First-rate."

I was getting fed up with him. You don't throw yourself under a bus and come out looking like Little Lord Fauntleroy and he ought to know that. Come to think of it, of course, he didn't know it was what I'd been doing.

"There may be some other papers," he said.

"Where?"

"With Kirinski."

A bus came in and filled the place with noise. It had the name Balkhash on the illuminated sign over the front. I supposed the lake was frozen now, though it hadn't been when I'd flown over it to the north. Christ, that was a long time ago.

I shut my eyes and let them water. The exhaust gas had been the worst, though I still couldn't feel my fingers.

"Opal Light," he said after a while, "was our operation."

I woke up very fast.

"It was *what?*"

He slipped the file back into the envelope with the films, and didn't say anything. Someone came to the open doorway.

"Excuse me, comrade. Is this the one for Alma Ata?"

"No," I told him. "This is for Ust'Kamenogorsk."

"Thank you."

He went away, lugging a canvas bag with a hen in it.

"Is that the one," I asked Ferris carefully, "where the wheel came off?"

"Didn't you look at the file?"

"Yes, but there wasn't anything specific."

"That was the one."

I sat back and tried to think, but my clothes still stank of that gas and my stomach was sour with it and I wanted to sleep, sleep for days. Fat chance.

"Kirinski," I said, "was doubling for two sides. That's why—"

"Three."

I looked at him. They'd got neon lights in the roof of this place and the windows of the bus we were sitting in were tinted, so that his face was grey-blue and mottled by the spots on the glass. But it wasn't just that he *looked* like death: I think there was more on his mind than he'd ever had before, and it was wearing him down, even Ferris.

I said: "Three?"

He took a breath. "Kirinski is our executive for Sinkiang."

I shut my eyes again, and let them stream.

The passengers were getting off the coach that had just come in and I could hear someone laughing. It was a shrill sudden laugh that echoed under the enormous roof, and I can still remember it.

"How long," I asked Ferris, "has he been working for the Bureau?"

"Eighteen months."

"What's his status?"

"Third-class. He doesn't know anything about us."

"He knew enough," I said wearily, "to blow Opal Light."

"Yes. And he's beginning to know more."

I started to listen carefully.

"Who got on to him, Ferris?"

"We sent three people out, one after another, with Chechevitsin to liaise for them."

"What happened?"

"They sent some stuff back, but couldn't get actual evidence."

"Where are they now?"

"They were found dead."

He shifted on the seat, crossing his legs the other way and turning his head to look past me at the passengers out there. "What sort of chap is he?"

"Kirinski?"

"Yes."

"Untrained, aggressive, physically strong. Nerves like castanets. Christ, so would mine be, trying to keep *three* in the air."

"Would you call him pyschotic?"

"No more than the rest of us in this trade."

I was still listening carefully to what he was saying, and to his silences. I was beginning to hear something that was only, as yet, in his mind.

"Do you want me to go back to his place," I asked him, "and see if he's got anything on the Bureau?"

He thought about this.

"No. He can't have anything we'd want to destroy. But he's been making too many contacts, and—"

"Not Chechevitsin?"

"No." He looked at me with a wintry smile. "We wouldn't have sent you to investigate a man and give you one of his contacts for your liaison."

"You bastards'd do anything." But it didn't sound funny. This was the end phase, and the end phase is never funny.

"London," he said absently, "is still working on your case, naturally."

"My *case?*"

"Novikov."

"What are they doing?"

"Pressure," he said with slightly more articulation than usual, "is being put on the Prime Minister to make the Yard see the point—the point being that even in a Cold War there are sometimes casualties."

It was all they could do. If you kill someone it's murder, but if you kill someone who is a potential enemy working within the gates, there is a difference. Not that I'd slaughtered that man in the Queen's name, but that was the argument the PM would use to get the thing wiped off the records.

"Still got the shits," I said, "have they?"

"Until the case can be closed," he said sharply, "the Bureau will remain at risk."

I didn't know at first why he'd brought the subject up. But now I knew, and I could feel the slight acceleration of my heart-rate under my ribs.

"Ferris," I said very carefully, "did they *plant* Novikov on me in that train?"

He looked away from the window. "Surely," he said with a certain impatience, "that's rather too extravagant."

"I wouldn't put it past them," I said and he heard the edge of my voice but refused to look at me.

Wings crashed against the window and I looked out. That bloody hen had got loose and they were all trying to catch it, running all over the place.

I thought it was time to ask Ferris.

"What is the actual objective for Slingshot?"

Immediate reaction as the tension came into him, though there wasn't anything to see: He was poker perfect. I had to wait quite a long time.

"As you know," he said with his voice a shade too bright, "we had to work out a suitable access. That's why we had to get the air photographs, and we'll be passing on some of these documents to certain organisations. But they were only the ticket for the trip."

They'd caught that bloody thing down there and it was flapping and squawking, trying to get away again. Some children were laughing, and clapping their hands. Then a man tucked the hen between his knees and took the head and gave a jerk and the squawking stopped.

"The actual objective," Ferris said beside me, "is less complicated. They want you to kill Kirinski."

18

Silence

She sat hunched on the stool, shivering, cupping the bowl of soup in both hands. Two men came in and I looked up at the fly-stained mirror and down again.

"Because I'm afraid of him," she said in a moment.

I'd asked her why she carried a gun.

"But you had it on you when he was away."

"I always carry it. There are the others, too."

The two men were all right: They were railway workers. I'd checked Liova all the way in from Gromyko Prospekt, three blocks from here, and it had been satisfactory. This place was behind the station, not inside it, and of course if the KGB wanted to drop on me they could do that: I wouldn't be able to stop them. Wherever they wanted to drop on me in this city they could do it, unless I went to ground; and I couldn't go to ground because this was the end phase and in the next few hours I'd have to get out of Yelingrad and get out of Russia before the pressure reached the point where the whole thing blew.

"What others?" I asked her but of course she meant the KGB.

She put her bowl down onto the counter and I noticed she'd stopped shivering. I didn't know her well enough to know whether it had been her nerves or the intense cold or both. When I'd called the apartment an hour ago she'd said Kirinski was there, but I'd wanted to talk to her, not him: If he'd answered I would have hung up without speaking. She said she'd meet me here.

"I mean the KGB," she said.

"You weren't afraid of them when you called them up and put them onto me, the first time we met."

She closed her eyes and for a moment looked younger, a child asleep. "Yes," she said, "I was."

It could be true but I didn't rely on that. I didn't rely on anything now, even Chechevitsin, even Ferris, even London. They'd got me to the point of the wedge again where the risk factor was a hundred per cent and I'd have to get out alone if I could get out at all. This girl and I had made love yesterday and today she could pull her gun and blast me off this stool and show her KGB card to the proprietor and walk out of here without even paying for the soup or she could make a signal and any number of agents could close in on this place before I had time to see them coming, but there'd been no way of diminishing the risks without diminishing my last few chances of getting out of Slingshot alive, and even those were thinning out the longer I sat here drinking this bloody stuff.

But there was no other way because time was too short now to plan anything foolproof.

"Do you belong," I asked Liova, "to the KGB?"

She looked up. "No. They asked me to watch Alexei for them."

"When?"

"A month ago."

"Why?"

"I don't know. They just came to me. They asked me to report on his close friends, and anyone I saw him talking to."

"And any visitors."

"Yes."

I stirred the soup with my aluminium spoon, and found some more meat at the bottom. "Why are you afraid of him?"

"Because of what he's doing. I don't understand it." She spread out her hands suddenly—"Listen to me, I am a doctor's daughter and I work in an office for the Agricultural Department, and I'm not used to the kind of things Alexei is doing. He's suffering under an enormous strain, and that's why he's on this—"

I waited.

She looked away and picked up her bowl, shrugging with her head. "He frightens me."

"What *is* he on? Heroin?"

She looked startled. "No. How did you—"

"Cocaine?" I'd heard there was traffic across the border.

Hesitation. "Yes."

"Is he mainlining?"

She looked puzzled, I suppose because I'd used the Moscow *argot*. "Does he inject himself?"

"I think so."

"How often does he get high?"

"I don't want to talk about it."

He'd been high in the car, in the Trabant. It had been like struggling with a tiger. He'd probably been high when he'd killed the three people London had sent out here.

"Are you on it too, Liova?"

Her dark hair swung and her eyes were wide—"It's killing him! You think I want to die too? Like that?" In a moment she said quietly: "There hasn't been any sex for almost a year. It takes that away first. First sex, then life. I know about it."

A man came in and sat down at one of the little tables, where the food cost ten per cent more. He looked all right but I went on checking him.

"Is he jealous?" I asked her.

"Yes," she said bitterly. "He doesn't want other men to do the things he can't do." She pushed her bowl away and turned on the stool to face me, sweeping her hair from her eyes. "I want to see you again, Andreyev. Not at the apartment."

I was getting out some money, to pay for our soup.

"I would've liked that," I said.

She was watching me. "Isn't that why you asked me to come here? So that we could talk?"

"Yes. So that we could talk."

I put down a ruble and five kopeks.

"We haven't said anything, Andreyev."

"I'm going away."

She slipped off the stool and we went to the door together.

"When?"

"Soon."

We walked with her hand in my arm; the pavement was slippery. It was three or four minutes before she spoke again.

"When will you be coming back?"

"I don't know," I said.

Chechevitsin had got me a Wolga, the medium-sized model, and I'd picked it up from the car park outside the football stadium last night after Ferris had gone. It was waiting for me halfway down the street that ran at right-angles from this one, at the next corner.

"When you come back," Liova said, "will you let me know?"

"Of course."

We turned the corner and I looked along the street and saw the Wolga standing where I'd left it. It was in the open, with no cover anywhere near; there was good cover farther along, where two trucks were still unloading into a warehouse, but I hadn't used it.

"Where are you going?" she asked me.

"I'm never quite sure."

Bitterly she said: "You're like him. Why can't you stop?"

"We don't know how." We were nearing the Wolga. "And we don't want to know."

There were five other cars standing against the kerb in this area and the dark green Syrena was the farthest away; but even from this distance I could see that he was still sitting there behind the wheel.

When we reached the first corner I said: "I'm going this way."

She stopped and I kissed her cold mouth and felt her gloved hands tighten in my own. She said nothing, and I let her go, watching her into the distance. She walked with her head down, taking care on the treacherous surface, a lock of dark hair lying across one shoulder, Liova, a Russian girl, last seen in the street of a city under snow.

I turned and went back and got into the Wolga and started up and waited for the tyres to find a grip on the ruts, checking the mirror when I crossed the first intersection to make sure he was behind me.

He needn't have come: I hadn't counted on it. There'd been two alternative procedures I could have used if this one hadn't worked, but they were now academic: He was here. I turned west, soon after the park where the Lenin Monument stood, and took the major road out of the city so that he could follow without any trouble. There was sand along most of the route and we drove at thirty miles an hour, keeping up with traffic. This was the way I'd come into the city after the woman at the farm had cleaned my injuries; the farm was below the caves, six or seven miles into the foothills of the Khrebet Tarbagatay range, where I'd sheltered for a time, coming down from the mountain.

Of course I'd told Ferris to go to hell.

He'd expected that.

"I don't think you've got any option," he'd told me sharply.

"You know bloody well I've never done an execution."

"Things have changed, you see. The man in the train—"

"I killed him for my *own* reasons and I'm *damned* if I'm going—"

"The position taken by the Bureau is that you are expected to do for *them* what you readily did for *yourself*."

"I won't kill a man in cold blood. I never have."

"Novikov was—"

"I was in a rage when I did that!"

"You can't be particularly fond of Kirinski. He destroyed one of our major operations down here and he killed three—"

"I don't give a *damn* what he did. He didn't do anything to *me*."

"There are, of course, certain other aspects. You are the subject of a manhunt throughout northern Europe, and Parkis believes he can get you reinstated at the Bureau if—"

"Fucking coercion. He can't use me like a—"

"What do you think we're running, Quiller, a garden party? You've been placed in the centre of a situation in which this man has to be eliminated, for the sake of—"

"Tell them to send out someone else."

"They sent three people out, and they didn't take enough care."

"That's their bloody lookout, if—"

"We think you can do it for us."

"Christ, I've never done it before, so how can they—"

"It's not *technically* difficult, of course."

"You bloody directors never go near the edge, do you, you're—"

"It simply requires skill in making your approach, doesn't it?"

"You're as bad as that bastard Loman, you talk like a—"

"I wouldn't throw this chance away, Quiller. I really wouldn't."

"Tell them to get someone else."

"If it's a question of morality, you should—"

"Conscience, is that what you—"

"Not quite, after the incident in London."

"I've told you before, that was personal."

After a bit he'd said with enforced patience: "Very well, I'm obliged to put the matter into the simplest terms: *We would expect you to defend yourself, if attacked.*"

That one shut me up and we'd left the bus station without saying anything else. Ferris hates having to spell things out but I'd been groggy from all that exhaust gas and not cerebrating too well.

He would have signalled London.

I checked the mirror again and saw the dark-green Syrena sliding about and trying to keep up, so I slowed a little. There were no more buildings now: The last thing we'd passed was some kind of processing plant with steam pluming into the grey winter sky. The caves were two miles ahead and the traffic was thinning out after the road forked, with the military stuff taking the southern route towards the border.

The foothills were coming up on the right, a sloping waste of snow with dark crags exposed on the lee side. The first of the farm buildings were now spread out on the left of us and I passed them at the same speed and then began accelerating. We had a mile to go and I didn't want to let him pull up behind me when we stopped because he'd have a gun and he'd use it at once.

The sand was patchy along this stretch and the Wolga was breaking away at the rear all the time until I got the nearside wheels stuck well down on the camber and used the grass verge as a cush. I saw him twice in the mirror, a long way behind but still on the move, and I kept my foot down until I came to the caves.

They were high on the hillside, their entrances strung out along a ledge that ran a hundred feet or so above the lower slopes. At this point the road had no particular border but the ground was obviously flat and I ran the Wolga through virgin snow and left it angled against the bank higher up. The stuff I'd taken from the consigne this morning was on the floor in the rear and I left it there, slamming the door shut and starting the climb on foot. The Syrena was still half a mile distant and the air here was quiet, giving me privacy.

I suppose there were other places as convenient for what we had to do, but I'd made my way instinctively from the city, seeking the wilds as animals do when the presentiment of death is on them. And I suppose there were alternatives: I could have gone to ground and spent the rest of my life in uneasy hibernation, or I could have lain low for a year or two and then gone back to that bloody place to ask them for a job in one of those offices where the halt and the lame and the superannuated finish up, complete with a pen and a pension; to hell with that.

The thing that had brought me here was the fact that a mission was still running and I was the ferret they'd sent down the hole and they were waiting for me to come up with something, and this was the situation that had shaped my whole life since I'd first gone into the trade, and it had become a habit.

I watched the Syrena coming.

Kirinski had contacts and by this time he might have found out I was from London, and that would be sufficient incentive for him to kill me, as he'd killed the others. He knew I'd taken a copy of the material, and he would want that copy and would kill for it if he could, at the same time destroying the information stored in my brain. But I had wanted to make absolutely sure he would attack me, so I had kissed her there in the open street while he was watching.

I climbed higher, and reached the ledge where the caves made holes in the snow. The car had slid to a stop below me, not far from the Wolga, but he didn't get out immediately and because of the reflection on the window glass I couldn't see what he was doing; his gun would already be loaded, and he was probably using the needle. Cocaine works fast, within a minute of the injection, and he would have left it until now, so that by the time he reached me he would feel that overwhelming power flowing through him. Without it he could look after himself well enough:

he was bigger than I was, and heavier. With the cocaine in him he would be galvanised, unstoppable.

The door of the car snapped open and as he got out I could see him clearly enough to recognise that great wedge of a nose sloping down below the eyes, and that odd backward-tilting walk of his as he came across the snow, his knee-boots kicking at it. He looked upwards now, and saw me; and I had the thought that in different circumstances I would have waved to him.

It was at this point that conscious linear cerebration broke up suddenly into random flashes, as if a bare wire had been dropped across an electronic circuit. I'd been briefed for this mission and I'd been given enough information to see it as a logical attempt to achieve logical goals, but there was always the unknown background to any mission and as I stood here watching Kirinski climb the slope I was thinking of Parkis . . . *It would save us the unpleasant task, later, of ensuring that the threat to security he would continue to present was nullified* . . . Parkis and Novikov . . . *Did they plant him on me in that train?* Novikov and Ferris, and the way Ferris had looked away when I'd asked him if they'd worked out an escape-phase for me once I'd reached the objective.

Uninformation, and a background to Slingshot that could make total nonsense of the understanding I thought I had of it: For all I knew I could be one unimportant component of a design so complex that only Parkis could make the changes necessary to remove that one component and render it harmless to the overall plan. My instructions were that the objective for this operation was Kirinski's death, but who was Kirinski—the objective, or a reliable Bureau man with instructions that the objective for *his* operation was to kill *me?*

In this trade we see the world in mirrors and I'm used to that but when I go out it's got to be someone from Moscow or Peking or Havana who finds me in the dark or pulls me into a trap or centres me in the crosshairs: someone in the *opposition*, not someone in London putting a small black cross at the point where the expendable executive is required to cease functioning, *not someone I thought I could trust.*

A final thought flashing through my head as I watched the man climbing the slope: *You can't trust Parkis.*

When Kirinski was halfway from the road below I turned and moved towards the mouth of the nearest cave and the shot smashed into the rock close to my face.

"*Rashidov!*"

Even at this distance his voice was loud enough to echo in the cave as the second shot chipped fragments away and sent them whining past me. I went right inside now, and felt my way along the rock until faint light came into the darkness ahead of me: These weren't isolated caves but a whole network tunneling the hillside above the ledge, parts of it broken from above and blocked with boulders that had rolled down from the heights—I'd lost my way when I'd come here before, and had to climb back up the slope to get out.

Light from the noon sky gave a leaden sheen to the ice that had formed below the snow mass, covering the walls where the arched roof had fallen in, and I moved again and noted distances and widths and gradients, listening for him as I went forward.

"*Rashidov!*"

It was the bellow of an animal, much closer now but impossible to locate because of the echoes. The cocaine was roaring in his veins and he would be feeling invincible and would behave accordingly. The heart rate and breathing would be accelerated and the body temperature raised, with increased blood sugar and muscle tone; but it was the psychic effect of the drug that would give him the strength to deal with anything that got in his way and leave it broken behind him. Anything.

I picked up a stone and threw it against the angle of the rock face where I'd turned, and the light of the explosion flared as the shot crashed in the confines and left the mountain singing.

Three.

I moved again as the reek of cordite came on the air. There were faint regular sounds and I noted them as being less than immediately threatening, until I realised that my ears were still half deafened by the noise of the shot and that he could be much closer than he sounded.

The walls narrowed and the ground rose and I couldn't see the light any more but there was no point in going back: He was close now and quiet, listening. I could be moving into a dead end but the risk had been calculated: To kill Kirinski I had to empty his gun and I couldn't do that in the city streets and I couldn't do it across open ground so I'd thought of the caves and I would have to do it here, where there'd be a chance of dodging him long enough to wear him down and come up on him from behind.

I didn't think I could do that. I only thought there was a chance.

The ground was steep and I waited, keeping still. If I tried to go higher I might slip and he'd hear and fire. The silence was total except for the singing of the blood through the aural membrane. A minute later I heard a sound but it was brief and I had to examine it in retrospect; it had been sharp and metallic: He'd probably caught his gun against a jutting rock. I couldn't hear his breathing, although he'd just climbed the slope from the road and was under the influence of the cocaine; but the acoustics in here were deceptive and I didn't think he was far away.

He was waiting for me to move.

The retinal nerves were switching from cones to rods and a faint area of light was forming to my left, higher than where I stood, and as I watched it I could feel the gooseflesh reaction along the arms because if Kirinski was this side of the corner where I'd turned a minute ago he would see my silhouette forming gradually against the light. It was possible that I was part of the rock's configuration and that he wouldn't identify the human outline, so that if I kept still he wouldn't shoot; but I couldn't be sure of that. If in fact the outline was becoming recognizable he would now be selecting his target—the head or the torso—and tightening his finger, and I must move in the hope of distracting him. But if I moved I might *present* the target by showing him that this configuration was not rock.

I listened.

Silence.

The light became stronger as the retinae accommodated, and I watched it. I could have been alone here in the mountain, in the stillness, a single creature isolated and without movement; but I knew he was close.

Tidal breathing.

Heart-beat.

Nothing more.

He was waiting, and so was I.

"*Rashidov!*"

Explosion of light and sound and I flung myself down with my hands going out and as the echoes rang around the walls I went forward, pitching across the open space I'd seen when he'd fired, hands and knees and then running until my shoulder hit the rock and I bounced, spinning and going down and kicking upright as the dark burst into light again and the mountain boomed.

There was more room here and I rolled sideways and found rubble and lay there while he ran past me with his boots scattering stones and the sixth shot crashing somewhere ahead of me and numbing the ears. It was the cocaine: He was overwhelmingly confident and functioning without resource to reason, hurling himself into the confines with the certainty I was there.

"*Rashidov!*"

Christ how he hated me . . . it was in his voice.

Stones scattered again and I lay with my face to the rock because my clothes were dark and he wouldn't see me here unless he came back and I didn't think he would do that because his mental process was unidirectional: He thought I was somewhere in front of him and therefore I would always be in front of him until he found me and killed me.

I could still see the faint area of light and the silhouette that was now moving across it, until suddenly his clear figure was standing there at the bottom of what must be a shaft open to the sky. He stood with his head cocked and his nose jutting, his feet spread apart and the gun moving in a slow arc as he looked for me.

"*Rashidov! Where are you?*"

The echoes ran from cave to cave and died away.

I couldn't tell how much he was still capable of reasoning. Cocaine doesn't dull the brain: It stimulates it, but to the point where confidence takes over from reason. He was standing there with a monumental arrogance expressed in his stance and the set of his head: He was omnipotent, lord of the mountain, and his question to me had been meant as a command—I must come out of hiding and show myself, so that he could shoot and this time kill.

"*Rashidov!*"

He was getting impatient.

When he moved next I would know by how much he was capable of reasoning. If he moved away it would mean that he still thought I was somewhere in front of him; if he came back it would mean that his brain could still follow logic: the logic that if I had gone ahead of him he would have seen me passing through the light where he was standing now.

He called my name again and swung round, circling the gun, his boots kicking at the stones under the snow. He was twenty feet away and I could see the light in his eyes, manic and obsessed, as he looked for the thing he was here to kill. I don't think he'd meant to shoot again before he saw me, but the gun jerked and the shot glanced off the rock and whined across the shaft in a ricochet as the smoke rose in the light, clouding against him.

Seven.

Perhaps he thought he'd seen me, or heard me.

Lie still.

"Rashidov! Come out!"

He was enraged, as I had been in London; but he was losing control to a chain reaction he couldn't stop: The set of his head, his shoulders and his legs expressed total determination—he would hurl himself bodily at the mountain and bring it down if he had to, in order to find me.

"Come out!"

He swung his head away from me and took a step, swinging the gun and then pausing, to turn and listen. Watching him, I could see the return of reason to his mind: He was looking slowly around him to find the tunnel that had led him there, and when he was facing me he began coming back.

Decision.

I had to make a decision because if he came too close to the rock he'd trip on me and he had at least one shot left in his magazine and I wouldn't have a chance but if I got to my feet and began running clear he'd hear me and fire blind.

"Rashidov!"

Enraged.

He was coming out of the light and walking faster now, his boots leaving the patch of snow and grating across the stones towards me as his dark figure grew in size and I heard his breathing. He was coming close to the rock where I was lying and I believed he'd trip against my feet so I took a breath and rolled face down and drove my hands and feet against the rubble and flung myself forward into a lurching run as the tunnel exploded with the gun's sound and its light flashed, throwing my shadow in front of me as I ran headlong between the jutting buttresses.

"Rashidov!"

Darkness again and the risk of smashing into the rock face but if I stopped he'd be on me and I wouldn't be ready.

His boots crashed over the stones behind me.

It was unlikely that he had more than nine shots in the magazine and he'd fired eight and I had to let him stay close so that I could stop him reloading if he had to but if I stayed close he would fire again if there was a ninth shot left and it couldn't fail to kill if it caught me now.

Feet thudding and the stones scattering, the echoes running ahead of us into the dark. This was where it was going to be: I could hear the sawing of his breath and knew how close he was and knew that if he had one shot left he'd fire it as soon as there was light behind the target and that if the magazine was empty he'd drop the gun and use his hands and demolish me, destroy me with that demoniacal strength of his before I could do anything against him. So this was where it was going to be.

Stones flew upwards from our feet.

"Rashidov!"

Light came ahead of us and the ninth shot crashed and span me round by the shoulder and I went down and reached for his legs and trapped them and felt his body swinging across my back before it hit the ground and the gun rattled against the stones *get it get the gun* and my hands groped, sweeping over the ground left and right left and right *get it get it before he*—got it and flung it as far as I could because he might have a spare clip and I wouldn't survive another nine, *get up and run* with the light spreading ahead of me and the first white flash of the snow as I reached the cave mouth and saw the gun and picked it up and threw it across the ledge, a whirling of bright metal as it disappeared.

He was coming for me when I turned round.

Shoulder burning from the shot but no paralysis.

He was coming fast with his head down and his hands reaching out for me and I went low and swung him down again but this time he caught at me and locked one arm and I twisted over and used the elbow in a curving strike against the side of his head and missed and hit the snow. His strength was appalling: If I left my arm in the lock he'd break it so I hooked back to the groin with one heel but didn't connect because he was rolling over and heaving his body upwards, dragging me with him until I brought off a sword-hand against his knee and he screamed and came down again with his free hand clawing for my face.

Blood from somewhere: my shoulder perhaps. Spots on the snow.

He moved very fast and pain flared in my arm as the pressure came on—he was going to break it and I curved a thumb-shot for the eye and missed and struck again and missed and went on striking until his head rolled back and I felt the softness of the eye and struck again and dragged my arm free and went for the throat but he was strong in his rage and heaved himself up again with an animal sound, his big hands reaching to hold me while his boot crashed down on the snow beside my head, going to be no go because he wasn't human, he was a crazed mind empowering muscle and motor nerves with the force of a monster and its intention was to kill and it would do it because it was programmed to do it.

I would need more than my own strength and my own skill if there were any hope of survival and I rolled over as he came for me again, trapping his right wrist and working on it and feeling him react because I'd damaged it before in the Trabant yesterday and the joint was sensitive. He had to move with the strain and I took him halfway over and got clear and ran for the ledge because that was the tool I was going to use, the weapon that could arm me against the cocaine, against the rage, against the monstrous strength of the man as he kicked upright and followed me with his boots flinging the snow aside—

"Rashidov!"

His name for hate, for death.

The leaden light was deceptive and the ledge was in front of me before I saw it but I dug my feet in and span sideways as he came headlong for me. I think he would have gone straight over but there were small rocks beneath the surface and he scattered them, breaking his run and pitching across me and dragging me with him as the edge gave under the weight and we went over together, the air freezing against our faces and a cloud of snow drifting over

us from the ledge. The drop was less than fifty feet but there
would be boulders below and we couldn't choose where we hit
ground.

Weightlessness.

The earth tilted, the ledge angling over and pushing at the sky
until the horizon was vertical and I was falling headfirst with one
leg hooked round Kirinski's neck and my arm locked in a hold
that worried me because if he were on top when we hit ground I'd
be crushed and he'd finish me: I went for the eyes again and he
began shaking his head from side to side as we clung together in
the rushing of the air with my fingers darting again and again until
the hold went slack and I dragged my arm free, kicking against
him and watching him float clear in the instant before we hit snow
and rolled, its crust absorbing the momentum.

He was staggering to his feet with a boulder in his hands and I
span clear as he brought it down with his shoulders forward and
his neck exposed, and I used a vertical sword-hand and felt the
spine flex under it but it wasn't strong enough to snap the vertebrae: The force dropped him and I followed up and he rolled
over and locked my left leg and reached for my face with a claw
strike before I could stop him. We were close now, clinging together, and neither of us moved.

The snow half covered us, its blue-white crystals absorbing the
crimson as it seeped from my shoulder, its colour spreading and
diluting, blood-red, rose-red beside his face as he lay motionless,
resisting my force isometrically as I brought pressure against his
hold.

Then he jerked an arm free and hooked it across my throat and
I whipped my head back but the snow stopped me and I stared at
the sky, feeling the slow closing of the windpipe and the first
throbbing as the breath was blocked.

"Rashidov . . ." he said through his teeth, "Rashidov."

The lungs dragged for air and found none: His arm was strong.

The sky was darkening.

"Rashikov . . ." he said softly.

Darkening.

The snow numbing the nerves, chilling the blood.

It would save us the unpleasant task, later, of ensuring . . .

Parkis.

Pressure and the sky darkening and the last throbbing of life, and night coming.

"Rashidov . . ." he whispered.

Not the way.

The death-bringing black of night.

This is not the way.

"Rashidov . . ." faint on the wind, his arm round me like a lover.

This is not the way to survive.

To survive you've got to move *but I can't move, he's*—you can move if you try *but there's nothing I can*—voices somewhere, voices in an argument, is this what it's like when—

Don't think.

Move.

Strength, no strength, he—

Move.

A hand. My hand. Where. Feel.

His face.

Eyes.

Move before—

Yes.

Fingers at his face, scrambling blindly, live things, live weapons, *move faster*, digging, clawing in the night, in the dark, *this is the way*, feeling the soft flesh, hooking down, hooking down deep, his body shifting, *yes*, his arm lifting to—*don't let him*—lifting to stop my fingers—*yes, this is the way* and a breath coming and the lungs bursting, imploding, dragging the air in as his whole body moved, the rage coming back, the pain in his eye scalding him and *now work, now do some work.*

Rage of my own as I went on hooking at his face but he was rolling sideways and when another breath went heaving into my lungs I used the oxygen and wrenched his arm away and brought a series of eye-darts against his face and felt him jerk and swung a wedge-hand across his throat: I suppose it was the sword-strike to the neck that had weakened him to this extent and I hadn't realised it *you should always be aware, you*—a quicker movement from him but I paralysed the nerves in the bicep with a centre-knuckle and found leverage and got to one knee and drove the wedge-hand down with all the strength that was in me and felt the vertebrae snap and the head come forward, fell on him, fell across him, closing my eyes and letting the breath come, letting it ebb and flow, life-bringing, ebb and flow, this was the way.

He didn't move.

After a time I raised my head and opened my eyes and looked down at him, Kirinski, the objective for Slingshot, a silence across the snow.

19

Flare

. . of similar threats in the past. The Soviet Union has been
steadily increasing its collusion with the United States of America
and its anti-China military deployment, intensifying its threats
against the Chinese Republic.

In spite of protests from Peking there have been more than
three hundred incidents along the Sinkiang border during the past
year, all of them provoked by the Soviet garrisons in the area.

Moscow must learn that it can no longer continue to flout the
warnings issued repeatedly by the Chinese Republic, and that
practical measures to normalise the situation will have to be un-
dertaken in the immediate future.

I kicked the door open, and it smashed back against the wall.

They swung round and stared at me, two lieutenants and a sergeant.

Meanwhile, it is learned that a serious lack of vegetables in Soviet markets is causing nutritional problems among the people.
Harvests have been—

"Switch that off!"

The sergeant moved so fast that he knocked the transistor off

the bench and tried to catch it before it smashed open on the con
crete floor.

"Leave it there!"

He straightened up.

"Get to attention!"

One of the lieutenants had gone pale. Everyone down here lis
tened to the broadcasts in Russian from Peking but in the armed
services you could be shot for it.

"Sergeant, write down these officers' name and numbers."

I went across the hut and kicked the red-plastic transisto
against the wall. "Who does this receiver belong to?"

None of them spoke.

"Answer me!"

"We don't know, Colonel. We all share it."

"Then you'll all share the responsibility. Sergeant, add you
name and number—come on, I'm in a hurry!"

The shoulder was stiffening. The wound had opened again and
I couldn't tell whether the blood had started seeping through the
uniform. It wouldn't look right: They'd call their headquarters.

I turned to the senior lieutenant with the ribbons and the pilot'
insignia. "I want an aircraft readied for flight—where is you
crew?"

"On standby, Colonel." His heels came together.

"Get them moving!"

He looked surprised, so I said: "Listen to me. I've been ordered
to the Mongolian border to lead an escort squadron: The Chines
have provoked a new incident there. This is an emergency, and i
you can get me airborne in record time I might forget you
receiver—you understand?"

"Yes, Colonel!"

He swung round and hit the klaxon on the wall as I snatched
the list of names from the sergeant. "Get me a helmet and flying
kit—come on, man, you can move faster than that!"

He broke for the door and I followed him out.

Half a dozen ground crew were tumbling out of the hut near the
dispersal bay. They didn't need any orders: The klaxon was still
going.

There was no actual hurry: I wanted to keep them busy so that
they wouldn't have time to ask any questions.

This was the nearest decoy field to the city, ten miles away to the south, according to the map. Kirinski had told me they flew two planes from each field, and these were both on the ground with their wing covers off and starter trolleys hooked up. They were MiG-28Cs, precursors to the Finback, their tail units higher and their missile racks bunched closer to the air intakes: There didn't seem to be any major difference in configuration but I didn't know how different they'd be to handle.

"Sergeant! Help me with this gear."

One of the officers was trotting across to the tower and climbing the steps, and half a minute later the klaxon was shut off and all we could hear was the whine of the first engine as it started up. The second one came in almost immediately afterwards, and the stink of kerosene blew back to us across the tarmac.

My head kept bumping. I didn't know quite what the trouble was: I'd had a couple of brief blackouts on the way here in the car and I didn't want another one at the wrong time. It was probably the result of whiplash: We'd gone down into snow from the ledge but the impact had been awkward and the head is a dead weight during a fall.

I let them help me into the cockpit because it was standard procedure and I didn't think I could have made it on my own: The shoulder was almost useless and giving a lot of pain and it wasn't easy to move normally—I'd told the sergeant I'd sprained it in the gymnasium.

Blackout again and the instrument panel faded and got lost altogether because my head had dropped and I was looking at my knees when I came to.

"You can check your trim, sir!"

Did that.

We were on internal power and I checked instruments and looked at the ground crew; there wasn't anything coming through on the headset and I didn't know whether I was going to be operation-controlled: No one seemed to be in charge of anything in this bloody place.

I saw them before I looked back at the instruments. There were four of them, all of them military except the last one, which looked like police: It had got its emergency lights swivelling.

The sergeant was still hanging over the edge of the cockpit, completing his checks. One of the ground crew was on the other side, plugging in the radio connections.

"Are you receiving, Colonel?"

"Yes."

The headset was still dead but I was in a hurry now.

The leading vehicle looked like a staff car, with a pennant flying from the front wing. They were all going flat out along the cinder-surfaced perimeter track and one of them had its horns blaring and its headlights on. The sergeant was watching them now.

Either they'd found Kirinski or Chechevitsin had been blown and given them the number of the Syrena or one of these people had decided to phone a report through to his headquarters: unfamiliar Air Force colonel demanding flight preparation, so forth, and some bright spark in the hierarchy had got the message: They'd been looking for an Air Force colonel ever since the Finback had come down.

"Sergeant!"

"Sir?"

"Get the chocks away."

He turned and called down to the ground crew and I heard the hollow drag of the wood blocks.

There was a change in the engine note and I looked at the panel again but couldn't see anything on the instruments; then I got it: The police car had its siren going as the convoy came heeling off the perimeter track and onto the tarmac. They were a hundred yards away and I pumped the brakes and pushed the throttles forward and started rolling.

The sergeant was shouting something but I motioned him to get clear and slid the canopy shut as the other man dropped to the ground. The systems for climb-out were running and I tugged at the ejection-seat pin and switched to continuous ignition as the leading staff car swung in a half circle across the dispersal bay.

The twin jets were screaming and I left the throttles wide open and moved in a curve to the end of the runway before the speed was too high. The tower was showing a red light and the headset was still dead but I was on my own now and the runway began blurring as the ground speed rose. Vibration was setting in but that was characteristic of the MiG-28 and I left the controls where they were and began waiting for lift-off.

The light was still fair and the cloud cover was high. The nearest airfield in Pakistan was Khanabad and last night the snow had started moving in from the south-west and it could push me higher and onto the radar screens, but the tanks were full and it was only a thousand miles and at Mach 2 with the after-burners switched on I could make it in thirty minutes: The chances were first-class.

The tower light was still red and the first shots hit the fuselage just aft of the cockpit: They sounded like stones. The third smashed into the paneling a foot from the canopy and I saw flakes of paint flick away in the slipstream. A red flare was floating across from the tower, trailing smoke as it buried itself in the snow beside the runway. The next came closer and left pink light dying against the windscreen as one of the tyres burst and set up a rumbling below the scream of the jets, the right wing dipping and correcting and lifting as I used the ailerons. They were shooting low and the nose went down and I brought the control column back: they'd hit the forward wheel and we were off the runway now and skating over snow, hitting a marker lamp and a second and a third until the whole of the aircraft was shuddering and I pulled the stick back another degree and waited and felt the lift coming into the wings.

Bad vibration, then it eased off, and the jets were the only sound.

A flare curved across the mirrors, dropping away below.

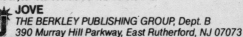